Paul Millard's
Time Travel Chronicles I
Fat Tony's Diner

Daniel M. Dorothy

Curtis Cove Publishing

ISBN-13: 978-0-9909002-2-1

Paul's Time Travel Chronicles I, *Fat Tony's Diner* is a work of fiction. Names, places, characters, and incidents either are the product of the author's imagination or are used fictitiously. Any resemblance to actual persons, living or dead, events or locales is unintentional and entirely coincidental.

Daniel M. Dorothy's new book "Paul Millard's Time Travel Chronicles I, Fat Tony's Diner" is so fascinating that I looked forward to the next chapter, and the next and the next and the next. The plot is nothing like you might imagine and I spent an enjoyable couple of evenings reading and becoming engrossed in the book and the characters the reader meets between the covers.
- Lang Reid, book reviewer, Pattaya Mail

This intriguing new book by Daniel M. Dorothy embarks on a remarkable ride through time travel. Even readers new to science fiction will find themselves swept up in this compelling, page turning adventure.
- Thomas Gingerich, freelance editor and author, *Headgame Solutions for Golf*

Fat Tony's Diner introduces the reader to Paul Millard, a young man who inherits a large sum of money, which, as you can imagine, changes his whole life. However, not in the way you may expect. Paul Millard becomes a time traveler and meets Albert Einstein amongst others, in a most readable and believable book. It is part of a trilogy and I am looking forward to the second of Paul Millard's Time Travel Chronicles, but in the meantime read this one!
- Dr. Iain Corness, author of best sellers *Farang* and *Farang The Sequel.*

Get in touch, I'd love to hear from you:
dan@dandorothy.com
or visit my website:
https://www.dandorothy.com

https://www.facebook.com/Dandorothyauthor-904614536394762/
https://www.amazon.com/author/danielmdorothy
www.facebook.com/MangoRainsDMD

Edited by Cyril Pringle: pachuck@gmail.com

"People like us, who believe in physics, know that the distinction between past, present and future is only a stubbornly persistent illusion."—**Albert Einstein**

ACKNOWLEDGEMENTS

Many people have given me ideas and encouragement throughout the writing of this book, and it would be impossible to name them all. Therefore, I would like to give special thanks to my mentor and friend Cyril "Chuck" Pringle who edited this work and provided invaluable advice; Tom Gingerich for his editing skills and providing me with vital input; my cousin David Sparks Jr. for trying his best to keep me on track; Dr. Karla Gingerich for lending her name and more importantly, for being such a good sister to her brother Tom, especially when he needed it most; and to my sister, Peggy Sanders for giving me legal advice. Without your help, this book would never have been completed.

Clarke's Law—By definition, if you are examining the unknown you can have no expectation of what you will find.

Prologue

Young William Vrill IV headed towards the attic high above the family diner on the edge of Little Italy. Bordering on the German section of Manhattan, locals came to the consensus the diner was once owned by an Italian Mafiosi Don who, during a massage, had been gunned down by a lone assassin after WWII for his refusal to pay a gambling debt to a powerful Jewish gentleman. The latter had taken the diner in partial payment, renamed it "Fat Tony's" as a sign of disrespect, and sold the place cheap to a German woman. This woman was William's great-grandmother who claimed to be a refugee from the hills of Southern Poland.

A savant, by the age of twelve William had mastered several languages including German, the language of his heritage.

Little Billy, as his family and neighbors called him, often took refuge in the attic, away from the taunts of local kids envious of his obvious intelligence and learning and being favored by his teachers, and the constant monologues from his parents and their well-meaning friends who would wax lyrical on the great things the young man might someday be capable of achieving.

Today he pulled down the folding steps from the ceiling and climbed into the attic with his sister's hamster, Cuddles.

William, as he now liked to be called while trying to discard the "Little Billy" tag that had weighed him down since birth, quite enjoyed the sneaky feeling of being alone in the attic, particularly since his parents tried to discourage him from spending so much time hidden away in seclusion. They wanted desperately for their son to make friends with other boys and girls his age and to become 'normal'.

Young William often pulled out his great-grandmother's steamer trunk from its resting place tucked away inside a fort he'd built of family boxes. Each box bursting at the seams, filled with items accumulated over the years that by now were obsolete, but too full of memories to let go. The steamer trunk, with its strange markings, was filled with magical writings, all in German; cryptic notes his great-grandfather meticulously kept while working on secret projects before his untimely death. This death, according to a note written by his great-grandmother, was carried out by an SS firing squad for his alleged collusion with the enemy, an American.

William had no trouble deciphering the German notes. Once he had, he began buying tools and parts, using his allowance and the small amount he earned tutoring other students who were helpless in math, science, physics and languages.

After his father gave him a laptop for his twelfth birthday, William went online to learn everything he could about how computers worked. He used this knowledge to max out the laptop's capabilities to levels way beyond anything commercially available. Once he had everything on his list, he began building a miniature model of his great-grandfather's project.

The model was not a quick build. With great care and secrecy, he started by gathering as much black model paint as his allowance would buy. He used the paint to cover one side of hundreds of small, square pieces of glass left over from a bathroom refurbishing project and stored away in the attic. This converted them into tiny mirrors that he glued to two bicycle rims. Using store-bought lasers, electric motors, the two mirror wheels he'd made and a primitive program he'd written for the computer, William created what he thought might be a prototype of a miniature time machine.

Today would be his first test. He decided no way was he going to jump in himself, even after all this effort. Besides, the vortex he was trying to create would be too small. He wouldn't fit in even if he wanted. Hence, Cuddles.

William switched on the lasers, the motors, and the laptop. After typing random parameters into his program and clicking enter, the machine sprang into life for the very first time. The young scientist stared in awe as the lasers hit the spinning mirror wheels and reflected off into a single point, creating what looked like a small vortex.

When he thought everything was running at full capacity, William sat Cuddles in front of the vortex, flicked him on the butt, and watched in amazement as Cuddles the hamster ran straight into the vortex and disappeared.

The event sent sparks flying and caused the power to cut—and after sputtering and clanking, the model shut down.

"Wow!" William said, his face covered in soot, his hair standing on end. "I think it worked!"

No sooner had this happened when his sister called up to him from the bottom of the attic stairs. "Billy, have you seen Cuddles? He's not in his cage."

"He's not up here," William called back. He let out a slight gasp and his eyes bulged when he realized what he had done. 'Little Billy' scrambled to hide his model before his sister reached the top of the stairs and had only just finished when she peered into the attic.

"What are you doing up here?"

"Nothing." Now out of breath, William used his body to conceal whatever he couldn't hide behind boxes and old curtains.

"You're not playing with great-grandma's stuff again, are you? Mom and dad told you not to."

"I'm not playing with anything. I like being up here alone. Everything was fine until you showed up."

"Well, if you see Cuddles, be a sweetheart and grab her for me, will you?"

"I promise," William said, then mumbled, "Phew, that was close."

"What did you say?"

"Nothing. Just talking to myself."

"You're so weird, Little Billy. Why can't you be like other boys your age and play outside? Find some friends, or a girlfriend or something. You shouldn't spend your whole life up here hiding away."

"Thanks Sis, I'll try my best."

Sis shook her head and headed back downstairs. "Don't forget to grab Cuddles."

"I promise."

1

A dozen years later.

I didn't set out to save the world. I'm just a normal guy from humble beginnings and I never thought in my wildest dreams I would play a role in securing the very existence of the human race. My goal was to help some unfortunate women and children who found themselves trapped, victims of an endless cycle of abuse.

I have to admit I was thoroughly unprepared when all the rest was thrust upon me, starting one hot July morning.

* * * * *

As I sat on the porch at our family cottage on the shores of Randal Cove in Harpswell, Maine, looking through the tall evergreens doing their damnedest to hide us from the ocean, I sipped my lukewarm stale coffee from my favorite mug, blissfully unaware this balmy summer morning would change my life forever.

I worked as a sternman aboard the Lochinvar, Johnny Toothaker's thirty-two foot lobster boat, picking, baiting, and stacking lobster traps. But this was Sunday, my day off. Other than a dozen voice and text messages from Peggy L. Sanders of Sanders Law Group that had been coming in over the past week or so, each call and text message filled with more urgency and weighing on my mind, life couldn't be better.

On this day I sat alone. The rest of my family and friends were off doing something. Some went to church, others were visiting friends and family, others perhaps just puttering around their houses. The peace and relative quiet were unsurpassed anywhere.

Being a man of action, however, and filled with three large mugs of coffee, there was a limit to how much peace and quiet I could take. After deciding to see what the rest of the world was up to, I rummaged around and found my mobile phone, turned it on and found more unanswered messages from Lawyer Peggy.

I'd been avoiding her as I thought it might have something to do with my unpaid taxes. Before you start thinking I'm an un-American deadbeat, let me explain. Paying taxes on time is not an uncommon struggle for men working in the lobster industry. The bulk of our money is made in the summer and early autumn. If we don't make enough to last the winter, and if employment is hard to find once the lobster season is over, money gets tight in the spring. This makes it difficult to pay income tax when due in April, before the next lobster season starts.

Given the lawyer's persistence, however, I thought it might be a good day to settle the matter, or at least find out what she wanted.

Her latest message read: "Mr. Millard, we need to meet as soon as possible to discuss details of an urgent message from Mrs. Merriman."

Mrs. M? Didn't I hear she passed away a week or two ago? Curiosity aroused, I called the number. A woman's groggy voice muttered, "Hello?"

"This is Paul Millard and I'm returning your call. Sorry I haven't gotten back to you sooner, but I've been real busy."

"Mr. Millard? Really? We must meet as soon as you can. I need you to sign some papers," she replied, now sounding wide awake.

"This isn't about my back taxes, is it? Because if it is, I'll take care of them right away."

"No, Mr. Millard, this has nothing to do with taxes. I need to talk with you about your inheritance."

"Inheritance? Did I inherit something?"

"If you only knew—" Peggy let the sentence hang. "Can you meet me at my office in Brunswick today?"

Now I was intrigued. "Sure, what time?"

"What time is good for you?"

The clock on the kitchen wall read 11 a.m. Returning my gaze out into Middle Bay, for a moment I considered whether this might be a trap, like I saw on television when the police would fool criminals into coming to the station under the promise of an expensive prize, and lock them up after they got there. Was this a trap on account of my unpaid taxes? Would this be the last time in a long, long time I'd be porch sitting at our cottage, known to our family as "the camp", looking out over the gorgeous scenery before me? Maybe I should have tried harder to pay those taxes.

In spite of my fears, curiosity got the better of me. "How about noon?"

"Noon would be fine," Peggy said.

After receiving directions to her office just around the corner from the Brunswick police station, which to me seemed to be a suspiciously odd coincidence, the conversation ended.

2

I hopped into my beat-up old Camaro and headed north up Route 123 towards Brunswick. It's always best to leave a little early when headed up to town, as Harpswell is a close knit community where people still wave to each other when passing by on the road, honking when passing a friend's house and seeing them outside. People don't hesitate to stop alongside the road for a chat in cars or pickups, window to window, to catch up on anything missed at the local store—the meeting place where people sit around outside, sipping coffee, telling and re-telling stories.

After an uneventful thirty minute trip north, with only a few honks and waves, I found myself outside the Sanders Law Group offices in Brunswick, Maine, right about noon. This surprised me, as usually I arrive either early or late and rarely at the appointed time.

Peering inside, I saw no one at the reception counter but I glimpsed a woman sitting behind a desk off to one side. She kept her nose down, preoccupied with reading and sorting official documents. Her wrinkled shirt and unkempt hair led me to surmise she'd just got out of bed and dressed hurriedly in order to make it in time for our meeting. After all, today was Sunday—maybe she had a late Saturday night. Whatever. Today she sure didn't look like a lawyer.

Cautiously opening the door, I didn't see any police lurking about, or any FBI, or whoever might lock me up for not paying my taxes. The place had a new smell, though, as if it had recently been set up.

The woman at the desk didn't look up when I entered the lobby. As I peered around the corner at her through the open door to her office, I realized if I spoke to get her attention, if this *was* a setup, there'd be no turning back. When no one jumped out at me, I crept further inside. Curiosity usurped paranoia. "Ahem." I cleared my throat to announce my presence.

When Peggy looked up she saw a tall young man with piercing blue eyes, perhaps in his mid to late twenties. She thought the man might have movie star good looks, although if he did, they were hidden behind a face weathered by years of working the salty sea. His strawberry blond hair winged out from under his bait-stained Boston Red Sox baseball cap, his New England Patriots Super Bowl Champions t-shirt fit tight on his wiry, muscular frame, and his blue jeans were loose, torn in places and generally tattered. She wondered why he had let himself go like this.

"You must be Paul Millard," Peggy Sanders said. Did she catch a faint whiff of fish?

"How did you know?" I asked as I continued my surveillance of the room, looking for curtains or hidden doors.

The woman paused a moment, perhaps to gather her thoughts as to why this man standing before her would think, that she would think, he could be anyone *but* Paul Millard. "You're right on time."

"Right," I said. I thought about how lucky I was not to have a desk job. I knew for sure sitting inside behind a desk would drive me batty.

Peggy offered me a seat and watched as my unkempt character approached cautiously like a wild animal unwilling to be caged. She began to wonder why Mrs. Merriman, the extremely wealthy Mrs. Merriman, would have willed him anything.

"Are you Paul Daniel Millard?"

"Yes."

"Do you reside at 1 Sunrise Place, South Harpswell Maine?"

"Who wants to know?"

"I'm sorry, my name is Peggy Sanders, Attorney at Law PLLC." She reached across the desk and gave me a firm handshake.

I cringed, for she inadvertently squeezed my swollen knuckle from yesterday's misstep. A rogue wave had caught me off guard while I was swinging a lobster trap from the rail to the trap rack, smashing my hand against the bait box. My knuckles were badly bruised and I might have broken a bone or two. Just another day as a sternman.

Returning to the task before us, Peggy said, "I am the managing attorney for Sanders Law Group, Edmonds WA, with an office here in Maine. We are experts in estate planning and I have been appointed the executor of the Will for the widow Mrs. Merriman of Ash Cove Road, South Harpswell Maine. Did you know her?"

"I used to mow her lawn."

"Do you have any identification?"

I reached into my back pocket and pulled out my old leather wallet. It occurred to me Mrs. Merriman had given it to me on one of my birthdays. I slid out my driver's license and handed it to my new-found acquaintance.

"Very good," Peggy said. "We've been trying to contact you because the late Mrs. Merriman left instructions to make sure you were present for the reading of the Will. I wish you had contacted me earlier, for I believe the proceedings would have gone much smoother if you were present.

"Her children filed a motion to read the Will right away and won. Once it was read the children entered a challenge against the outcome, specifically your share. But witnesses swore that Mrs. Merriman was completely sane and well aware of what she was doing when she signed it. The probate court made quick work of the challenge and her Will stands, leaving one-third of her estate to you."

"To me?" I was stunned. Without realizing it, I took off my baseball hat and scratched the top of my head. "How much are we talking about?"

"Mrs. Merriman was a wealthy woman. Your share of her cash and investments amounts to seventeen million, four hundred and fifty-two thousand, six hundred and forty-two dollars and seventy-five cents."

I sat there staring at her across the desk. Where were the hidden cameras? When was someone going to jump out from behind the curtains and yell, 'Surprise, you're on candid camera!'?

Peggy waited, looking for a reaction. She received nothing but a blank stare. "Seventeen *million*, four hundred and fifty-two *thousand*, six hundred and forty-two dollars and seventy-five cents," she repeated, putting extra emphasis on 'million' and 'thousand'. Still no reaction.

I gave my neck a firm rubbing, then the back of my head a good scratching. "What's the catch?" was all I was able to muster as I threw my hand into the air for emphasis.

"No catch," Peggy said, relieved I had finally said something. "Sign these papers and you're a multi-millionaire."

Still in a daze, I accepted her gold plated pen and signed the papers without reading them. "What now?"

"Now, cash, stocks, bonds, Treasury Bills and Certificates of Deposit, everything in your share will be transferred into your name. We'll keep in touch, but by the end of the week at least the bank accounts should be settled. The stocks and bonds will take a little longer to transfer. In her last few dying weeks, Mrs. Merriman cashed in many of her investments and deposited the funds into her bank accounts. Her portfolio still contains a hefty amount in CDs, Treasury Bills and whatnot, but most of her wealth was liquidated into cash. We will, of course, take out our lawyer's fees, but soon you will be the sole account holder of over fifteen million dollars in cash."

"What about taxes?"

"Those have been accounted for. What you are receiving is all yours, to do with what you wish."

"Why me?"

"Only God and the late Mrs. Merriman know."

As I sat back in the office chair, I felt faint. What was happening? I often played the lottery but never dreamed of inheriting a fortune. In fact, I wouldn't have predicted Mrs. Merriman liked me all that much. She had lots of other people who had worked for her whom I thought she liked better.

I guessed I'd better call John and tell him I wouldn't be going out hauling in the morning.

3

Everything finally cleared after about a week. The IRS put a lien on the inheritance until I paid my back taxes, with interest. Once done, I was the proud owner of a very large bank account.

After the legalities cleared and the full fortune was mine, I did what any self-respecting, formerly indigent, income tax challenged ex-lobster sternman would do: I went on a spending spree.

I proceeded straight to Goodwin's Chevrolet on Pleasant Street in Brunswick and bought a bright red Silverado 1500, four-wheel drive, extended cab pickup with the biggest engine and most modifications the salesman could think of. Bought it right off the showroom floor. Paid cash. Drove it home. Life was wicked good!

Next on the agenda was Tess's market, also on Pleasant Street, to order a dozen kegs of beer. Even though they had long ago switched over to selling wine, they still had the connections for the number of barrels I had requested.

The plan was to throw a huge keg party at the ball field, just like old times. There was room for parking, it was off the main road and out of sight of prying eyes, and there were enough fallen trees and scrap wood out back to build a roaring bonfire suitable for such a momentous occasion.

Problem was, more than a few years had passed since the last keg party, and the final one was not remembered fondly by the town constabulary. Something to do with building a fire without a permit, or because some of the drunker, more boisterous members of the crowd gave deputies from the Cumberland County Sheriff's Department a hard time when they came to extinguish it. Perhaps it was the handful of minor accidents—fender benders really—blamed on drunken driving in the wee hours of the morning.

Whatever the case may have been, the law was not about to allow another party there—ever. They made this perfectly clear with a visit to the Jersey Lodge, the old family house built in 1855 where I lived when not at camp, as soon as they learned of my plans. I was told any attempt to contravene these orders would be dealt with quickly and severely.

Undeterred, but most certainly perturbed, I began to make plans to buy the damn ball field, something I managed to do over time, even though the purchase cost me a chunk of my inheritance. "That'll teach 'em!"

I hoped a side effect would be to move the bean hole suppers back to the front of the ball field where I remembered them being held for many years during my childhood. If successful, this would also take time, which I still thought I had plenty of.

While I waited, I also put in motion plans to buy the house next door to the camp. If successful, since there was no electricity or running water at camp, I wouldn't need to run up to the Jersey Lodge to shower and watch the Red Sox, Patriots, Celtics or Bruins on TV. Listening to the games on the battery powered radio, sitting in the darkness on the porch at camp was fun, too, but every now and again I enjoyed watching the action in living color.

The owner did not want to sell, so once again I parted with another sizeable chunk of my inheritance to convince him.

Then came the matter of the missing half a million dollars. Half a million! I couldn't believe I would've mislaid such an amount and suspected some kind of fraud. But the bank insisted I withdrew the money and they had video footage as proof.

I had to admit the man in the video did look like me, but I have no recollection of being there or performing the transaction. The bank was adamant there was no way they would have assembled and released such a large amount of cash unless they performed rigorous security checks. The man (I still say it wasn't me, no matter what he looked like) had passed them all, with current driver's license, social security card, birth certificate, passport, and all other means of identification.

Who knows? Maybe I was hypnotized, or fell victim to some other scam, as I know I don't have half a million dollars in cash sitting around anywhere, nor have I made any recent investments for that amount. So my only choice would be to hand the matter over to the authorities and wait.

Then the accusations came in, the investigations, allegations of hidden offshore accounts. The taxman cometh, talking of massive gains unreported, although with no proof. It was driving me crazy. Is this what all wealthy people have to go through? Or is this treatment reserved for the newly rich?

There was not much I could do except plead ignorance, for I had no memory of anything going on remotely resembling what they were talking about. I decided the best thing to do would be to ignore the whole affair and try to enjoy my wealth in spite of them.

I finally managed to have my party at the ball field, although a couple years later and, of course, with a new bundle of beer kegs. The party didn't turn out quite how I planned, though, for, as with anything lost over the passage of time, sometimes memories grow in status and turn out to be less than remembered, best left alone while continuing to move on to new ones.

Town folk left the bean hole supper where it had been for the past few years, more towards central Harpswell in Mitchell Field where the old fuel farm used to be.

Over time, I put the ball field into a trust, giving it to the town of Harpswell, making sure no one else could do anything with the land should I die. Provisions in the trust stated people could use the land as a public park, as long as no structures were erected, except for perhaps a dugout on either side of the baselines along the softball diamond.

This came with a caveat—I and my friends could assemble a softball game at any time we chose, followed by a keg party complete with bonfire, along with pre-approved permits and an open invitation to members of the all-volunteer Harpswell Fire Department. Parties need not follow softball games if no one was interested; plus, keg parties and bonfires need not be preceded by softball games.

My new house, although small, came with an expansive yard out front, acres of woods behind, and a connection along the shoreline with the land behind the ballfield. This plot of land, on the shore of Randal Cove, was tucked away far out of sight of Route 123 and anyone who might hear us, so the parties migrated there instead.

These sometimes raucous parties became famous, or infamous, depending upon with whom one might be talking, attracting people from far and wide.

My lobster and clambakes became legendary, too. With plenty of room for camping, each summer a small tent city popped up filled with travelers from far away, some with strange names from places spanning the globe. From June to September the land was transformed into a mini-Woodstock, sometimes even with big-name live music. On 'quieter' nights, which was most of the time, guitars, bongos, and singers were plentiful, and jam sessions often continued well into the hot summer nights.

Despite advice from other new money in the area to rent, not buy, anything that flies, floats or fornicates until I became accustomed to being a multimillionaire and all that goes with it, I went ahead and bought one of the most beautiful boats I ever laid eyes on. She was long and sleek with elegant lines. The builders claimed she would do seventy-five knots if given enough room. Not that I would ever go that fast between the rocky shores of the Calendar Islands in Casco Bay.

Once I bought the boat I realized, in spite of this being a dream come true, at seventy feet she was way bigger than I was ready to handle, much less at such high speeds. I was a nervous wreck each time I took her out. It was still fun for everyone else on board, but to avoid calamity I never got her going past an idling speed. So she spent much of her time on the mooring in Randal Cove. Even this caused consternation; being so big, she tended to bump into other boats moored in the cove at mid tide. At full moon low tides, she would sometimes bottom out, listing heavily to one side or the other. Luckily, the floor of the cove was mostly mud, so no real damage was being done.

The *Miss Louise*, named after my grandmother, was used more as a floating getaway than an open water cruiser. The vessel served as an occasional party house, but for the most part, I would putter out from shore in my Boston Whaler, often alone, to climb aboard the *Miss Louise* on her mooring so I could hide inside and away from all the wild hangers-on this fortune had accumulated over the past few years.

I also used the vessel as my private office, holding court with the plethora (in the true meaning of the word) of people asking for money to fund their particular projects. I donated to worthy causes, with children's cancer research through the Jimmy Fund and Alzheimer's research being substantial beneficiaries. Occasionally I found myself roped into funding a startup that sounded like a great idea, but more often than not turned out to be a complete flop.

One of these startups came from a man named William Vrill IV whom I met at one of the crazy shoreline parties. William, who seemed sober at the time, claimed he was on the verge of building a full-scale workable time machine.

I might not have believed a word he said, but as my inheritance dwindled, desperation set in, so just about anything promising, no matter how crazy, seemed like a good idea. The later the evening progressed into night and the more booze I ingested at the party, the more reasonable it sounded.

Eventually, with too good a buzz, William wore me down with his technical jargon. I relented and said I'd finance his miracle invention.

Barely noticeable at first, the meeting would become one of the two biggest turning points in my life.

4

The second big turning point came a night or two later as for once, instead of mingling in the middle of the party next door, I was sitting quietly overlooking Middle Bay with close friends on the wooden deck between the camp and the shoreline below, built precisely for this purpose. I had just returned from my after workout shower in Brunswick where I had taken up Thai boxing—one can never be too prepared nowadays. Showing up wearing new clothes and sporting an expensive haircut, I was a tad embarrassed when my friends kept telling me how I had "cleaned up real good" and "shined up like a new penny."

"So don't I," was my reply in typical local parlance, trying to deflect the attention. Just the same, my new look was one I decided to keep.

I had dozens of friends before my riches, and many more after. But this core of friends sitting here on the deck had been with me from the start and always kept me down to earth.

The unceasing party continued in the field next door without me, but something was in the air. Every now and again, even on party nights, the tension was palpable.

My cousin Russ walked down the short trail to the deck, approached the group and came straight to me. "Can I speak to you a minute?"

"Sure, what's up?"

"Follow me, we'll talk along the way."

As soon as we were out of hearing range, Russ paused. "A woman up in the parking lot says she wants to see you right away."

"Who is she?"

"I don't know. If she's been here before I don't remember seeing her. I was out back when I heard a commotion in the parking area."

"Out back? You mean in the outhouse?" I asked with a grin.

"Yes, but that doesn't matter. A man and woman were arguing and it didn't sound good for the woman. I heard a couple 'smacks' and a 'crack', so I hurried up there just in time to see a dark-haired, bearded man climb into a pickup and speed off. I didn't recognize him, either. The woman was crying and holding her face. She was also having trouble standing, and I thought perhaps she was drunk, but she wasn't."

"Is she ok?"

"Better look for yourself," Russ said and began jogging up the short trail through the tall evergreens and forest brush to the parking area. About halfway, he turned to look over his shoulder. "I tried to help but she said she only wanted you."

"Me? Why me?"

"You'll have to ask her."

When we reached her, Chrissy Woods was leaning against one of the parked cars. The growing darkness made it difficult to see, but I could tell she was trying to hide her face.

"Are you ok?"

"Are you Paul?" she asked.

"Yes, who are you?"

"I want to borrow some money."

Russ dug out his phone and found the flashlight, turned it on and shone the light toward her face. She continued to hide behind her hands and hair.

"What for?" I asked.

"I want to buy a gun to kill my husband." As she said this, she dropped her hands revealing her bloodied face. One eye was swollen shut. I couldn't tell, but she may have been missing a couple teeth and her long blonde hair was matted with blood.

"Oh gawd, did he do this to you?"

"Yeth," she tried to say. Drops of blood misted out of her mouth when she spoke. "No more. I can't take it anymore." Her breath was deep and fast. Her eyes, filled with a mixture of terror and hatred, glared at the light.

I looked at Russ and gave a slight shake of my head. He took the hint and killed the light.

"You're not going to kill anyone," I told Chrissy. "But I promise we'll work something out. First, we need to get you to a doctor."

"No doctors," she said with a lisp. Once our eyes adjusted to the semi-darkness, the half-moon above us provided enough illumination for me to see blood drool out of her mouth and down her chin when she talked. "They only ask questions and call the police. I do this and get it over with tonight, now or never, with or without your help."

"I understand, but you're in no condition to shoot anyone."

"I know a doctor everyone calls Dr. Lynn," Russ said. "She helps women and children like you. No questions asked. She won't call the cops. She'll know what to do."

"Russ wouldn't lie to you," I said. "Will you please at least let us take you to her and see what she says?"

Chrissy began sobbing. "I don't know."

Russ put his hand on her shoulder and she fell right into his big, gentle bear hug.

I took my cue, climbed up into the Silverado and fired it up. I maneuvered it around to head the nose out towards the main road, then reached over the seat and opened the passenger door to let Russ and Chrissy climb in.

Not wanting to attract attention from any law who might be out that night, I drove at or under the speed limit all the way to Brunswick, across to the Mere Point Road, and followed Russ's directions to Dr. Lynn Reid's private office tucked away down a dirt road deep inside thick woods.

A light came on over the front door as we approached. Pulling to a stop as close as I could, we sat and waited a few moments for something to happen. When no one appeared at the door, I slid out and walked over towards the house. I was only a step or two away when the door opened and a woman stepped into the light.

"Who are you and what do you want?" Dr. Lynn said. Her voice had a slight tremble, cracking, almost growling at us. This was one angry woman.

"I'm sorry to bother you, but we have a—" I started to say.

"I'm the only one here, no one else but me," she said. "Now be on your way or I'll call the police."

"You don't understand, we—"

"Go. Go now." She stood fast, blocking the doorway until her attention turned towards the pickup where Russ had opened the door and brought out Chrissy. "My god. What did you do to that poor woman?"

"We, uh, nothing," I stammered. "We need your help."

Dr. Lynn didn't hear me as she pushed past to help Chrissy. As she approached, she looked up. "Russ? Is that you?"

"Yes Doc," he said. "Her husband beat her up pretty bad."

"Is that her husband?"

"No, no, he's my cousin Paul. He brought her here hoping you could help her."

"Why didn't he say so?" Dr. Lynn took hold of Chrissy's arm and led her toward the house. "You poor girl. You did the right thing coming here. We'll fix you up like new."

As they passed me near the front door, Dr. Lynn turned and said, "Sorry, I misjudged you."

"No problem," I said as I turned and began walking back towards the pickup. At that point I just wanted to get out of there.

"Please wait. We need to talk. I'll come back out after I get her patched up and settled in. Do you know her name?"

"She told Russ her name was Chrissy Woods."

"Come on Chrissy, let's get you inside."

5

Russ and I sat outside Dr. Lynn's private office for a couple of hours, chatting in the cool night air, stopping to listen to the spooky screams of a mother fox somewhere deep in the darkest part of the woods. Every now and again we'd debate whether to leave, but when an angry woman, no matter who it is, but especially a woman of authority, says 'we need to talk,' it would always be in a person's best interest to do as asked and wait.

"How do you know Dr. Lynn?" I asked Russ.

"She was a guest speaker a couple times in my psychology classes at the University of Southern Maine."

"You must have made an impression if she remembers you."

"I did some extracurricular work with her in school."

"Like what?"

"Nothing major. Sometimes I went with her when she visited troubled families in rural areas. She said she took me along just to keep her company, but I think I was extra security in some of the more dangerous neighborhoods. I learned a lot on those trips. So much of what goes on in this world stays hidden to everyone but people like Dr. Lynn, who go out and meet the challenges head-on. She's a real champion."

"She's brave," I said. "If she didn't see you, she wouldn't have let me near her house."

"Yeah, well, I guess she has to be. Someone needs to stick up for those who can't stick up for themselves."

"Damn! That mother fox sounds spooky," I said while attempting to wave away mosquitoes in the darkness. "Sounds just like a baby crying. It's getting closer, too."

"I think that one came from inside the house," Russ said. We both stopped to listen. When the noise stopped, we went back to idle chatter.

"Do you suppose more women like Chrissy are inside?"

"I would be willing to bet on it," Russ said.

"The house isn't very big."

"I suppose not," he said.

I thought for a minute. "The money Mrs. M. left me hasn't exactly been put to good use for the past few years. Perhaps now would be a good time for me to stop being so selfish and start doing something better with it."

"Like what?"

"Like building a place where the Chrissies of the world can be safe, away from people like her husband."

"A noble thought," Russ said. "But I don't imagine it would be easy. Or cheap."

"Yeah, well, I still have enough left to get something started."

I was unable to finish this thought before the front door opened and Dr. Lynn appeared alone. "Thanks for waiting guys."

"How is she?"

"She'll be fine. But it will take time. I gave her a sedative and laid her down on a cot in the back room. I stayed until she fell asleep, then took the battery out of her phone in case her husband tried to call."

"Did she tell you what happened?" Russ asked.

"Yes, and apparently this isn't the first time. I'm won't go into details, but I'll just say her husband is not from around here. Not even from this country. She said she fell in with him at a young age. Too young." Dr. Lynn shook her head. "She really is a beautiful young woman. Such a shame."

Russ and I stared at our feet.

"So, Paul," Dr. Lynn changed the subject. "Russ told me you're rich. He said you've inherited a substantial sum of money."

I looked over at Russ, who by now was not only looking at his feet, but shuffling them as well. Did I detect a quiet whistling?

"Yes," I said without elaborating.

"I can only keep Chrissy overnight, maybe a day or two at most, and then I'll have to send her back out on her own," Dr. Lynn said. "I could be much more help if I had a bigger place somewhere to help her and women like her, including their children to stay for a bit longer."

"Funny you should mention—" I started to say, but she cut me off.

"We might not need much," she continued. "Just enough to begin. Maybe more later."

"Like I was saying—" I tried again, but again couldn't finish my sentence.

"Think about a plot of land someplace big enough to build on," she said. "There are plenty of good people around here, and I'm sure we could convince some of them to chip in their time and money to build a shelter somewhere."

I decided not to interrupt and let her finish, nodding in agreement after every sentence.

"We need startup money. I know of a huge plot of land for sale, cheap. It belongs to one my former patients who won it in a settlement against her abusive husband. I believe he's fled the country and now she wants to help. She has kids to take care of and can't afford to donate the land but will sell it for less than market value. What do you say?"

I waited in case more was coming. When she finished her nervous pitch, I smiled. "Yes, I would be happy to help. We were just talking about this before you came back out."

"You were?"

"Where is this place and when can we start?"

* * * * *

Over the next few months, the land was purchased in my name. For tax reasons, it was designated as a medical facility for patients with special needs. Some of the area's best construction workers lowered their costs and built a beautiful post and beam lodge, four stories high with dozens of rooms, each en-suite with full bath and kitchenette. A reception area dominated the front center, and the lower floors included medical facilities and meeting rooms. The lodge was built deep inside a densely wooded area. One road led in and out.

No expenses were spared in the setup and furnishings, all funds coming from my dwindling inheritance.

Peggy Sanders was brought on board, at first for her legal expertise, but she soon took to the project as if it were her own and became its guiding light. She was an expert at getting over, around, under, or through legal hurdles that might have caused a lesser lawyer to give up.

She was amazingly good at tracking down and prosecuting abusive boyfriends, husbands, fathers, stepfathers, and even abusive women. Her perfect conviction record was legendary. Some believe this became a major deterrent, perhaps saving women and children from abuse. No man or woman wanted to suffer her wrath.

Peggy also had experience with fundraising and began to put it to use. And none too soon.

Within a year, Dr. Lynn's Clinic for Special Needs Patients began filling up. More funds were needed for food, accessories, utilities, and intangibles. I didn't complain. In fact, I took immense pleasure in seeing my inheritance going to such a worthy cause. I continued writing checks, even when the funds to cover them approached dangerously low levels.

6

Mark Whitten decided now was finally the time to install a swimming pool behind his house. He was a manager at Ace Hardware on Maple Street, across the bridge over the Raquette River in Potsdam, NY, and now he was on the edge of retirement, content to let the younger generation take control of the family business.

After his kids had grown, moved away and had kids of their own, the Whitten family sold the old, rotting farmhouse out on Route 11 where his grandparents, parents, brothers and sisters, and his own children had grown up.

A while back he had bought a 24.3-acre plot of land over on Sweeney Road. An old house rested near the center of the land, but it was even more decrepit than the old farmhouse. Some considered the house haunted, but even the saner residents of this upstate New York college town gave it a wide berth, for a murder had taken place there a long time ago. The body was left to rot, causing the entire house to smell like death, a stench time could diminish, but couldn't extinguish.

Gossip was rampant about the victim, with most agreeing he was a gangster from the city who owed someone a lot of money. True or not, no one would make an offer to buy the house, even though the town had long ago repossessed it in lieu of back taxes and would have almost given it away.

Mark considered it was worth taking a chance, bought it for a pittance and tore down the old house, replacing it with his dream home—a log cabin replica hunting lodge.

Before long, his grandkids, fourteen of them spanning ages from six to sixteen, veritably took over the place, with its expanse of land and all kinds of fun things to do. Their parents liked it because Mark had rules about how much time could be spent on computer games and cell phones, a five to one ratio—if five hours were spent playing outdoors, they were allotted one hour of computer games.

Now that the grandkids were getting older, this five to one ratio was getting much harder to enforce, especially with teenage girls who claimed they couldn't function without their cell phones.

Hence the swimming pool; for surely it would be better to swim during the heat of the summer rather than talking on the phone, wouldn't it?

One day Mark stood looking out of his back window at the construction crew digging the hole where the pool would reside. The workers had stopped and were engrossed in something they had uncovered.

Fearing the workers might have brought the gangster rumors to life by unearthing a dead body, Mark headed out the door to see what was going on.

Instead, the crew had unearthed a metal box. Inside was stack upon stack of old cash, and upon close inspection, they found the cash was dated from the middle of the last century. Most assuredly, it belonged to the dead gangster.

Mark had the workers bring the cache inside and put it on the dining room table where he and his wife Ann could count it. All the grandkids, along with a handful of Mark's adult children and a few of the workers watched. Mumbles were heard each time a new bundle of bills was counted, rubber banded, and placed on top of the stack.

The total came to a tad under a half a million dollars, with all the banknotes dated from the late 1930s to early 1940s. None were dated after 1944.

Silence pervaded the room. The assembly stared at the pile of loot sitting on the table in front of them, trying to decide what to do next.

A loud knock on the front door caused everyone to jump. Could this be the gangsters coming back to claim their lost loot?

Cindy, Mark's fourteen-year-old granddaughter, was the lone brave soul who ran over to open the door before anyone else had a chance to stop her.

Luckily, they weren't gangsters. Instead, the local TV news crew had caught word of the event and came to film a report for the nightly news. One of the workers must have called someone, who called someone else, who called a contact in the media.

The story broke that night on the local station. From there, the news about how a family in upstate New York had uncovered hundreds of thousands of old dollars, blood money for sure, left over from the heydays of mafia reign in New York, was picked up by the local CNN affiliate. The next night it went national. The night after it had become an international sensation. Never mind the lack of proof about its origin.

It should have been expected that such wide-reaching publicity would attract less-than-desirable elements.

7

Fifteen-year-old Kevin had the hots for Cindy. She repeatedly turned him down, though, because he smoked too much dope and didn't take care of himself.

Kevin's older brother Skip was a small time drug dealer who also picked up extra money to supply his drug habit by breaking into houses and stealing anything he could take across the border into Ontario and sell to his fence, a bombastic little man who called himself I.M. King.

When the brothers found out about the Whitten family discovery, it took Skip no more time than the wink of a gnat's eye to launch his plan to relieve them of it. After all, the loot didn't belong to them just because they found it behind their house. It obviously belonged to gangsters from the city. The brothers would be doing them a favor by taking it off their hands and getting rid of it. Not that either brother was the least bit burdened by a conscience.

With so much loot, the boys could buy enough dope to keep them supplied for years to come, and might even allow Skip to enter the big time, no longer needing to risk getting arrested for breaking and entering.

That night, at about two in the morning, the boys made their way down Sweeney Road with their car lights off. They parked on the paved road, walked up the short dirt road to the Whitten's house and found a spot where they could watch to make sure no one inside was stirring.

When they decided it was safe, they continued to the front door, opened it and walked inside, knowing full well that no one in this neck of the woods locked their doors. They had taken just two steps when Kevin tapped Skip on the elbow and pointed. Right there out in the open was the entire loot, tin box and all.

The brothers quietly put the money back in the box, picked it up and walked back out without anyone in the house having had any idea they were there.

After struggling to lug the heavy box back down the dirt road to their waiting car, off they went into the darkness.

An hour of excitement followed by 2 hours of, "Now that we have it, what do we do with it?" later, Skip stuck to habit and decided he and Kevin should try and do the same thing Skip always did with his stolen booty.

Next stop: across the border into Canada to the pawnshop owned and run by the vertically challenged man with questionable morals.

* * * * *

Iglesias Montesero King hobbled over to his pawnshop near the river in downtown Ottawa, Ontario, his back and legs still hurting him. Damn this getting old, he thought. Being a small person didn't help.

As he reached down to click open the padlock holding the folding metal gate closed, he noticed a familiar car parked across the street. 'Looks like Skip is back,' he thought, 'but who is that with him?'

When the two got out of the beat up old Ford Fairlane and began walking towards him carrying a heavy metal box, he saw the younger boy was a carbon copy of Skip, but a head shorter. Both wore the same style flannel shirt, buttoned up to the throat and with the sleeves cut off at the shoulder, dirty jeans and expensive running shoes. Skip sported vestiges of a scraggly beard. The younger boy appeared to have tried to accomplish the same, but enjoyed minimal success. Both had dirty blonde almost shoulder length hair sticking out in all directions and in need of a wash.

Must be Skip's younger brother.

King pretended to ignore them as he opened up the pawnshop. After closing the door behind him, he flipped the hanging sign over to show 'open' from the outside. Knowing the boys would be entering at any moment, he climbed up on his stool behind the counter, flipped open the tin box containing his .38 snub-nose, checked to make sure it was loaded, and put it back. He left the lid up to keep the weapon out of sight but within easy reach. There was no telling what these druggies might do if they were high and wanted cash.

Soon enough, the door swung open and the two entered, fighting gravity as they brought the rusted tin box inside. "King, my man!" Skip said. "How the hell are ya?"

"I was doing good until I saw you."

Skip feigned hurt feelings.

"What are you doing here so early in the morning?" King said. "Have you been driving all night?"

"In fact, we have. Just to bring you something we think you will be most interested in."

"Stolen?" King asked.

"Now why would you say that?" Skip once again tried to act indignant but it was a difficult emotion to pull off when both parties knew the truth.

"Because I know you," King said. "What is it?"

"Wait till you see this," Skip said as the two boys lifted the hefty box and clanked it down on the counter.

"Careful boys, don't break my counter."

Skip lifted the lid to reveal the old cash.

"What's this?" King asked.

"Old money, what does it look like?"

King gave him a scowl and looked inside. "How much is in here?"

"I don't know," Skip said. "A million dollars."

"There's not a million dollars in there," King said.

"Two million."

"You have nowhere near one or two million dollars in that box."

"The TV guy said there was half a million," Kevin said. Skip poked him in the ribs and told him to shut up.

"The TV guy? So, this is the money the family in upstate New York found in their back garden? How did you end up with it?"

"My girlfriend Cindy," Kevin said, ignoring Skip's glare.

"Who is 'your girlfriend Cindy'?" King said, mocking the young boy's accent.

"Cindy Whitten. Her family found it, and she gave it to me."

"Gave it to you?" King turned to Skip and chuckled at Kevin's innocence.

"She told me her family wanted to sell it but don't know how. She said she knew I would know how, so they wanted me to sell it for them."

Skip nodded his head, proud of his younger brother's quick thinking.

"She did, eh? How much does she want?"

"How much will you give us?" Skip said, intent on taking over the negotiations.

King took out a few stacks of bills and flipped through them. As far as he could tell, all the money was from the late 1930s & early 1940s. "I'll give you a hundred bucks for the lot."

"A hundred bucks? No way José. I could get at least ten thousand for all this."

King flipped the lid shut. "So go get ten grand for it. When you can't, c'mon back and we'll talk."

Skip didn't know any other fences, anywhere, much less one who would buy this lot of cash. He also knew that King was well aware of this. "Ok, a thousand bucks then. We need to pay for gas to get home, and we should make a profit for doing all the hard work."

"Hard work?" King reached under the counter and began putting items up on top to sell, his way of telling them he wasn't interested. "My guess is the only hard work you did was driving that beat up old Ford out there from Potsdam. Five hundred Canadian, my last offer."

"You've got me by the short and curlies you rotten sumbitch," Skip said. "Seven-fifty American and you'll never see me again you cheap bastard."

"No!" Kevin said. "It has to be worth lots more than Seven-fifty. Let's just get outta here."

King looked at Kevin, then Skip, shook his head slowly and cracked an arrogant smile. "Ok, Seven-fifty US."

When neither boy protested, King turned around, slid a counter sized grandfather clock to the side to reveal a safe on the back wall, and punched in the combination. He only kept small amounts of cash in this safe for buys like this. He kept larger amounts in a much larger and better-hidden safe out back in case he was robbed, which seemed to happen about once a month. Local druggies always seemed to get the drop on him.

King counted out seven hundred and fifty American dollars. He paused a moment as if he was having second thoughts, then slid it across the counter. "Have a nice day, boys. Drive careful back to the other side of the border."

Kevin started to protest but Skip grabbed him by the arm, scooped up the money and forced him out the door.

King mumbled obscenities as soon as they were out of earshot.

Once outside, Skip told his brother, "We're lucky to get this much. If King knows about this money and where it came from, everybody does. I mean everybody, from the pawn shops to the kid throwing newspapers off his bicycle. We had to take what we could get and be rid of it. He wasn't going to budge and there was no way we were going to take that money back with us. If we got caught, we'd be going to jail for a long, long time."

"But Seven-fifty?" Kevin complained. "There was a lot of money in that box."

"Seven hundred and fifty dollars was more than we had at this time yesterday and we got it for free. So stop whining."

8

I had just left Peggy Sanders' law offices where we were discussing ways to find new sponsors to help finance the shelter and to try to stretch out the remainder of my inheritance, when I received a panicked call from Dr. Lynn.

One of the young women at the shelter had gone missing during the night. She was known to take long, lonely evening walks in the forest, but was always asleep in her bed in the morning. Today she was nowhere to be found and her bed had not been slept in.

"I called the police, but since it hasn't been twenty-four hours they said they can't do anything. I don't want to wait any longer," Dr. Lynn said. "Can you come out and help look for her?"

"I'll be right there," I said. I shoved my phone in my pocket and raced back into Peggy's office.

"We have a developing situation. One of the girls has gone missing. I'm headed over there now, do you want to come with me?"

"Of course I do!" Peggy said. She grabbed her laptop bag and bolted through the door right behind me.

I screeched the tires out of her parking lot and onto Pleasant Street, narrowly missing traffic, and nearly slid sideways making the turn south towards the shelter. Peggy held tight, but kept a determined stare forward towards our destination. Breaking several speed limits along the way, we reached the shelter in record time.

Dr. Lynn, Chrissy, Russ and another young woman who was introduced as Suzie were waiting when we arrived. Suzie showed signs of having been crying.

"What's the plan?" I asked no one in particular.

"We need to go find her," Suzie said. "She might be hurt or in danger."

"Does anyone know where she usually goes?" I asked.

"No, she always wants to be alone," Chrissy answered.

"Who knows these woods the best?"

"No one knows them like Angel does," Dr. Lynn said. "She's the only one to go out there."

"Angel? Is that the name of the missing girl?"

"Yes," Chrissy answered. "She does this a lot but always comes back and never stays out overnight."

"I fear she might harm herself," Dr. Lynn said. "She's been falling further into depression. Every day, I ask a different person to look after her, follow her everywhere. Last night it was Suzie's turn, but she fell asleep."

"I'm so sorry," Suzie said and began crying again.

"Come on, Suzie, it's not your fault," Chrissy told her, but with little effect.

"Angel, like so many young women who arrive here, thinks that somehow it's all her fault," Dr. Lynn said. "She and many like her are so young they fall for the 'bad boy' persona. When the abuse starts, they think it's all part of the act and if they want to stay with him, they just have to put up with it. Most are convinced he will change. But when he doesn't, it leads to poor self-esteem, deep depression, and makes it so much more difficult to get out from under his spell. Angel is a classic case. Until we can get her back here and under our care, she is capable of doing anything. It's a very dangerous situation."

"Let's not waste any more time talking then," I said. "Let's form a search party, split up and head out into the woods."

"Hold on a minute," Peggy said. She had her laptop out and opened to a web page showing a satellite image of the shelter and woods surrounding it. "Everyone should take a long look at this, pick a route and study the terrain. We don't want everyone to get lost."

The hastily assembled search party huddled around the computer screen. After we divided up the area into six pie slices, one each for me, Dr. Lynn, Russ, Chrissy, Peggy and Suzie, we agreed to meet back at the shelter every hour for updates.

Before heading out, I walked over to the pickup and pulled out my trusty knapsack. I hardly go anywhere without it, mostly because it has a compass, first aid kit, a couple bottles of water, healthy snacks and some basic survival gear.

My slice of the pie chart was sometimes thick with brush, brambles and tangled branches, other times open and easy through a grove of evergreens. Deep in concentration, I nearly jumped out of my trainers when a rabbit thumped across my path. No sooner had I caught my breath when a bright red fox raced by me in hot pursuit, nearly running right into my legs. I had to think it was so intent on catching its meal, it didn't even see me.

After about forty-five minutes I spotted what looked like a jean-clad, barefoot leg sticking out from behind a tree. I tried to remain quiet as I crept closer, a nearly impossible fete given the fallen sticks and undergrowth in the forest.

Peering out around a tree I was trying to hide behind, I noticed a young woman was still attached to the leg. What's more, she had another leg, two arms, head, neck and body. "Are you Angel?" I dared ask.

"Don't come near me," she answered. She scooted around to the other side of the tree, out of sight.

I'm not sure why, but I looked away, making sure not to make eye contact. Relieved that she was still alive, I sat down on the forest floor and leaned against a particularly uncomfortable tree.

"Boy am I tired," I said, still not looking at her. "And thirsty."

I reached into my pack and pulled out a bottle of water. "You must be thirsty, too. Would you like some?"

"No," she said. "It's drugged, isn't it? You're going to knock me out, beat me and drag me back."

I didn't answer. Instead I tried to be as loud as I could while taking off the bottle's plastic safety covering. I wanted to make sure she knew it was new and not refilled. I twisted off the top and took a long drink, consuming about a quarter of the contents, followed by a deep, satisfying sigh.

"I needed that," I said. I recapped the bottle and gently rolled it over in her direction. Still not looking directly at her, I watched in my peripheral vision as she picked up the bottle and began to drink.

"I'm kind of hungry, too." I reached into my pack and pulled out two energy bars. Opening one, I took a bite and began to chew. This time I did look at her and noticed how, with her mouth closed, she subconsciously stuck her tongue slightly to wet her lips. A tear formed at the corner of her eye.

I reached down to pick up the other energy bar but before I had a chance to throw it over to her, she scrambled over to me, balled herself into a fetal position and buried her head firmly in my chest. She began sobbing while rocking back and forth in my arms.

I didn't say a word, holding her, letting her get it all out. Her crying lasted a long time; I wasn't sure how long, but at least fifteen or twenty minutes. After she finally began to slow, and when she was able to catch her breath, she squeaked out, "I want to go home," so quietly I almost didn't hear her.

"Ok." I slowly rose and helped her to her feet. I took off my jacket and wrapped it around her shoulders, and held her tight as I led her out of the forest.

It had been more than an hour, so Dr. Lynn, Russ, Peggy, Chrissy and Suzie had already returned to the shelter. I could see them talking and pacing near the Silverado, trying to figure out what to do.

When they saw us emerge from the forest edge, they began running in our direction. Their intentions were good, but the noise and excitement was too much all at once, and little Angel started to pull away from me to get away from the rushing horde. I hugged her gently but tight, if there is such a thing, and gave a slight shake of my head 'no' to the others to stop them from coming in too fast. They stopped immediately, every face wrought with concern.

"Look," I told Angel. "They love you, see? We all do. You're safe now. We're your family and you are part of ours. We'll take care of you, not because we have to, but because we want to. We'll never let anything happen to you again. I promise. Ok?"

Angel looked up at me with wet eyes, then over to the waiting welcome party. She looked back up at me and smiled as best she could before she broke away, ran over and hugged Dr. Lynn, safe at last.

A few days later, after another grueling stretch at Dr. Lynn's, I escaped to my personal Valhalla aboard the Miss Louise. Last night a man managed to find the shelter and was trying to break in. Hopped up on crack, he said he had a shotgun in his truck and would use if we didn't allow him to be reunited with the love of his life.

Adding to the intensity, the woman he sought had already left the shelter weeks before. Of course he didn't believe us and insisted she was there.

Dr. Lynn called the police, but since the shelter was so far out of town, it would take them a while to get there.

Russ and I had brought some supplies to the shelter that evening, and were still there when he arrived. We stood in the doorway, unwilling to move. We had some success talking the man down, telling him he didn't want to do anything that would put him in prison for many years to come. But our occasional success was always short-lived as the drugs would again take over, turning the man into a crazed animal who would yell at us incomprehensibly. He would even growl. I'd never seen that before, a grown man growling like a wild beast.

The situation came to a head when he yelled, "You'll all be sorry when I get my shotgun!" and began running towards his pickup.

Dr. Lynn scurried inside and told everyone, "Get down! Stay away from the windows."

Russ stood half in and half out of the doorway, prepared for anything.

Without thinking, I ran toward the man and his pickup, intent on tackling him and keeping him away from his weapon.

The man was fast, though, and before I could catch him he ran around to the other side of the pickup, swung open the driver's side door, jumped in, and spun away down the dirt road. He didn't return.

The police finally caught him somewhere up near Damariscotta. It would be a while before the man, whoever he was, would see freedom again.

Later that night when I got back to camp, I escaped the madness on shore and sat alone on the stern deck aboard the Miss Louise. Facing away from the noisy parties where dozens of people were raging-on without me, I tried to relax by watching the sun disappear behind Freeport.

I hadn't been to one of the shoreline parties for quite some time, but it didn't matter. They continued unabated.

Mid-summer sunsets in Maine vary, and on that tranquil evening the sun disappeared at a little after 8 pm. But this far north, on a clear night dusk lasts over an hour, painting the sky in vibrant pinks, oranges and purples. As I stared off into the distance, Middle Bay was glass calm, and thankfully the Miss Louise effectively blocked out the party noise, allowing me to hear the sounds of the sea past Randal Cove.

The view in front of me was grin-inducing idyllic. Whaleboat and Little Whaleboat Islands to the left, Lower Goose Island straight ahead, with Upper Goose somewhat to the right. Cousins Island Power Plant's beacon near the horizon warned all low-flying aircraft of its whereabouts and unceasingly announced it as a landmark to seagoing vessels.

Freeport and Cumberland occupied the horizon. Even as clear an evening as it was, 'Cloud' Washington, also known as Mount Washington, the area's highest mountain that spends most of its life hidden in the clouds, was still not visible. Must be too hazy.

With the party sounds muted behind me, I was almost mesmerized by the sounds of an occasional seagull squawking or dropping a mussel onto the rocks, the plaintive cry of a lonely osprey, and the intermittent splash of seals chasing pogies. At times, the whine of an outboard engine pushing a wooden skiff from one island to the next would grab my attention. Was it someone I knew?

I had become absorbed in the sights and sounds before me until some minor fireworks, bottle rockets and such, broke the mood. I called ashore from my iPhone and asked them to stop, which they did.

I wanted it to stay like this throughout the night and hoped the tide wouldn't go super low, causing the Miss Louise to bottom out on the mud and list to one side, rolling me out of my bunk.

Caught up in my thoughts, I didn't notice the skiff pull up until it nudged the side of the boat as it came to rest with Cousin Russ at the controls. The passenger, some guy in his mid-twenties, looked vaguely familiar. The two climbed aboard, with the stranger clutching a stack of notebooks.

"Good to see you again, Paul," the spindly young stranger said as he adjusted his round wire-rim glasses before extending his hand. I took it, but looked over at Russ, giving him my best, 'who in the hell is this?' look.

Russ smiled and tilted his head. "This is Vrill the Fourth, don't you remember?"

"It's William, thank you," Vrill the Fourth corrected him.

"Bill Vrill?" Russ said and chuckled, "Like Kill Bill the movie?"

William ignored the comment and turned to me, "I thought you were going to blow me off. It's almost 9 p.m."

Now I was most assuredly out of my element. "Sorry fella, remind me again who you are—"

"William Vrill the Forth, we met a while back at one of your parties. You agreed to fund my project to create a portal to travel through space-time, but then I didn't see you again until late last night when you got back to the bonfire. You told me to meet you at the camp around 7 p.m."

"A time machine," Russ said. His smirk betrayed his disdain and showed how much he regretted bringing this strange person out to the Miss Louise, but William wouldn't take no for an answer. Russ was confident I would tell him to take a hike after hearing what it was about.

I had to admit last night was a blur. I tried to explain to William Vrill IV how there was some trouble at Dr. Lynn's—someone's boyfriend or husband found the place and was determined to get inside. "Russ and I had to stand in front of the door and talk him back," but I realized it was futile to try and retell the story, especially since I might have already tried last night after two or twelve bottles of amber 'calm me down' liquid.

"First off, forget about 'William Vrill the Fourth', too much to remember. From now on you're Vrill. Sets you apart from all the other Williams and Bills that seem to be showing up every day and night asking for something. Next, let's start over. What is your portal thing? What does it do? How does it work?"

"If it makes a difference, Vrill works fine with me. I don't mind."

Thus began a long conversation between what some might call a fool and his money, with an ambitious genius who wanted a chunk of said money, and a third party attempting to be the voice of reason.

What could possibly go wrong?

10

"I'm the great-grandson of Colonel William Vrill Sr., whose wife and son were immigrants from Germany," Vrill began. "Don't hate me for revealing this, but Col. William Vrill Sr. was a physicist in the Nazi SS. He was part of a team of scientists working on, shall we say, 'unusual experiments'. Their lab was in the Owl Mountains in Southern Poland, close to the Czech border.

"His particular project was called 'Die Glocke', which translated from German means The Bell. When this information became known many theories sprouted as to what it was. An engine with unusual strength, perhaps a way to travel faster than the speed of light, or possibly some sort of transporter. But when I first started reading his notes about it as a kid, I was convinced it was a way to alter the space-time continuum to create a portal through space-time."

I gave Russ what might best be described as an incredulous look: head tilted, eyes widened, a lifting of my shoulder and eyebrows raised. Russ nodded his agreement.

Vrill continued, either not noticing or choosing to ignore the looks. "William Sr. disappeared towards the end of the war. Some say he was executed by firing squad and left in an unmarked grave with all the other scientists working on mysterious projects in Poland. It was thought to be Hitler's way of making sure the advanced scientific technology they discovered and developed would not fall into enemy hands.

"There is another theory which does seem to have some validity. According to one account, the apparatus exploded when they tried to use it, leveling the entire base and killing everyone within a two mile radius. There are some written accounts testifying to this, but if this really did happen, I managed to work out how it could have, and I have designed failsafe measures to keep it from happening here.

"Finally, others believe he managed to finish his project and traveled to the future so he could find the perfect weapon to bring back to win the war for the Fatherland.

"This last possibility, although the strangest, is what I lean towards. For whatever reason, he never made it back. I believe this because after the war his wife, my great-grandmother, didn't wait around for his return and instead escaped to America with their only son, my grandfather William Jr. When she escaped she also managed to smuggle out William Sr.'s collection of handwritten books describing all his experiments, which she kept locked away in a steamer trunk.

"She ended up in New York City, and strangely enough, she took refuge with people of German Jewish heritage. She told them she was Jewish and had escaped persecution in Poland. I guess she was a quick learner, as the local population took her and my grandfather in, protected them, and made them part of their community."

Vrill stopped for a moment to see if I was still listening to his family history. I was, so he continued. "When she passed away, William Jr. inherited the trunk. He opened it, saw the books were stamped with the Swastika, and closed the trunk, locking it, never to open it again. I guess it was too soon after the war and he realized no one should find out he was the descendant of a Nazi. By then he had grown up in the

Jewish faith and was an active member of the local synagogue.

"For whatever reason, he kept the trunk and left it to my father, William III. My father was an intelligent man and saw the books had scientific value, but he never bothered to learn how to read or write in German. He, too, saw the Swastikas and decided perhaps it should be left alone."

Russ shifted his feet and accidently kicked a gaff leaning against the Miss Louise's port side washrail. It clanked and clattered onto the deck. The noise echoed throughout the cove.

Vrill hardly missed a beat. "I grew up speaking four languages, American English where I lived, German, which was still spoken in my community, Italian, which many of the families in the adjoining neighborhoods spoke, and Science. You might not consider Science a language, but I do—you could call it math and be correct, too—but science is so much more than that. I speak, read and write all four fluently.

"My father gave the trunk and all its contents to me after I earned my Master's Degree in Quantum Physics at M.I.T. Even though for most of my youth, and against my parents' wishes, I had been reading and experimenting with the contents, now I could do so in the open.

"I translated William Sr.'s notes and planned to use them as a starting point to write my thesis to earn my doctorate, also at M.I.T. But when I mentioned I was determined to build a time machine for my thesis, my friends and colleagues advised against it. They told me, and probably rightly so, I would be laughed out of school and more than likely never earn my Ph.D.

"So instead I used my adaptation of the notes, combined them with scientific breakthroughs by Dr. Ronald Mallett, and combined these with advanced applied mathematics to write a computer algorithm to, in theory, create a wormhole—which, in reality, is exactly what is needed to travel through time.

"Since, theoretically, creating a wormhole would be something that someday might be useful for interstellar travel, it seemed more palatable than trying to tell the adjudicators I was creating a way to bend the space-time continuum for time travel."

Vrill stopped to shuffle through a few pages in one of his notebooks giving me the impression this was a rehearsed speech. Perhaps he forgot what came next. A quick read and he returned to his sale's pitch.

"I did earn my Ph.D. and the kicker is, I know it works because I built one when I was a kid, although on a much smaller scale. Either that, or I killed my sister's hamster." Vrill produced a sheepish grin as he tried to pass this off as a joke, even though he knew it might be true.

"Now I just need funding to build a full size version."

"What do you need to finish?" I asked.

"I can't believe you're actually considering this," Russ said.

"Let's hear him out. It sounds like he knows what he's talking about. After all, he has a Ph.D. from M.I.T."

Russ shook his head and looked down at the deck. He couldn't believe he was hearing this from his cousin.

Vrill ignored him; after all, it was I who had the money. Encouraged by my response, he continued. "I tested the theories on a small scale," he said, leaving out the details, "and determined the proposed theory was solid, lacking only the proper materials to make it work. William Sr. and his colleagues didn't have computers or lasers and were trying to make do with equipment available at the time.

"According to the notes, they used a large, heavy bell-shaped apparatus tethered to concrete poles set up in a circular configuration and connected at the top. Why a bell? I don't know.

"Powerful airport runway lights with different colored filters provided the light source for their attempt at creating a vortex, which they calculated would create a wormhole and use it to travel to other times and dimensions."

"All this was during World War Two?" I asked.

"Yes, the project ended at some time in 1944, September or October I think," Vrill said, momentarily bumped off his train of thought. "William Sr. wrote about how light is directional. It may be all-encompassing, but it can be pointed at an object or objects. For instance, notice how light makes patterns on your wall when peeking through spaces in your curtains in the morning. William Sr. and his team tried to use this phenomenon to create what we now call an Einstein-Rosen Bridge, a wormhole through which time is bent around itself, much like taking a piece of paper and bending it so the two ends meet.

"If we want to accomplish this wormhole, we need to create a vortex of light, space and time, and we now have the technical knowledge and can obtain the proper materials.

"We start with two rotating rings, perhaps two or three meters in diameter. These circles are lined with thousands of tiny angled mirrors. At a predetermined distance away from them, we would install hundreds of laser strobe lights in five different wavelengths: the three primary colors red, yellow and blue, along with white and black. We aim these strobes at the circle of mirrors and pulsate them, synchronized at designated speeds determined by a computer algorithm I wrote by slightly altering quantum computer algorithms developed by David Deutsch.

"The computer also controls the speed of the motors that rotate the mirrored circles, one clockwise and the other counterclockwise. Using quantum harmonic oscillation, we can create a carefully controlled vortex, leading to an Einstein-Rosen Bridge, aka, our wormhole.

"The mirrors are aimed at a small target. This determines the time and date along the space-time continuum we would visit. All this is controlled by a powerful computer programmed with my algorithms to control the rotational speed of both the laser banks and mirror wheels, and the precise rhythm of the laser strobes."

Seeing blank stares from both me and Russ, Vrill changed tactics.

"If, say, we wanted to go to, oh, Portland, Maine on January 1, 1900, at 8 a.m., we'd enter the date and time into the computer. The program would then dial in the correct coordinates to alter the speed and the pulse rate of the laser strobe and the speed of the wheels' rotation, as well as which lights are being used in which intensity and frequency, to aim the vortex at the exact point when space-time can be bent back upon itself to create a 'door' if you will, to open in Portland Maine on January 1, 1900, at 8 a.m. A traveler would step through this door and walk out into this particular place, date and time."

"How would a time traveler get back," Russ interjected, hoping there would be no way to make this happen, thus ending the conversation and any further discussion. Maybe then he could go back to the hot new girls at the party back on shore.

Undeterred, and perhaps even encouraged by the question, Vrill misinterpreted him. "I have that covered. I designed plans for a return module, a homing device if you will, no bigger than your smart phone. The device is an advanced recording mechanism to save all the variables at the instant a person or object goes through the wormhole. To get back, push the return button and all the variables are reversed. The person would return to the exact time he or she left. To anyone observing this, it would appear as if the person had never actually gone anywhere, even though the person may have experienced hours, days or even years in the alternate time.

"The homing device may be the most important part of this project. Whomever shall visit the past must protect it at all costs. It's imperative to keep it safe, as it is the only way back."

After a pause to let this new information sink in, Vrill began again. "I am now very close to making this a reality. All I need is funding to buy the rest of the materials, and computers powerful enough to run the required software. Along with time, and perhaps some help, to put it all together and test it."

Much to Russ's chagrin, I was tired enough to launch into a monologue about how only a few hundred years ago, everyone knew the earth was the center of the universe. "And the world was flat. And no one in their right mind would own a computer in their own home. It was foolish to think anyone would ever want a cellular phone. Maybe William Vrill the Fourth is onto something, and the two of us would be pioneers into this new world-changing invention, like Bill Gates, or Steve Wozniak and Steve Jobs, or the guy who invented the cellphone. And social media. Could this be the next big thing? The kind of thing everyone would want to be a part of? A thing that would change history and ensure our names would go down in folklore, remembered forever?"

The more I talked, the more incredulous Russ became and the more it excited Vrill.

"We can build it in the barn at the Jersey Lodge. We've had it renovated, including the apartment upstairs. If you want, you can stay in the apartment. We'll have the downstairs barn sealed off, making it dust free, and we'll make sure we can supply enough electricity and everything you need."

I had made my decision and was as excited about it as Vrill, blind to the far-reaching consequences of such an undertaking.

It wouldn't take long for the invention to open my eyes.

11

Nighttime porch-sitting at camp could not, by any stretch of the imagination, be considered merely as a way to pass time.

Sitting in complete darkness, looking out through the sparse evergreens towards the ocean ahead, which on this night was glass calm and visible only as a lighter shade of dark, bordered on being a religious experience.

Russ and I watched as Cousins Island power-plant methodically flashed its warning lights off in the distance. An occasional smaller green or red light blinked slowly across the water's far edge, marking a passing vessel heading either inland (green light) or offshore (red light), navigating between the islands along the coast. A few minutes later, a slight buzzing sound might betray its engine.

Times like these are meant for solving the world's problems, feeling confident whatever one comes up with had to be the perfect solution for whatever problem was being addressed.

"I just had an idea," I said after taking another slug off my Lynyrd Skynyrd, a mixed drink we invented at some time in the not too distant past. It was made of Jack Daniels, Rock Star energy drink and Coke, the liquid kind sold in stores, not the powdered form which once was an ingredient in the liquid kind.

"What?" Russ said, hardly turning his attention away from packing another onee, his term for a one-hit herb pipe.

"I've been thinking a lot about Vrill."

Russ looked up, "Who the hell is Vrill?" he said before returning to the task at hand.

"William Vrill the Fourth, the guy I gave money to build a time machine."

"Oh, that guy." Suddenly the line of questioning wasn't such a mystery. Russ knew I had been debating the pros and cons of my investments into this outrageous idea. As far as Russ could tell, it was all cons and no pros.

"What if he can do what he says he can do? What if he can transport someone back in time, then bring them back, all under control?"

Russ flicked the lighter, which, with the pervading complete darkness being the mainstay of porch sitting, looked like a small explosion. He inhaled deeply, held it for a few seconds, and slowly let it out. He kept silent for a moment or two so as not to cough and finally came up with his brilliantly profound, well thought out response. "So?"

I don't often partake in Mother Nature's organic life enhancements, but the mood tonight seemed like the perfect night for it. "Gimmee one of those," I said, ignoring his question.

After the exchange, a few minutes of preparation, another small explosion of light, deep inhale, slow exhale and moment of reflection, I now felt prepared to reveal my brilliant plan. Ideas were flowing. I only hoped my creativity wouldn't disappear up in smoke overnight.

"Let's say he builds the damn thing, and it actually works. How about if I were to gather some old money—"

"How old?" Russ interrupted.

"I don't know. Twenty years old."

"I think I have a twenty-year-old twenty-dollar bill in my pocket. Do you want it?"

"Yes. Hand it over." When nothing was forthcoming, I figured it was safe to continue. "How about, I study up on the stock market from twenty years ago and figure out what stocks were around back then that are not only still around today, but have significantly increased in value." I admit, at this time of night I was having a bit of a struggle pronouncing 'significantly'. But I figured I'd gotten my point across.

"Something like Google, or Microsoft or even gold. I'll bet those stocks were like ten dollars a share back then, and now they're like $500 each. So I take your twenty and a bag full of other old money back to, say, 1994, and buy a bunch of shares. I bet I could buy a lot of them and they would be worth a fortune today. It might solve my funding problem for Dr. Lynn's place."

Not overly impressed, Russ replied, "So, what would you do, put them in a retirement account or something? How would you cash them in today?"

"That's the beauty of it. I wouldn't buy them online like we do nowadays. I'm not sure I could in the 1990s. I would need to find a broker, preferably down near Wall Street in New York, and buy the actual stock certificates. I'd buy as many as I could with however much money I could muster to take back with me. Wrap them in plastic, put them inside a sealed plastic tub, and put it all inside some kind of metal box, perhaps a small safe, to keep it intact over time. Then I'd come back into Maine, right here in Harpswell, sneak down here to camp, making sure no one sees me—I have no idea what would happen if me back then would see me from now, back then, if you know what I mean."

"I have no idea what you mean."

I have a habit of scratching my neck in an odd way. When it itches, which is often—and it's debatable whether I'm scratching an itch or performing a nervous tick—I raise my chin and with the palm of my hand facing inward, flick my fingers upward and out from underneath in a rapid motion, scraping the back of my fingernails against the itch.

It was something I'd seen my father do. My poor deceased father who couldn't find his way out of a bottle, dying when I was still so young. Unfortunately, the scratching wasn't the only habit I've picked up from him, as I, too, can drink anyone under the table.

More often than not, I didn't realize I was doing it. "The whole paradox thing," I said, scratching my neck this way while deep in thought. "If I, in the 1990s, saw me, from today, during my time travel visit, who knows what would happen. The entire universe could collapse or something." I stopped scratching as it was derailing my train of thought.

"Anyway, I'd sneak back here at night, and when no one was around, I'd dig a hole in the woods out back, bury it, and cover it up so no one would ever find it. Then I'd come back to the present and go back there and dig it up, take the stock certificates to a broker and cash them in. Rich again and loving it."

Russ thought for a minute. Fffffssspt. Hold, slowly exhale. "Pretty hard digging back there. Too many roots."

"I'd figure something out."

"So, if you could do such a thing, and end up doing it, which in theory would mean you've already done it, then wouldn't those stock certificates be there now?"

A long, pregnant pause ensued, followed by an inspiration, albeit short-lived. "Good point. Shall we go look?"

"Too dark," Russ said, unwilling or unable to leave the comfort of his seat.

"Maybe in the morning." I then thought a minute, shook my head in the dark and said, "I'm confused. If I go ahead and do this in the future, meaning it's already there, and if we go and dig it up and find it, then why in the future would I bother to go back in time and go through all the trouble of buying stock certificates, sneaking back here and burying them? And if we find it tomorrow morning, meaning I don't need to bother going back in time and go through all the trouble, how would they have gotten there in the first place?"

"Hell if I know," Russ answered eloquently. "Maybe you did. Maybe that's where the old numbers carved into the wall behind the couch come from."

"Ooh, spooky," I raised and shook my hands and head in my best ghost impersonation. For naught, of course. It was too dark for Russ to see.

Russ flicked on his phone. "Hey, it's after midnight, we're missing Dr. Drew's Loveline. Turn on the radio."

Evidently listening to sex advice on the radio trumps confusing talk of profiting from time travel, especially when high.

12

The next morning I decided to head up to town for a workout and another Thai boxing lesson to get the cobwebs out, then head back to the Jersey Lodge to see how Vrill was getting along and feel him out. I wanted to get an idea of what his views might be about the stock idea. I was fairly confident he would not be open to the plan, but perhaps I could probe around the edges and gain some insight.

I found him working on his project in the barn. When I entered, he looked up and greeted me with a smile. "How's is going at your shelter up in Brunswick?"

"The shelter is doing great, thanks for asking."

"And the girl, Chrissy? Is she ok?"

"She recovered well. She's now taking counseling classes at night and working at the shelter during the day. She wants to be a full-time counselor there."

"I'm sure you're paying for it all, too," Vrill said.

"It's the least I could do after what she went through at one of the parties at camp."

"It wasn't your fault," Vrill said.

"Maybe, but I still feel responsible. I'll tell her you asked about her," I said and winked.

"No need for that. I, uh, I was just, you know, hoping she was ok."

"Sure you were."

"Not to change the subject, but is there something on your mind?" Vrill asked, changing the subject.

"Yeah, we'll get back to that later. You should call her. I noticed her watching you yesterday when we were all eating lobsters down at camp. I also saw you looking at her."

"Coincidence," Vrill said. "What's your point?"

"You're a good man, Vrill. Intelligent, hardworking, caring, and there isn't a malicious bone in your body. You're a credit to our gender and you'd be a good influence on her. You two should hang out, show her not all men are abusive."

"Playing matchmaker today?" Vrill asked. I could tell he was a little embarrassed and perhaps a bit annoyed, too.

"No, I'm just stating the obvious."

"I'll consider it," Vrill said. "Was that your question?"

I had to smirk. "Go ahead, be that way. My question? No, my question is, what should we do with our time machine once it's finished?"

"Many things, I suppose. The best might be to set up tours for the rich so we can earn enough money to keep developing the technology."

"But what about people who want to go back and change things? Or go forward to learn things to change their lives for the better?"

"That *is* a dilemma. We want to make sure people who travel through time only do so to observe, not to change anything. Like Star Trek's prime directive. We need to write up strict rules prohibiting travelers from altering the past or future in any way, and have them sign off on them before we allow anyone to go on a time travel vacation."

"Can we guarantee this?"

"I don't know, I guess we could stress its importance and try to screen potential travelers to keep out anyone who might want to ignore this prime rule."

I thought for a minute, debating whether I should approach the subject of the plan I conceived last night while under the influence of Lynyrd Skynyrds and onees. Given the current direction of this conversation, I decided against it.

"There are bound to be those who could trick the screening process, which might lead to them trying to change the past or future for their benefit," I said.

"Yes, it could happen. I—*we* hope it wouldn't, as it would tend to prove the doubters right."

"What do you mean?"

"It has been taught how, yes, time travel is possible, but only in one direction. According to Einstein's theory, if a man or woman was able to travel at the speed of light and left earth for a foreign extra-terrestrial place, they might be able to travel there and back in a matter of, what, a few years? But it would be in their time. Days, weeks or months in the travelers' time would equate to years or decades for the people left here on earth, which, if you think about it, probably wouldn't be much help when searching for an alternate planet where humans could relocate once we used up all the life-sustaining natural resources here, or if there were an imminent extinction level event bearing down on us."

Vrill paused for thought. "However, I believe what you say is precisely the reason quantum scientists deny all predictions of reverse time travel. They don't want people going back in time and changing anything because of the effect it might have on everything. The most common example put forward about this is the grandfather paradox. If a time traveler was able to go back in time and kill his grandfather, either on purpose or by accident before his grandfather met his grandmother, then the two never would have married, meaning one of the time traveler's parents never would have been born. Since the time traveler wouldn't have been born, he or she could not have killed granddad.

"It makes sense," he continued. "Imagine if someone were to travel back in time and accidentally kill someone like Albert Einstein. Not on purpose, but because they were so excited to meet the twentieth century's greatest mind, they, oh, caused him to die in an auto accident. Think what it would mean for everything he gave us, his theories we now depend on, leading to so many scientific advances. Including his theory of relativity which has led us here, and now, to the possibility of time travel."

While weighing all this new information and still thinking about finding more funds for the shelter, I asked, "So, what would happen if someone jumped back in time and did change something? Would the whole world collapse?"

"No, I don't think so," Vrill said. "Some theorists say, if this happened, then whatever he or she did would already have been a part of history. They call this a temporal causality loop, meaning that a person who goes back in time and changes something, had to go back in time to change something to create the conditions for said person to go back in time to change something. It sounds confusing, but let's say a man wants to go back in time to save the life of his girlfriend who was tragically killed in an auto accident. The man goes back to warn her, only to cause the accident that took her life."

"I don't understand," I had to admit.

"Ok, the accident that killed his girlfriend caused the man to go back in time to save his girlfriend, but by doing so he caused the accident that killed his girlfriend. If he hadn't gone back in time, the accident wouldn't have occurred, so his going back in time became a part of history. But he couldn't change it because he was caught in this causality loop which could go on forever."

"What if I wanted to go back in time to win the lottery?" The thought just occurred to me.

"Did you?" Vrill said.

"No, but I mean, what if I wanted to try?"

"Like I said, did you? Physicists predict whatever you do in the past is already part of the past. If you were able to go back to win the lottery, you'd know by now. Your name and face would have appeared in the newspapers and online. Your bank account would already be, and have been much larger all along. You would know."

"What if I shot ahead six months, saw the numbers, dipped back a couple days and bought the ticket with the winning numbers, then returned to wait for the drawing?"

"I suppose it's possible, but not probable. The future is filled with anomalies; events and their outcomes change due to events and their outcomes leading up to them. There is no guarantee—in fact there is very little probability the conditions existing today would remain unchanged for the next six months. The numbers you find and buy six months from now based on today's conditions would have little chance of being winners given all the changes happening over that time period."

"How about two days?"

"Same thing, smaller scale, and in my opinion, the same chance of success."

"Boy, you're a real buzzkill, aren't you?"

"People will try," Vrill said.

"I suppose they will," I said, trying not to raise any suspicion about my plan. "Does this mean what we are doing now, well, we shouldn't be doing?"

"No, I refuse to believe what we're doing is a mistake. Any scientist worth his mettle who gains knowledge about something with the potential to change the world, not only should proceed but is obligated to proceed. Damn the consequences. If we can do something, not only should we, we must. Think of Oppenheimer—he was a brilliant man who, with his team, managed to figure out how to create the most terrible bomb ever conceived. It ended World War Two, saving perhaps millions of people. But it killed hundreds of thousands. Did he set out to kill all those people with his research? Maybe, although I'd like to think he didn't. At least not in the beginning. It was used militarily for destruction on a scale never before seen, and hopefully never to be seen again, but his discovery of how to split atoms led to other advances in technology. These advancements are the foundation we depend on today for things such as nuclear power, quantum physics, splitting atoms for non-military uses, and so much more.

"So no, or yes, I forgot your question ... Yes, it is possible for someone to try to abuse the system, but if someone does try to cheat and change things, I have to believe they'd be caught up in a temporal causality loop, not an earth-shattering paradox. Either way, I believe we need to continue what we're doing, as I truly believe it has the potential to change the course of all mankind, and therefore we have the obligation to continue."

Vrill convinced me, then and there, I was part of something much bigger than myself. It could be argued I purposely misinterpreted Vrill's speech when I decided, not only should I go through with my plan, I was obligated to do so.

Therefore I resolved to try and find the old money I would need, feeling confident Vrill had the technical knowledge and full commitment needed to make all this happen. To quote Vrill, damn the consequences.

13

I began asking around for anyone willing to trade old paper money for current. I even took out a classified ad in both the Brunswick Times Record and the Portland Press Herald, but only let them run for a week on the advice of a friend or two who, after no small quantity of free beer, debated the legality of doing so.

Being as popular as I was, for everyone loves a rich person who seems as though his life's mission is to share this wealth with his buds, my friends were coming out of the woodwork with old bills of various denominations. Unfortunately, they were mostly small bills.

Many people, both friends and otherwise, wanted to help me in my quest to gather old money, even though not one person knew why I was undertaking this project. Maybe they thought I was eccentric, or perhaps beginning to lose my mind. Whatever. It seemed perfectly normal at the time, and many were willing to try and help a friend, especially a wealthy friend fitting the description mentioned above.

After a couple weeks a Canadian fence showed up at camp with a suitcase full of what he described as old money. He was a man small in stature, but large in character.

Russ and I towered over him. Not menacingly, as there was no malice in our intent; we were tall men, and this man was quite diminutive.

When asked his name, the funny little man from Ontario raised his chin, stuck out his chest and replied in a heavy French-Canadian accent, "My name is Iglesias Montesero King. I. M. King." He spoke with a slight pause for effect between the I and the M.

Russ and I looked at each other, both automatically and without prompting tilting our heads to one side, each raising an eyebrow.

"O. K." I said, with a slight pause between the O and the K. Looking back at King, head still tilted, eyebrow still raised, I said, "What can we do for you, I. M. King?"

"Not you, me!" he said. "I M King!"

"What can we do for you, U. R. King?" I asked.

"Don't you ever forget it," he said. His laugh was arrogant and triumphant, bordering on a sneer. "It's not what you can do for me, but what I can do for you."

"What can you do for me?"

The little man clumsily plunked his case on the table, popped open the latches, lifted the lid and swung it around so we could see what was inside.

"What's this?" I said.

"Word on the streets is you're looking for old money. This is old money."

I looked down at the cache. I didn't recognize any of the bills, but the coins looked fresh and new. "How old?"

"I don't know, really old. Like early last century."

Russ reached down, picked up and studied a ten-dollar bill. "This is from 1941. What are we supposed to do with this?"

"Hey, I heard you were looking for old money, and here is old money. What do you want, *gros bedaine*, money a little bit old and not too old? C'mon, this is worth a fortune."

"Where did it come from?" I asked.

"Don't ask."

"But I am asking."

"Some guy in upstate New York found it in his back garden when he was digging a hole or something. The kids say he told everyone."

"What kids?"

"The ones who sold it to me."

"How did they get it?"

"I don't know, and why should I care? They were drug addicts so they sold it to me cheap. I'm offering it to you at a small markup."

"How much is in here?"

"Four or five hundred grand, more or less. It's old but in pristine condition. You can sell it for millions. But I only want ten grand."

"How much did you pay for it?"

"None of your damn business. Do you want it or not? I'm offering you a great deal. I'm sure I can sell it for a lot more to a collector somewhere."

"A collector who doesn't care that it's stolen?"

"Who says it stolen? Maybe the kids dug it up themselves."

"Two drug addicts own a house in upstate New York, dig up a king's ransom in 1940s money, jump the border with it and sell it to a fence in Canada?"

"*Mon Chris du tabarnak.* Who cares who they were? You asked for old money, here is old money. At a discount. Untraceable, and it's yours for the low, low price of ten-K. What do you say?"

I turned to Russ and said quietly in an aside, "If I take this money back to the '90s, there would be two identical sets of this collection. I would have to find a buyer, some collector somewhere, and since it's stolen, any collector would be sure to check the serial numbers. For certain, I'd get caught."

"Maybe it's stolen money now, but not back in the '90s," Russ said. "Who's to say the guy who it was stolen from didn't buy it from you in the first place?"

"Hey, I don't care. Take it or leave it. There's at least 400 grand in old bills and coins, maybe more. It could be worth millions to collectors. I just want to unload it and go home."

"Ok, alright. I'm running out of time, so I guess I need to take what I can find. Will you take a check?"

"What do I look like, an idiot? I may be small, but my brain is full size, bigger than yours."

"Ok, ok, five grand cash," I said. When he agreed immediately, I started to think I should have bargained lower.

"Wait for me here. I'll go to the bank and be back in about an hour. Help yourself to some leftover lobster rolls."

14

After returning from the bank and settling up with I.M. King, I headed to the Jersey Lodge to saddle up to the computer in the upstairs loft. The plan was to search for viable companies into which I would invest this money, should I in fact be able to go back in time.

However, being a formerly tax-challenged lobster sternman, I never really had much interest in the stock market. My entire knowledge was gained via the occasional five minute segments about the economy on the nightly news. Even they were spotty at best and centered on how stock x or y was doing and what effect bond rates were having on the economy.

Sure, I knew that Microsoft stock was way up, Amazon was making Bezos a zillionaire, and Buffet the stock broker, not the pot smoking singer, became one of the richest men in America via stocks, while some other guy names Soros had destroyed economies with his speculations. But how all this came about was still a mystery to me. So I did what anyone else would do in the information age, I googled it.

Thinking I would need to target the mid to late 1980s and search out companies like Microsoft, Apple and Google, what I found was surprising.

I stumbled upon an old website extolling the virtues of Google, saying only nine companies had performed better over the past (at that time) nine years. There was a graph showing how stocks like Priceline had increased over four thousand five hundred percent from August 2004 thru August 2013. After checking several times, I was convinced the figures were genuine. Priceline's stock price did increase over an astounding four thousand five hundred percent during that time, from twenty dollars in 2004 to nine hundred forty dollars in August 2013. The graph showed ten thousand dollars invested on August 18, 2004, would have been worth four hundred sixty five thousand one hundred and fifty dollars on August 19, 2013, not including dividends.

The site listed twenty such companies, with the company ranked twentieth on the list having gained six hundred thirty three percent. Google was ranked number ten after its stock price "only" increased by nine hundred and eight percent. Only. Phew!

And the beauty was, the prices of the stocks the website listed, at least the top ten, had risen even further since 2013. A lot further. Some even doubling or tripling or more.

Since some of these stocks were listed on the sheet Lawyer Peggy had given me of stocks Mrs. M had sold, it became obvious she knew her stock market.

Going all the way back to the 1980s now seemed foolish. Microsoft was no doubt a great deal in the 1980s, but Apple from 2004 to 2013 increased over three thousand percent, and Google wasn't even listed until August 2004. This showed how I would need to go back no further than about a decade and a half, say sometime in 2004, to enjoy tremendous gains.

I checked further and saw that Amazon's stock price in 2004 was only about forty dollars, increasing to over sixteen hundred dollars in 2018, also making 2004 a good year to invest.

It became obvious I shouldn't have bothered to make a deal with I.M. King from Ottawa. I might even be able to take my current currency back, although maybe I could try to sell the old money and make a profit. After all, I needed all the money I could muster.

As I didn't know what resources would be available once I got back to 2004, I printed out the chart with the intent of taking it with me. I crawled into the storage space at the top of the stairs and peeled back some unassuming boxes and suitcases until I found the one I was looking for. The old cardboard box the computer came in was filled with knickknacks and the LL Beans knapsack with all the cash I had stored up for the trip. I opened it, slid the graph inside with the old and new money, then zipped it shut and put the other boxes and suitcases back on top. I was only just finishing when I heard loud pounding. Someone was at the downstairs door.

I managed to extricate myself from the crawlspace and shut the door behind me in record time. Good thing, for as soon as I did, two men in dark suits, white shirts, and thin black ties had already made their way up the first set of stairs and started up the second level leading to the loft.

"May I help you?" I asked. I stood at the top of the stairwell, blocking the upper entrance to the apartment. This kept the strange men in black below me, halfway up.

"I'm Special Agent Robert Carpenter and this is Very Special Agent Steve Catlin." As he said this, a grin spread across his face.

"Very Special Agent?" I said.

"Never you mind," 'Very' Special Agent Steve Catlin said. "It's an inside anecdote. We have more serious matters to attend to. We're with the Treasury Department and we'd like to ask you a few questions."

"What about?"

"May we come in?"

"It seems you're already in. No doubt with a search warrant in your pocket or a made up excuse claiming probable cause."

"Now why would you say that?"

"I guess it's a distrust of men in black suits claiming to be from the Treasury Department." I didn't budge, and at six foot five, two hundred and thirty pounds, I did present an immovable object, even more so with the advantage of having the high ground.

"We seem to be getting off on the wrong foot," Catlin said. "We only want to ask a couple questions."

"Shoot."

Carpenter reached into his pocket and pulled out a photo. "Do you recognize this man?"

The man in question had straggly hair and a few days' growth of beard which made him appear a lot different than when he was here a few days ago, but it was unmistakably I.M. King. "Never seen him before. Why, is he a criminal?"

"We have reason to believe he might be involved in the disappearance of some mid-last century money found in upstate New York. You wouldn't know anything about that, would you?"

"No. Why would I?"

"Well, we have reports he was seen in the area this past week. We also have a copy of a classified ad you ran offering to pay cash for old money. Putting two and two together, we think he might have tried to sell you his stolen cache. So again, do you know this man?"

"No, never seen him before." I lied.

"Do you mind if we have a look around?"

"Do you have a warrant?"

"Now why would you ask that?"

"We've been over this. I have an innate distrust of men in black suits claiming to be from the Treasury Department, particularly those who invite themselves into the privacy of my own home, unannounced and without a search warrant or probable cause."

"We can go get a search warrant if that's what you want."

"If you want to search my house, then I guess that's what you'll need to do."

Very Special Agent Steve Catlin smiled and nodded his head. "Ok, then. Stay here and we'll be back."

"Not gonna happen. I'm going back down to camp to eat dinner. I'm starved."

"Where's your camp?"

"About a quarter mile down the road. Dirt road, past the church and cemetery. If you want me, that's where I'll be."

"Cemetery? We can't stop you, but we'll be in touch." The two men turned, walked back down the stairs and out the door.

"Have a good day, boys. Don't get lost."

"You can count on it, Mr. Millard."

15

I hurried down to camp and gathered anything I thought I might need, including my old driver's license from 2004 that I kept in a pile with all the other old documents I couldn't bring myself to throw away. I stuffed into a bag my social security card, some snacks and, just in case, a couple boxes each of Crystal Light grape and strawberry energy drink, along with a couple boxes of fruit punch and anything else I could think of that might help me once I arrived at my new time destination. I said goodbye to Russ without elaborating and headed back up to the Jersey Lodge.

Even though it had started to rain, heavy at times, it was time to go. Now or never. I only hoped Vrill had finished the time machine enough for me to jump back to 2004, away from the Feds, and get all this underway.

I parked my car out back behind the barn, hidden from view. I used the rear entrance upstairs to gather the old money and my list of stocks to buy. I packed all this and a few extra changes of clothes into my well-used knapsack, and was about to bring it out from the crawlspace when I heard someone coming up the stairs. I quickly put everything back under boxes, hiding it as best I could.

Exiting the crawl space on my hands and knees, I closed the door behind me and was relieved to see Vrill peeking his head around the corner. For whatever reason, I still had my iPhone in my left hand.

"Why do you do that?" Vrill asked as he began to climb the stairs.

"Do what?" I asked. Did Vrill know I was rummaging around in the crawl space? Did he know what I was hiding in there, and what I was up to?

"Scratch your neck like that. Isn't that an insult in some cultures?"

"Oh that," I said, relieved. "I don't know, I didn't realize I was doing it. Anyway, what's up?"

"I hate to ask, but I could use a bit more money. I need a few more parts."

A passing car caught my attention. I turned to look out the window behind me and was happy to see it wasn't the Feds returning. It was then Vrill's words sunk it. Was the time machine not finished? If my plan is going to work, I needed Vrill to be confident his project would be one hundred percent ready. "Oh? What do you need?"

"The problem I'm working on now is factoring in the earth's rotation and wobble. This is important because we don't want our time traveler to end up in the middle of the Sudan if he wants to go to Miami.

"I've worked out the best way to keep time travel terrestrial; in other words, a time traveler doesn't need to shoot off into space for the system to work. This is important since the earth is traveling through the solar system at about thirty kilometers per second— that would be about nineteen miles per second, or about 67,000 miles per hour. If we missed our target by just a half hour, it would put our traveler out into unfriendly space 33,500 miles away from earth. Not a good thing; we wouldn't want that to happen. It was a tough one to determine, but I've managed to find a way to keep a time traveler from the need to leave earth."

I nervously looked out the window. Vrill was on another one of his rolls again, and there'd be no stopping him now. I had to admit it was refreshing to see someone so enthusiastic about his work. But now was not a good time.

"I did this by basing time travel calculations on light, not earth. Earth might travel at 67,000 miles per hour, but light travels at over 186,000 miles per second. Do the math. You'd have to travel great distances through time at that speed to miss our target by half a second, much less half an hour.

"But I still need to factor in how much the rotation has slowed or sped up over time, and based on historical figures, predict where a certain arrival point will be at that particular time given the earth's wobble on its access.

"In theory, going back in time would be easier to control, as we have historical data for it. NASA has all this on their computers and online should anyone ever need it. Believe me, I've made good use of this information and have backward time travel all calculated. Future travel, not so much."

I spontaneously let out a sigh of relief and immediately hoped Vrill didn't notice. He didn't.

"At best, we can make an educated guess about these variables going forward, which might not always be completely accurate due to unknown variables, including leap years and variations in the atomic clock. What if earth's poles change, as some scientists theorize might happen someday? Without first going ahead in time, we have no way of knowing these types of things. All we can do is make best guesses based on current and historical data and hope it works."

"So, you're saying we're all set up to go back in time, but we need a few more parts if someone wanted to go forward in time?" I asked.

"Yes, that's basically it."

"How about rain? Would heavy rain like we're having now affect it?"

"No, it shouldn't," Vrill said. He thought for a moment, "Why?"

"No reason—this rain outside got me to thinking."

"As long as we're inside, it shouldn't make any difference," Vrill replied.

"I have one more question, for now," I said, hoping for a quick answer. "I was watching TV the other night and there was a show about time travel. A guy on the show said he used to work on a government project where tests were being conducted at a facility on an island near New York City. Do you know anything about this?"

"Sounds like sensationalist TV to me," Vrill said.

"Maybe, but he did bring up an interesting point. The guy said the project scientists had already sent many people on a time journey, but not one of them survived. He said they all ended up dead, embedded in rocks, or walls, or something like that, killed instantly upon arrival at the time travel destination. Could that happen?"

"I see what you're getting at. First, how would anyone involved in the project know that all the people they sent on a time travel ended up embedded in a rock wall unless they time traveled with them? This would, by definition, make the claim false. If someone went with them and came back to tell the tale, then the 'fact' no one survived would immediately be proven false. The people on those shows should really think things through.

"However, the scenario he talked about has certainly been a concern of mine and you can rest assured I made compensations to keep it from happening. The computer has algorithms built in to keep the vortex from pointing at a solid object. I call it a solid object deflector program, making it impossible for the vortex to end up in things like rocks and buildings.

"I've also made vortexes 'allergic' to water. They will always veer away from bodies of water more than two meters wide and one cm deep. We don't want people drowning. If we can't guarantee this, I doubt there would be very many people willing to take a trip, now would there?"

"No, I'm sure that would be comforting to know," I said.

"Our time traveler will be unaware of any changes in trajectory. Jumps will appear to be instant, no matter how long they take. It will be like falling asleep on a train or plane at the beginning of a long journey, and waking up upon arrival."

"Cool," I said, looking at my watch.

"Even better," Vrill said, gaining momentum. "Travelers won't age during jumps. The theory is, time travel will reverse aging by a tiny amount, no matter which direction in time is traveled. Most often it will be unnoticeable, although depending on the length of time traveled it might become noticeable. Jumping 1,000 years forward or back might result in a somewhat noticeable reverse aging."

"Ok then, what do you need?" I said, thinking the Treasury men in black could show up at any time.

"I need some hardware and connectors to rig up another device to make scientifically sound predictions of these unknown variables. Plus I know a website with some algorithms I need. The guy says he doesn't want to charge for them, but he's a genius, and broke, and asking for donations, and I thought, well—"

"Ok, ok, how much?"

16

With Vrill happily refinanced and on his way up to Sparky's Electronics Warehouse in Brunswick, and with the law closing in, I knew it was now or never. As I watched from the upstairs apartment window while Vrill started to pull out of the driveway, a blur of passing cars caught my attention. A black sedan led the way, with a sheriff close behind, whizzing past, temporarily blocking Vrill from leaving. The entourage headed towards the camp road and even though I only managed a quick glance, I was certain the two men in front were those badges from the Treasury Department.

Sure enough, they entered the camp road but instead of continuing on, they stopped, backed out, turned around, and headed back towards the Jersey Lodge.

I dove back into the crawlspace, knocking boxes out of the way, not caring where they fell. As fast as I was able, I grabbed my knapsack full of money and plans.

When I emerged and looked back out the window, I could see not one, but two sheriff's cars had arrived and two deputies had joined the Treasury men. They began pounding on the downstairs door, trying to open it, prevented by the security locks Vrill activated by habit when he left.

I had to act fast before they could surround the house and cut me off. I slipped out the back apartment door, across the balcony, ran down the stairs and stealthily made my way to the back barn door, gaining entry unnoticed but soaking wet from the rain.

Once inside, I was relieved the front windows had been left closed with curtains drawn. I sat my iPhone on the computer table next to the return device, and once again observed how much they looked alike. I'd have to make sure not to mix them up. Instead of putting it back in my pocket, I slid my iPhone a couple inches further away, just in case.

I turned on the computer and waited impatiently for it to start. Once it warmed up, I switched on the lasers and mirror wheels, which made a loud whirring noise that I hoped was being drowned out by the rain outside.

To my surprise, as everything began warming up, the Chamber Brothers song "Time has come today" began to play through the computer speakers. Vrill must have been listening to it at full volume before he left. In the confusion, I couldn't figure out how to shut it off.

Instead, I tried to ignore it while I did my best calculations as to what would land me back in time to 2004, and just as I thought I had it figured out, the front barn door slid open. All four officers had their guns drawn and pointed at me. "Freeze!"

Proving Einstein's theory of how time is relative, the next few seconds seemed to take an eternity. I kept my eyes on the handguns pointed in my direction as I reached for the return device on the computer table and discretely shoved it into my pocket. I then stood frozen, looking like a deer in the headlights. All four lawmen kept their steely gazes and their weapons trained on me.

What should I do? Would these men shoot me over some stolen old money?

With cowbells in the Chambers song simulating the tick-tock of a clock blasting through the speakers, adding more confusion to this bizarre situation, I began to back towards the vortex.

The whirring sound behind me was getting louder. I turned to look at it, then turned back to look at the men in front of me. Two strangers had joined the fray behind them. Something about them didn't look right. Something menacing.

"Don't do anything stupid," Special Agent Carpenter said. "Put down your backpack, get down on the floor and put your hands behind your head."

As I turned toward the mirror wheel again, I could hear a man's voice yell, "Now!" That one word sparked an inner trigger I didn't realize I had and one which I had no control over. My mind told me to do what the officers were telling me, but my body moved towards the vortex.

Everything was happening in slow motion. I thought I heard someone behind me yell, "Stop or I'll shoot," but it didn't sound normal.

Was it my imagination? Two more steps and I would make it into the vortex. I heard a pop and a ping.

One more step. A thud, more whirring, louder. I had made it in.

As the psychedelic musical break in the Chamber Brothers' song blared at ear-splitting volume, complete with screaming and laughing, there was a blinding flash of light, a sonic boom, and a massive shockwave, followed by silence. The room filled with smoke as the apparatus ground to a halt. The men stood stunned, for a moment unable to move.

The event knocked out electricity in over half the Harpswell peninsula.

17

The next thing I knew, I found myself half sitting, half lying on solid ground, pavement perhaps, awkwardly leaning against my pack. Everything was dark and tinted green as if it was night and I might have been looking through infrared night vision goggles. At first I thought my heart was pounding but soon realized it was my entire body. I was being beaten by strong blasts of air, the frequency of which was increasing.

The air smelled like peanut butter, or bacon, or both, and my mouth was filled with a strange metallic taste. I couldn't move a muscle, stuck in that uncomfortable position, paralyzed. The air blasts turned rapid fire then suddenly stopped and when they did, my surroundings returned to normal daytime color.

The smell and taste dissipated too, and for the first time I was able to move. Despite being soaked from the rain just an instant before I was now completely dry.

I still had my knapsack with me, as well as both legs, arms and all fingers. I didn't know about my toes; as far as I could tell they were still in my New Balance sneakers.

There were also tiny shards of glass on the ground around me. I guessed the deputy's shot missed me and hit one of the mirrors.

I was in an alleyway somewhere between brick buildings. One end was closed, guarded by filthy old dumpsters. A rickety fire escape climbed up one side of the alley appearing as if certain death or injury would result should anyone need to use it.

I rose to my feet, dizzy and unsteady, but at least my breathing returned to normal. I slouched down, picked up my pack, steadied myself and headed toward the open end of the alley.

As I exited into the street my first thought was, did the broken mirror knock Vrill's machine off target and land me in the middle of a Hollywood set? The street was lined with old cars, antique street lamps and power lines, a cafe, newsstands, and what could be a boarding house or cheap hotel.

I couldn't put into words what I was expecting to find; in fact I hadn't given it much thought, but whatever it was this couldn't be it. While looking around for movie cameras, a movie star I might recognize, or a golf cart ferrying people around, I found nothing of the kind.

After making my way over to a street side newsstand & cigar shop, I approached the burly, gruff-talking man behind the counter. "I know this is going to sound strange, but, well, where am I?"

"New York."

New York? I took a moment to consider this. Why New York? Must be the wobble thing in the earth's orbit Vrill talked about. No wonder it looked like a movie set. "What day is it?"

"Monday, August 21."

"What year?"

"What do you mean, what year? Are you fractured or something? Did you get injured in the war?"

"No, I fell and hit my head over there. I'm a little confused right now," I started to point towards the alleyway but decided against it.

The burly newsstand clerk smiled for the first time. "Ah, yes, so many boys get hurt over there. Welcome back. Do you need a doctor?"

"No, thanks, I think I'll be ok if I can just figure out a few things. What year is this?"

"1944."

"Excuse me?" I looked down and noticed the New York Times. The headline splashed across the front page, written in all capital letters read, "THE OFFICIAL PEARL HARBOR REPORTS". Photos of three military officers appeared below, and below them was a picture of three more men dressed sharply in suits.

"1944. Did the bump on the head hurt your ears, too?"

"No, thanks, it's just, well, never mind." It occurred to me what 'over there' meant, and it didn't mean the alleyway around the corner. World War Two must have been raging 'over there'. I remembered my grandfather singing songs about the 'boys over there'.

The clerk nodded, glad to be able to help this brave soldier back from the war and all mixed up. "Welcome home son. I heard it was really bad over there."

I returned the nod and walked away, picking up speed until I got back to the ally where I arrived. 1944? Not 2004? I need to get out of here.

I turned out my pockets and searched the ground looking for the return device so I could go home, damn the consequences. Whatever the Feds had in store for me couldn't be worse than this.

All I could find was my iPhone, which I remembered being on the computer table next to the return device before I left. Did I grab the wrong one? I dropped to my knees and flung open my pack in desperate hope I'd put it in there. I hadn't.

I tore through my clothes, every possible pocket, every fold in my clothing. Still nothing. After several minutes of futile searching, I slumped to the ground, engulfed in a strong mixture of terror and despair.

Now what?

I reached over and reopened my knapsack. Everything I had packed was still there, including my stock list and the old and new money. I picked up an old bill, read the date, and was relieved I had, indeed, met and did business with I.M. King. It read 1942.

I could put the old money to use here, if only to get a room in one of these old boarding houses.

18

For twelve dollars a week the no-name boarding house offered an old, square, wooden room, no windows, a lumpy bed, small closet, and a noisy, ineffective table fan, its frayed power cord plugged into a single wall socket. The bathtub and toilet were down the hall, shared with whoever else might have rented a room on this floor. The furnishings were a far cry from the luxury aboard the Miss Louise, but it was the best I could do for now. I resolved that if I end up being stuck here, I will need to seek out better lodgings later.

Earlier, while checking in with the wall-eyed, unshaven, unwashed, singlet attired clerk downstairs, I noticed a ragged "Dewey or Don't We" poster on the wall. A dark-haired, mustachioed man with eyebrows connected in the middle stared out from the poster. The words "Thomas E. Dewey" were printed across the bottom.

Meanwhile, behind the clerk, a crackling radio about the size of an apartment Frigidaire buzzed out a voice admonishing people "Don't swap horses in midstream". The clerk hardly took notice.

Next up was food. It was getting late in the day and I was famished. Before I felt safe enough to leave, I took the Swiss army knife out of my pack, rolled back the ragged piece of carpet under the bed, and managed to loosen a floorboard enough so when I gave it a mighty tug, it peeled back. It revealed an empty space big enough to hide my belongings. No wonder the floorboards creaked so much. After grabbing out some cash and flattening the pack inside the hole, I draped the carpet over it, hiding it as well as I could. Since I couldn't replace the board, it found a new home standing in the corner behind the cloth wardrobe. As long as no one moved the bed and walked on the floor underneath, or tried to remove the rug, what little I had should remain out of sight.

After a quick trip to the WC down the hall and a splash of water on my face, I headed out to try the diner I had seen not far away up the street.

As I passed the newsstand, I noticed an 'I Want You' poster partly tacked to the wall, flapping in the breeze. The white-haired, goateed avatar of Uncle Sam with his star clad top hat pointed sternly at anyone who might be caught looking at it.

After seeing a neon sign for Tony's Diner, I found a booth near the window and settled in. The place was empty except for the cook in the back and the waitress busying herself wiping down the counter.

While looking around, I thought this place could be a set in an old movie. Red cushioned booths stretched along the windows on three sides. In the center, a long counter formed a barrier to the kitchen in back, lined with sentries of red cushioned swivel stools.

Red and white tiles checkered the floor, their colors matching the booths and swivel stools. Tucked up against the window in my booth was a glass sugar canister topped by tin, the old-fashioned kind with a hole and a trap door to keep the flies from getting in. A small pitcher, filled with coffee cream, sat behind a glass ashtray. The salt and pepper shakers were solid enough to use as weapons. The handy napkin dispenser rested against tin clips holding up a laminated menu with cartoon drawings of cowboys and Indians waging battles amid words that described the most often ordered dishes. I couldn't help but think how it wouldn't be out of place in an episode of *Leave it to Beaver.*

While staring out the window, trying to figure out what to do, my thoughts were broken by the waitress.

I looked up and was quickly taken in. There was something about her eyes. They were almost—alien. Two emeralds floating on bright white clouds. Dark at the edges, the emeralds subtly lightened as they progressed towards the center until they crashed into her coal-black pupils.

I couldn't break away from her gaze. I sat staring, mesmerized until she finally broke the silence. I didn't even realize she spoke when she said, "I'm Karla, what can I get ya, sailor?"

When at first I didn't answer, she said, "Jiminy Cricket stranger, you're not from around here are you? Nobody around here dresses like that."

"No, actually I'm not." For the first time, I looked away from her hypnotic eyes. I could see she had a striking resemblance to Cookie, Blondie and Dagwood's daughter in the comic strip. Her bright smile, impressive figure and 1940s hairstyle clinched the impression.

"Well, ya going to order something or stare at my nose?"

Maybe it was the time travel, or perhaps I was tired, but I found myself stammering for words. "Your nose? What? No, I, um, coffee please."

"You look like something's troubling you. Is everything ok?"

"Yes, thanks."

I tried to regain my composure. I didn't want to let on this could possibly be the worst day of my life. If I couldn't get home, what would happen to the shelter? What would happen to me? "It's only jet lag."

"Jet lag? What's that?"

The question caught me by surprise. Perhaps the phrase hadn't been coined yet. "It's an idiom. It means being tired after a long trip."

"Oh yeah? Did you just get back from over there?"

"No, I just got here from another long trip."

"From where?"

"I came down from Maine."

Karla studied me from head to toe. "That is a long trip. Do all people in Maine dress like you do?"

I was wearing my New Balance running shoes, Levi jeans, and a Red Sox 2013 World Series Championship t-shirt, an official one Russ gave me, which included a holographic sticker on the left shoulder. It was then I realized almost everyone else I had seen since my arrival was dressed as if they came straight out of an old black & white gangster movie. Black suits and ties, pressed white shirts, and most of them either wore or carried some style of fedora. "Some of us do."

"What brings you here from Maine?"

"It's a long story, and you wouldn't believe me if I told you."

With no customers to keep her busy, Karla slid into the seat across from me. "Oh yeah? Try me."

"I'm not sure it would be the wisest thing for me to do."

"And why is that?"

"Because you might think I was a nut case."

"I already do, so why not humor me?"

I began by telling her I used to be a lobster fisherman but inherited a lot of money and retired. Since then, I had donated a lot of my time and used a lot of the inheritance to fund a shelter for abused women and children. "I left Maine to try and raise more funds for the shelter. Something happened out of my control and I ended up here by mistake. Now that I'm here, some of the investment money I brought with me is relatively useless."

"Why? Is it German—or Japanese?"

"No, US dollars, but it might as well be foreign."

"I still don't understand. Why would American money be ok in Maine and useless in New York?"

I tentatively tested the waters, mentioning how it's not a matter of where, but when.

"You lost me."

I hesitated. This was the hard part. As I started to tell her I was from the future, 2018 to be exact, and how I came here by mistake in a time machine, another customer walked in, a well-dressed man in his late thirties or early forties. He had a sinister aura about him, one which I thought he could use to get work as a James Cagney double in the movies. "Tell me Karla, does everyone here dress like him?"

"Of course they do. How else would they dress?" As she got up to leave, she turned back to me, "I have to get to work. You might be the strangest person I've ever met and I don't believe a word you say, but this sure beats the usual chatter."

I had to agree. I watched intently, once again mesmerized as she brought a menu to the new customer in the next booth.

"What can I get ya, Frankie?"

"The usual, doll."

"One black cup a joe comin' up." Karla winked at me and turned towards the counter to fetch the coffee pot.

Francesco Marciano, aka Frankie the Mole, was a second generation immigrant from Sicily and a top earner for the Napoli crime family in New York City's Little Italy. He caught the wink and turned to see for whom it was meant. Seeing me, he also must have thought I was a strange sight, for in his world of suits and ties he'd never seen anyone dressed in jeans and a colorful t-shirt embossed with such elaborate writing.

I gave him a cautious grin and a nod. I sensed right away this man was not one to be trifled with.

Frankie held my stare for a minute, shook his head almost unperceptively, and turned back to his table without saying a word.

After pouring Frankie's coffee, Karla offered to do the same for me, eliciting a "thanks" and, "What's the special today?"

"Whatever your heart desires."

"What would you recommend the best thing a lobsterman from Maine should eat today?"

"Our Jolly Fryer out back can slop together just about anything, as long as he has the ingredients."

"How about steak and eggs?"

"Steak and eggs? It's four in the afternoon."

"Yeah, call it brunch."

"Brunch?" Karla looked at her watch.

"It's a portmanteau of the words breakfast and lunch. And I literally do not know why I know that. I must've picked it up somewhere along the way."

"Ok sailor, I know what brunch is. This is more like lunper. A portmanteau of the words lunch and supper. I might not have finished school, but I do a lot of reading you know."

"Sorry, I didn't mean anything by it. A 'lunper' of steak and eggs would be great if you can."

"Steak and eggs coming up." Karla turned toward the counter and as she walked away she yelled through a window to the grill out back. "Steak and eggs Fryer Tuckles! Make 'em tasty for our guest who came all the way here from future Maine to eat your cooking."

Moments after Karla put through my order, the unmistakable crackling sound of a hot grill being put to use was followed by a smell wafting through the air of melting lard. Soon after, the splash of cold meat hitting hot griddle caused me to swallow involuntarily as I anticipated my first meal in 1944.

19

After more small talk with Karla, which elicited a half dozen stares from Frankie, I returned to my room. After first checking that my bag was still in place with all its contents, including the money, I flopped down on my lumpy bed. What a great find this was, which led me to my first thought of the night: I need to find better accommodations, pronto. After all, thanks to I.M. King and poor aim by the Cumberland County Sheriff's deputy, I have enough money.

I resolved to start looking around in the morning to see what was available as well as see if I could track down a stockbroker. 'As long as I'm here,' I thought, 'I might as well at least try to go through with the original plan.' It may even work out better, for I would be gaining a much larger head start on any stocks I might recognize.

My mind turned to my new friend Karla. She had a way about her. Perhaps I could talk her into showing me around town if it wouldn't be too forward of me.

Lost in these thoughts, I could've sworn I heard my iPhone ringtone. Couldn't be though, not here, not now. I only bought the thing because my Nokia 6300 had stopped working. I hadn't quite figured out all the new phone was capable of doing but I had no trouble finding sports scores with it. Sometimes I was able to catch live games aboard the Miss Louise while getting away from the crowd.

Strange, but I heard it again. I rummaged through my pack and pulled it out. Sure enough, someone was calling me. I tried several times to answer, none of which worked. After only a few more rings, the iPhone seemed to answer itself. I could hear people talking with what sounded like a two-way conversation, but it was muffled and impossible to make out what they were saying. One of the voices sounded like me, but of course it couldn't be. Creepy, huh?

I tried to break into the conversation with no success, eventually realizing whoever it was on the line couldn't hear me. Must be some odd interference coming from somewhere. Then it occurred to me: it's 1944. The world is embroiled in WWII. Maybe my phone is picking up some kind of surveillance, radar, or some sort of espionage chatter.

Never mind, it's probably just a fluke. Just the same, it *is* 1944. WWII *is* in fact still raging on. It might mean Vrill's great-grandfather, at this very minute, could be working on his bell thing Vrill talked about. What did he call it? Dee Glockah? Something like that.

As crazy as it might be to pull off, maybe, just maybe, Vrill's great-grandfather would be able to find a way for me to go home. If I can remember enough about what young Vrill told me to be able to help his great-grandfather finish his work, I might be able to barter this knowledge for a jump through time back where I belong.

Of course, I'm American and Vrill's great-grandfather is a Nazi SS officer, so it might be nigh on impossible. Plus, he's somewhere in Poland. I would need to find a way to get from New York to France or England, then somehow get across many miles behind enemy lines, and somehow locate a secret Nazi base so I, an American, sworn enemy of the Fatherland, could meet up with an SS officer and try to convince him to trade my scant second-hand knowledge of time travel for a ride home.

To top it off, I don't speak German.

I guess I have to admit the odds are not exactly in my favor. In fact, they're humongous—make that incredibly, nigh even impossibly against me. Then again, I traveled from the year 2018 and now lay on a lumpy bed somewhere in 1944 New York. What were the odds of that happening?

How else would I get home?

There goes my phone again. What's going on? Again I tried to answer, again it kept ringing until someone else answered and began talking to someone else. I tried again to break into the conversation, but again either they couldn't hear me or just plain ignored me.

When the indiscernible conversation ended abruptly, it left me yelling into the phone, begging for someone to answer. When they didn't, I flopped back down on Mr. Lumpy and absentmindedly opened Google on the smartphone to the sports scores. The Indians beat the Red Sox seven to six in thirteen innings. Mike Ryba took the loss for the Sox. Who is Mike Ryba? Must be someone they called up from Portland or Pawtucket.

While scrolling through the box score to see how Peedee and Mookie did, I noticed their names were conspicuously absent. When I read how Bobby Doer played second base that night, it hit me—what I'm looking at is the score of today's game; August 21, 1944.

Being in New York, I decided, what the heck—let's type in Yankees and see what happens. Turns out they beat the Tigers five to one. There wasn't a single familiar name on the Yankees roster in the box score. Hersh Martin? Russ Derry? This is way too strange.

20

During an uncomfortable, oft-interrupted sleep, the earworm 'Mana Mana' crawled around my brain over and over. I can't tell you how difficult it is to try and get to sleep in a new bed, in a new place, in a new year, with that tune driving me to insanity. It was no help reminding myself that Sesame Street used the song even though it was written for an Italian softcore porn movie about sex in Sweden. I'll never think of the Sesame Street sketch in the same way again. By the time the sun came up I wanted to pull my hair out.

Finally, an hour or so after sunrise, I couldn't take any more tossing and turning and decided to get an early start.

At that time in the morning the bathroom was all mine so I put it to good use. It ended with a shave and a splash, the closest thing I could muster to a shower. Man, I was jonesing for my power shower back home. It must have worked, though, for my earworm was gone.

Somewhere in the distance, perhaps from the reception desk downstairs, I could hear a faint song crackling through the radio. I could've been wrong, but I thought I heard a woman singing, "Gonna wash that man right out of my hair," a song my mother used to sing during my bath time back when I was a terrible little two-year-old.

Fitting.

While dressing, I decided what the hell, might as well try to find a broker to invest the old money I brought from I.M. King. Who knows? If I'm able to find a way home, perhaps money well invested now might even serve me as well or better than if I had landed in 2004.

Armed with newly acquired confidence born from my brand-new plan, I grabbed my LL Beans knapsack full of cash and headed out to try and find a New York City broker during the dog days of summer, drawing many strange looks from the suit and hat-wearing men and swirling below-the-knee skirt-wearing women on the streets.

A couple hours later I had to admit I had no idea what I was doing. If there were any brokers who had hung a shingle outside their front door to announce their craft, I didn't see any, at least not in this part of town. I had never been in New York City, and certainly not in this time period. I was hopelessly lost more than once.

Tired, but not discouraged, I managed to find my way back to Tony's Diner for a bite to eat. The added attraction was that my favorite waitress might be in there too. I wasn't disappointed, although she seemed to be occupied with a couple of other waitresses I hadn't seen before.

One of them took my order and while eating my breakfast I thought of yet another brilliant plan. It must be my day for creativity.

I called Karla over and asked her to join me for a minute—I had something important to ask.

Initially hesitant, the impending important question must have piqued her interest. She made her way over and slid into the booth opposite me. "What's on your mind, sailor?"

"I was just wondering if I can hire you to show me around town."

"I'm not that kind of girl." Karla gave me stink-eye and started to slide back out of the booth.

Her reaction was like a slap in the face. Grin gone, I scrambled to save the situation. "I'm sorry, I didn't mean it that way. All I meant was I am new here, you live here and know your way around, and I would very much enjoy your company. I'm looking for a stockbroker. Would you happen to know anyone I might contact to find one? I offered to hire you because I didn't want you to lose wages if you were to take off work and help me."

"Why didn't you say that in the first place, dummy? You made it sound like I was some dumb skirt looking for a cheap date. It would be my pleasure to show you around. Let's go."

"You mean now? Don't you have to work?"

"Nah, Margie and Ellen are here, they don't need me. Normally today is my day off, but I had nothing better to do so I came in. There are no customers here, and, well, now I have something better to do."

The change in Karla's demeanor was immediate, as if she'd been waiting for some excitement in her life, or at least something to do rather than hanging around Tony's Diner on her day off. I guess to her I seemed harmless enough; in fact, I get the feeling she had begun taking a liking to me, the stranger from future Maine.

When Karla looked at me, I could tell the wheels were turning in her head. 'Do I have a girlish crush on this strange man from far away?' she thought. If she did, it would be her first time. 'Nah, it couldn't be.'

I paid my tab, slid my knapsack out from under the table, and off we went, disappearing into the busy streets of Little Italy, Manhattan.

21

There was a rather uncomfortable silence for the first block of our walk. Karla had asked me what I was carrying in my 'suitcase', and my answer was so cryptic it came out sounding like a snub, hurting her feelings. From that point on it seemed like neither of us could figure out what to say.

As we passed an Italian bakery with the smell of freshly baked cannoli wafting into the street, I finally broke the silence, although my question seemed to deepen the mood. "Tell me about yourself, Karla."

"What would you like to know?"

"Anything. How about, what's your last name?"

"Gingerich," Karla said, without elaborating.

"You mean like Newt Gingrich?"

"Who?"

"The senator? Never mind. Inside joke." I realized Newt was probably an obnoxious rug rat in 1944.

"Well, no, how you pronounced it doesn't sound right. I spell it G I N G E R I C H, it's pronounced ginger-itch."

"Ginger-itch," I said, trying to articulate.

The conversation went still again, this time for another half a block. The area was alive with sounds, though, as the streets were filled with traffic noise. Car horns blared, cabbies yelled obscenities out of their windows at each other, and an occasional radio broadcast could be heard from shops along the way where people had gathered to listen to Edward R. Murrow deliver the latest war news. Between his announcements, it seemed like every radio played the same song, "All day, all night, Marianne, down by the seashore sifting sand."

"How long have you worked at the diner?"

Karla stopped me dead on the sidewalk. By that time we were both sweating in the sweltering Indian summer heat. "Ok, if you want to know about me I'll tell you. I don't know who my parents were. They left me in an orphanage when I was three years old. Old enough to have a name, too young to understand why I was left at an orphanage."

After a slight pause, we began walking again. "I sometimes dream of people who I think might be my parents, but they're just dreams. I have no idea who they were and wouldn't know them if I bumped into them right here on the street."

"Sorry, I didn't mean to bring up bad memories. We can talk about something else if you want."

"No, you got me started. Since you're the first person in my entire life to ask me I'm going to tell you whether you like it or not."

"Please do. Nothing would make me happier than to learn all about—"

"Shut up. If you want to know, don't say anything until I'm done. OK?"

I pursed my lips and nodded to let her know I wouldn't interrupt, and at the same time hand over complete control.

"I hated it there. I don't know why. They were never cruel or abusive. I just, felt," Karla thought for a minute. "Trapped. Like I was in prison.

"I couldn't take it anymore. I ran away after I turned twelve. Looking back, I can see it was a mistake to leave so young. I nearly starved, but there was no way I was going back to that damn orphanage."

She giggled after saying the word 'damn'. "I joined up with some other homeless urchins and became pretty good at surviving on the streets. Hustling, stealing, it all seemed normal."

"A real bad girl."

"Are you going to let me continue, or keep interrupting me?"

"Sorry. Please continue."

"When I was, I don't know, maybe fourteen years old, my girlfriend Margie and I managed to steal a bunch of money from someone who turned out to be one of Don Antonio Napoli's collectors. It was too easy. He had a perversion for young girls and as Margie, who was the same age as me, was distracting him, I climbed into the back of his car and took a sack of money. It was more money than I'd ever seen before and if I got out without being noticed we would have been rich beyond our wildest dreams. But I tripped coming out of the back seat and landed loudly on the sidewalk. My hands slapped down hard on concrete and the noise caught his attention. He started yelling at me to stop. I was so scared I peed my pants. Margie pushed him off her, and we both ran.

"The pervert wanted to kill us. When Don Antonio found out, we thought for certain we were goners. But for whatever reason, he took pity on us, brought us into his home and took care of us. Of course we had to, uh, take care of him too. But it was a small price to pay for not sleeping with the fishes.

"Eventually the boys got tired of us and put us to work running numbers. But we were pretty awful at it so they set us up as waitresses in the diner. Been there ever since. You met Margie today. She took your breakfast order."

I remained silent, waiting politely in case there was more coming.

Karla gave me a long stare. While gauging my reaction, suddenly she seemed to perk up. "See that building over there?"

I followed her point and nodded yes. My lips remained pursed.

"That's the orphanage."

I nodded, again staying silent.

"It's ok, you can talk now." Karla could see my struggle to keep my mouth shut.

"Thank you." I let out a burst of air as if I had been holding my breath. "Yours is the most remarkable story I've ever heard. I still think you're the most beautiful person I've ever met, but now I realize you're also the most amazing person too. Having gone through all you did and still with such a positive attitude. How do you do it?"

"Wow, a man who actually listens to a woman? Are all men in Maine like this?"

"Pfffft. I wouldn't go that far. But I am from the future, remember?"

Karla ignored the last comment. "You know what? When I first met you, I didn't like you. You wear strange clothes, talk with a strange accent, keep saying things with no meaning, then say 'I forgot, never mind'. But the more I get to know you—"

Before she could finish, Frankie the Mole came running across the street to catch up with us, seemingly out of nowhere.

"What are you two lovebirds up to?"

"We're not lovebirds," Karla said in protest and with mock disdain. "What are you doing here?"

"Just making the rounds, taking some bets on tonight's game. Care to make a wager, Maine?" Frankie couldn't remember my name, only that I came from Maine.

I looked at Karla and decided keeping my mouth shut might be my best option at this point, but Frankie forced my hand.

"Do you like sports? How about the Yankees? You're not a milquetoast, are you?"

"I like sports, but I'm a Red Sox fan, not the Yankees."

"Well then, could I talk you into a little wager against them?"

"A bet? Is that what you do, take bets from out of towners?"

"Let's just say it's a side business. Are you in or not?"

I always kept some extra cash in my shirt pocket and pulled out two five dollar bills. I started to say, 'Ok, how about ten bucks on the Mets to win,' but for once I stopped myself from sounding like a fool. The NY Mets hadn't been conceived yet. "How about ten bucks on the Yankees to win."

"Ten bucks? A hundred bucks. Thousands, up to you."

Karla remained quiet. As the men talked about sports and gambling, she absentmindedly stared across the street at an Estee Lauder sign. I noticed it too, and I could've sworn the last e looked like an s. Must be the heat.

"Thousands? Too steep for me. Who are they playing?" I could've sworn I saw drool leaking out of the side of Frankie mouth.

"The Tigers. Newhouser is pitchin' for Detroit. He's their ace this year."

"Their ace, huh? Sounds like you know a lot about baseball. Even though I'm a Sox fan, I'll take ten bucks on the Yankees to win."

I tried to hand Frankie the two fins.

"No, keep it in your pocket. If you win, I'll pay you. If you lose, I know where to find you."

It didn't matter to Frankie he might lose the bet, what mattered more was he had a new lamb to bet with. In fact, he hoped I did win. Build up my confidence a bit, sucker me in for bigger bets later on.

Easy money. "Ten bucks then. We'll settle up tomorrow in Tony's Diner. Ok with you?"

"Ok with me Mr. Marciano."

"Please, call me Frankie. We can be friends, right?"

"Ok, Frankie it is. Go Yanks." I couldn't believe I was saying this.

Frankie cracked a sinister smile. "Don't push it, kid."

Once Frankie walked off, probably to try and find another sucker to bet with, Karla and I continued our walk in relative silence down Center Street from Little Italy to the financial district. It was obvious something was troubling her.

As we neared Wall Street, Karla stopped and gave me a stern look. "I must warn you, Paul. Frankie is one of Don Antonio's men. The Don is a bad, bad man. Whatever you do, don't cross him. Or any of his men."

22

When we reached the financial district, and with neither one of us having any idea what to do next, we wandered into a tall office building to look around. The information directory on the wall in the lobby showed the building housed a number of lawyers and brokers.

"You pick one," I told her.

"Why me?"

"Because I trust you more than anyone I've ever met."

Karla studied the directory and after a few minutes of deliberation pointed to M. Estes, Money Manager, third floor, office #314. "Good name, sounds like he might be trustworthy."

"M. Estes, Money Manager it is," I agreed.

We found an elevator being attended by a young man in uniform and hat. "Third floor please," I said.

"Third floor," the attendant said loudly with a rising tone on floor. He pulled the gate shut and pushed the lever to the up position. The elevator clanked as it lurched upward.

"This is an old building," Karla whispered. "New buildings have buttons in their elevators."

"Third floor," the attendant announced again when the elevator bumped to a stop. He pulled open the gate and let us out, all the while frowning at Karla. Elevator operators were rare in modern day 1944. He was proud to be one of them and glad to have a job.

We searched up and then down the hallway until we found the door to office #314. M. Estes Money Manager was stenciled onto the frosted window. The paint was still wet.

We entered and were greeted by a smartly dressed secretary. "How may we help you?"

"I'm here to invest some money," I said. This caught Karla by surprise. She felt a sudden rush of excitement and decided to play along even though she had no idea what I was up to.

The secretary announced our presence to someone in another office via a button on a wooden box intercom. A garbled response came back, and although I couldn't decipher what was said, the secretary announced, "M. Estes would be happy to see you."

She led us to the office door, opened it and motioned for us to step inside.

"Wait, you're a woman," Karla said.

"Yes, thank you for noticing," M. Estes said. "My name is Marianne Estes, and you are?"

"Stunned," Karla said.

"Paul Millard, it's a pleasure to make your acquaintance," I broke in.

"But your sign," Karla said.

"M. Estes. Yes, I know. Wall Street is a man's world, a real old boys club. It's the only way I can lure people into my office. Most leave as soon as they see I'm not a man. I can assure you I possess all the qualifications necessary and I have an impeccable investment record for all who are brave enough to trust me. Would you like coffee?"

When I answered yes, Marianne nodded towards her secretary who was still standing at the door. The secretary took the hint and disappeared.

Marianne pushed an ashtray across her desk, but as neither of us smoke we ignored it.

"How may I help you?"

"I'd like to buy some stocks and bonds."

"How much would you like to invest?"

"A lot."

"How much is a lot?"

I set my knapsack on Marianne's desk, zipped it open, and for the first time, Karla realized she had been walking down the street with me, unprotected, with a backpack full of cash. Her reaction let Marianne know she was unaware of this.

"At least a few hundred thousand dollars."

Marianne didn't seem fazed. "And what are your goals for investing so much money?"

"I want to make sure all my descendants are well enough off they don't need to work."

"An admirable goal," Marianne said. "What is your plan?"

The secretary returned with cups and saucers of coffee, along with cream and sugar, all balanced on a silver tray. She laid one set each in front of us.

"I don't have a plan, per se. Stocks and bonds I guess. Whatever would help me achieve my goals."

"What kind of bonds? War bonds?"

"Government bonds?" I said. My response was more of a question than a statement.

The secretary held the pitcher of cream in front of me, silently asking if I wanted her to add some to my coffee. I smiled and nodded yes.

She poured the cream then proceeded to make the same gestures to the women. They both waved her away.

"City, state, or federal government bonds?"

"Federal," I said, gaining confidence. "I guess with some war bonds too."

Karla sat and watched all this unfold, not knowing what to think. She wouldn't have guessed this strange man sitting next to her who claimed to be from the future would suddenly pull out hundreds of thousands of dollars as if by magic.

"May I suggest a seventy-five, twenty, five allocation? Seventy-five percent stocks, twenty percent bonds and keep five percent in cash?" Marianne said.

"You seem to know what you're doing," I replied. "Can you show me a list of stocks or something?"

Marianne slid open one of her desk drawers and produced a sheet of paper with a dozen or so company names on it. She said she was confident all the companies on the list had the potential for long-term gains. She also recommended some companies I didn't recognize.

However, I was familiar with three names: Hersey, Johnson & Johnson, and Coca-Cola. I knew all three would still be around when and if I returned home, and I was confident they would increase their value for a long time to come.

"I'll take two hundred and forty thousand dollars' worth of these three companies."

"Yes, they have potential, but I believe you would be better off with these other choices. The railroad stocks are up thirty-three percent since last year."

"Thank you, but as far as I know, railroad stocks will be losers by the 1960s or 1970s," I said.

"1960s? How far in the future are you planning?"

"2018."

Marianne, who had been leaning forward on her desk, sat back in her chair. "2018? That's a long time to hold onto stocks. These companies might not be around seventy-four years into the future."

"Oh, I think they will." I looked over at Karla as I spoke. "At least until 2018."

Marianne tried one more time to convince me at the very least to buy a few stocks in one or more of the railroad companies.

"Thank you, but no. I'll take two hundred and forty thousand dollars' worth of Hersey, Johnson & Johnson, and Coca-Cola, split evenly at $80,000 each.

Minus your commission, of course. By the way, how much is your commission?"

"Six percent."

"Ok then, I guess we have a deal."

"Yes sir. I'll get to work purchasing your investments right away."

"And don't forget, sixty-four thousand dollars in bonds," I reminded her. "The safer, the better, but with good yields too."

"You've done this before," Marianne said. "You fooled me into believing you were an amateur."

"I am an amateur, but I do occasionally read the business section of the newspaper. Most of it is way over my head, but for some reason bond yields seem to have stuck."

I wanted to say I heard talking heads on TV discuss bond yields and their effect on the economy, but I was well aware I hadn't seen a single TV since I arrived, and for the second time since I arrived, I managed to hold my tongue and not make a fool of myself by talking about something that was not yet commonplace. For all I knew, TV wasn't invented yet.

"I'll get right on it," Marianne said. "It's getting late. Would you like to come back tomorrow?"

"Tomorrow would be fine." I left enough cash with Marianne to purchase the agreed upon investments. I kept the rest of the cash I was carrying at the bottom of the knapsack, just in case. It amounted to quite a bit more than the five percent I was advised to keep. Even though I trusted her, if she did turn out to be untrustworthy, I didn't want to lose everything in one big gamble. Turns out I had no cause to worry.

We stood and shared a firm handshake, followed by Marianne offering a slight bow to Karla while sweeping her hand toward the door.

Once outside, Karla slugged me hard in the fatty part of my upper arm.

"Ouch! What was that for?" I ducked in case there was another one coming.

"You really are crazy. I hate you," Karla said. "I tell you my entire life story and all along you were carrying hundreds of thousands of dollars in that thing—what do you call it, a knapsack? And never even hinted about it? This is New York City. People are killed on the streets for a whole lot less. We even saw Frankie, too. It's a good thing he didn't know."

"I didn't tell you because I didn't want you to worry."

"Worry? Of course I would worry."

"See? I did the right thing by not telling you."

"No, you didn't. And don't ever do that again."

"Ok, ok, I won't."

"Where did you get all that money?"

"I inherited it from an older lady."

"What older lady?"

"I used to work for an older lady mowing her lawn and doing handiwork around the house. Come to think of it, I'm sure you would have liked her. Maybe you can go back with me to see where I used to work."

"Maine?" Karla asked. "You want me to go with you to Maine?"

"Yeah, sure. That would be fun. But first, we'll need to come back here tomorrow to pick up the stock certificates and bonds."

"*We* need to?" Karla said.

"I was kind of hoping you would come back with me, Karla. I like you. I like being around you. Please?"

Karla crossed her arms and huffed. "We'll see how I feel tomorrow."

23

The large overhead sign read Tony's Diner, but most people took guilty pleasure in calling it Fat Tony's Diner. Word had it, Fat Tony was the nickname made men gave Don Antonio during the early years when he was fighting his way up through the ranks. Only they could get away with calling the diner by that name to his face, no one else. Not even his own lieutenants or soldiers, much less anyone from the general public. But out of earshot most people called the eatery by this forbidden title.

The next morning I headed straight to Fat Tony's Diner. I could think of no better place to go. Sure enough, Frankie was sitting at the counter blowing on the top of his coffee. When he saw me walk in, he waved me over, handed me ten dollars and grumbled, "Beginner's luck."

"Yeah? How about we go a hundred dollars on tonight's game?"

I was sure it was the reaction Frankie hoped for, but, "There's no game tonight. The Bronx Bombers are traveling."

"So when's the next game?" I acted dumb, even though I had already looked up the schedule and scores last night on my iPhone, which mysteriously still maintains access to the Internet.

"A couple a days. They've headed to Washington to play the Senators. I'll let you know."

"Washington Senators? Are they any good?"

"They can be. It all depends on your luck."

I smiled and slid the ten dollar bill toward Karla. "Breakfast for my new friend Frankie and me."

"Oh, big spender," Karla said. She left the money on the counter.

"So Karla, are we able to go for another walk today?"

"Karla?" Frankie said.

"It's not like that Frankie. I'm helping show a new friend around town."

"Sure, whatever you say."

"That's right, whatever I say." Karla gave him an evil stare. "And yes Paul, I look forward to going on another walk with you. Right after I finish bubble dancing."

"Bubble dancing?"

"You know, washing dishes. Say, you really are from another world, ain't ya."

I shrugged and looked at Frankie for help. None was forthcoming. Instead, he asked, "So, Paulie, what do you do for a living?"

"I used to be a lobsterman, but I—" I stopped myself, remembering what Karla said about keeping my fortune a secret.

"I what?"

"What do you do?" I said, since I couldn't think of anything else.

"Who wants to know?"

"I do," I said.

"Who are you, Dick Tracy?"

"Forgedaboutit," I said in my best gangster impersonation. I immediately wished I hadn't—must've watched too many old gangster movies late nights at the Jersey Lodge.

Frankie gave me the strangest look. "You certainly are an odd man Paulie."

I stopped talking and stared at Frankie. He was no longer in focus. Everything around me fell out of focus.

The diner lights were blinding. My ears began ringing and my head started pounding. Within seconds the pain was so intense I slumped over, banging my head on the counter

Karla rushed over. "Paul, what's the matter?"

She received no coherent response, just a low groan.

"What did you do to him?" Karla pushed Frankie aside to get to me.

"I didn't do nuttin, we was just talking."

"Paul? Paul, can you hear me?" Karla asked.

Margie, who had been watching the event unfold from behind the counter, started screaming, waving her arms and shaking her head. "Get it off me, get it off me!"

"Now what?" Karla said as all attention turned in her direction.

"A rat! A rat jumped on my head!" With a frantic swipe, she sent the critter bouncing across the counter and crashing into one of the booths.

Frankie sat still, sipping his coffee as he watched the events unfold. He hardly flinched when the critter flew over his shoulder. It was just another day at the diner.

From the kitchen, Friar Tuckles looked out through the serving window with mild amusement. His life could sometimes be so repetitive it bordered on boring. Any change from routine was a welcome diversion and this was most certainly a change from routine. An exciting one at that.

With everyone but Frankie trying to get a better look at the now-immobile creature, I started to come around. Still blurry eyed, I asked what was going on.

"Are you ok?" Karla peered at me through the corner of her eye, keeping most of her attention on the intruder. Side to, still facing the critter, she leaned heavily into me when she said, "You blacked out."

"My gawd, the lights got so bright they gave me the worst headache ever."

When the offending beast ceased to move, Karla returned her full attention to me. After studying my face, she clenched her teeth and sucked in a breath. "Looks like you had a migraine. I had a friend at the orphanage who would get them. Does it still hurt?"

"It's getting better now, thanks, but a migraine? I suppose so. It was like I was in a dream or something. A very painful dream. I kept seeing something strange. I don't know what it was, I couldn't make it out. But it felt like I was in another place."

As the blurriness began fading, I looked around the room to welcome back my surroundings coming into focus. "I thought I heard Margie screaming. What was all that about?"

"A rat fell out of the cupboards and landed on Margie's head," Karla said, but added, "I don't see how. The cupboards are all shut and she's not even standing near them. It must be a good jumper."

"A rat?"

"Yes, it's over there. Margie really bashed it when she threw it against the booth. It's not moving and I think it's dead."

I looked over to where she pointed. I was still unsteady but managed to climb off my stool and bend down to get a closer look. "That's not a rat. It's a hamster."

"A hamster?" Margie said as she slowly rose from her hiding place behind the counter.

"Yes, look." I picked it up.

"No don't," Karla said. "If it's a rat, it might be diseased."

"It's not a rat," I said. "It's someone's pet. It's even wearing a tag."

I flipped the tag over, "See, it even has a name. Cuddles. Well, what do you know about that? Where did you come from, little fella?"

It started to move again, so Frankie reached over, grabbed Cuddles out of my hands and twisted its head, breaking its neck. "Don Antonio don't want no varmints in here chasing off customers." He reached over the counter and tossed the dead animal into the trash.

Karla, Margie and I looked at each other in disbelief, then back at Frankie.

"Whaaat?" he said with a thick Sicilian accent.

24

Once the commotion was over, the women went back to being waitresses while Frankie and I kept busy with small talk during the rest of breakfast. Every now and again I would peer into the kitchen and catch Karla watching me while 'bubble dancing'. After another cup of coffee and a trip to the men's room, I was ready to go. I tilted my head at Karla, silently asking if she was ready.

She returned an exasperated look as if she'd been waiting a long time, took off her apron and threw it down on the counter. "I'll be back in a couple hours," she said to Margie, then added, "Maybe."

Margie gave her a wink of encouragement. "Don't hurry back hon, I can handle things here. Have a good time."

Karla grabbed me by the arm and pulled me off my stool, dragging me through the door and into the street. It wasn't an easy task for her smaller frame against my much larger body, but I was a willing participant and offered no resistance.

"I didn't tell anyone about yesterday. I mean, not about your money," she said. I could tell she'd been waiting anxiously to tell me this.

"Thank you, but I guess it's ok if you do."

"No, it's not. You're new here and you don't know this town. Or these people. If word got out you were running around with hundreds of thousands of dollars, you wouldn't last until the end of the day."

"I'm sure glad I have you to protect me."

"You are such a fool," Karla said. "You'd better find a good hiding place for all your money and don't tell anyone. Not even me. If anyone finds out, and if they even suspect I might know where you keep it, my life would be in danger, too."

"I think you're overreacting. Nothing is going to—"

"I'm not overreacting," Karla interrupted. "Please believe me. Don't be stupid. We're going to go get your investments, you're going to hide them, and we're never going to speak about this in public again. Ok? Will you at least promise me this?"

"Ok, ok. I saw a couple banks near Marianne Estes' office. I'll choose one, rent a safe deposit box, and put everything in it. You're right; it would be the smart thing to do."

"Thank you," Karla said. She let out a sigh of relief.

"I repeat, I sure am glad you're around to protect me, if not from all the gangsters around here, then at least from my ignorance."

"Don't call them that," Karla said. "At least not in public."

* * * * *

Karla and I were able to pick up the investments without a hitch. Renting a safe box was also easy, and despite what Karla said earlier, while she waited outside I had the bank clerk put Karla's name with mine on the paperwork. With everything except my cash safely out of harm's way, the mood lightened.

During the walk back, we passed a movie theatre. The marquee announced Dumbo was playing a matinee. "I used to love that movie," I said. "My mother took me and my sister to see it on the boardwalk at

Asbury Park. It was one of my favorite movies as a kid growing up. It was so sad when—"

"As a kid?" Karla said. "How old are you? Dumbo just came out. I think this year or last, didn't it? How could you have seen it as a little boy?"

I thought I might try to defend myself, but I decided it would be better not to. Just let it go and enjoy the day with Karla instead of trying again to convince her I was from the future.

My silence prompted a response. "You're not going to start with the time travel line again, are you?"

Hit with a direct question, I felt compelled to answer. "I know it's difficult to believe, but it's true."

"You are one strange, strange man. If you really are from the future, what's going to happen to me?"

"I just met you, how would I know? It's not like I can jump ahead and find you, then jump back and tell you what you will be doing in X number of years."

"Why not? If you invented time machines, why can't you bounce around from time to time?"

"It doesn't work that way. First off, I didn't invent time travel. I hired someone else to do it. I jumped into it without telling him, and worst of all, I forgot the return doohickey I need to get back. So I'm stuck here, for now."

Karla rolled her eyes.

"This is going to sound like the craziest thing ever, but my plan is to go to Europe and find my time machine inventor's great-grandfather. I'm going to tell him about his great-grandson and hopefully remember enough about what he told me to help Mr. Great-Grandfather finish off his version of the time machine and return me to my own time."

I hesitated, then said, "I hope after I get home I can get the return device and come back here to see you again."

Karla actually started to laugh. "I'm going to say it again; you are the strangest man I ever met."

"Someday you'll see all this is true."

"Ok, so who is this Mr. Great-Grandfather in Europe you need to track down? And don't tell me he is an evil genius."

"Well," I said, again with much hesitation. "Actually he is."

I took a deep breath, unsure if I wanted to continue. I'd gone this far, why stop now? "He's a Nazi SS officer who works at a secret base somewhere in southern Poland."

"Oh," Karla said, with tilted eyebrows and a crooked smile. "Is that all? Why didn't you say so? It shouldn't be a problem at all to find him and convince him you're from the future, and that you want to build a time machine."

"You're mocking me. I think I better shut up while I'm behind."

"No, please continue. I want to hear all of it," Karla said.

"That's about it. Who knows, while I'm over there maybe I can assassinate Hitler and bring an end to the war. I'm a long way from this ever happening, though, so if you don't mind I would much rather enjoy the moment with you here in New York City."

Karla wasn't sure how to respond. "That would be nice," was all she could muster.

We walked back towards the diner much closer together than we ever had before. Occasionally, with our arms hanging by our sides, our hands would gently brush against each other. Each time they did, I felt a rush of excitement pass through me. I imagined she felt it too.

Thirty minutes of small talk later, we reached the front of my boarding house. Karla gave it a once-over. Made of old and crumbled bricks, wedged between a cigar shop and a rundown movie theater in the middle of a long row of three-storey shophouses, the only windows she could see were broken and covered with brown postal paper. Someone once tried to paint the rusted fire escape but only managed to drop splotches of black down onto the grimy sidewalk, turning it into a permanent Rorschach test.

"You're staying here?" She said.

"Yeah, it ain't pretty but it's home. Do you want to see my room?"

"I'm not sure," Karla said.

Even in the darkness through the front door, Karla could see where paint had peeled off the walls. The torn and matted carpet could have been a leftover from the civil war. The entire lobby, if one could call it that, reeked of dirty feet.

"Come on, where's your sense of adventure?" I led her inside and began to head for the stairs.

"Whoa, where do you think you're going?" The bug-eyed man who sat behind the reception desk called out. He had just finished his lunch of greasy chicken and wiped his hands on his unwashed formerly-white singlet.

"To my room," I said. "Why?"

"This is a respectable place," he said. "We don't allow no whores in here."

I turned and was about to jump over the counter to defend Karla's honor when she grabbed my arm. "I'm no whore."

"She's no whore—" I said, and once again Karla stopped me.

"Who are you?" Karla asked the clerk.

"Are you one of Don Antonio's girls?" the man asked. He won't be happy if he finds out you were cavorting behind his back with strangers in this hotel."

"First of all, I'm not cavorting," Karla said. "Second, you don't know Don Antonio. I do. And believe me, your life is going to be worth nothing when I tell him you called me a whore."

It was then the clerk realized Karla wasn't just one of the Don's girls. The woman standing right there in his hotel lobby was none other than Karla Gingerich, Don Antonio's unofficially adopted daughter.

Everyone knew the Don treated her like one of his own. Word on the streets was he put her to work in the diner to keep her humble. However, those who knew her thought she chose to work there to be with her friends, eschewing all the wonderful things the Don's blood money could buy. Either way, she did remain humble and always stayed leery of the Don and his men. She knew full well their devotion to her could turn on a dime.

With this new realization, the clerk, fearing for his life blurted out, "I'm sorry. I didn't recognize you. Go ahead. But please don't tell Don Antonio."

Karla pushed me toward the stairs and glared at the man once more.

Nothing more was said as we climbed the stairs and walked down the dark hallway to the door to my room. Inside, Karla took a quick look around. "Why are you staying here in this dump?"

I wanted to defend my choice but didn't get the chance.

"With all your money, you could stay in a much nicer place. You don't even have your own bathroom. It's disgusting."

I knew she was right. "It was the first place I found when I arrived.

"Pack up your things. We're getting you out of here."

"But I'm paid up for another week."

"So? You can't afford to throw away, what did you pay? Ten dollars for the week?"

"Twelve," I said sheepishly.

Embarrassed, I began gathering what little I had left to gather.

"Turn around," I told her when I dug under the bed to retrieve the sum total of my worldly belongings which consisted of the backpack with the money, a handful of clothes, and a small assortment of other things I brought from Maine.

"Let's go," Karla said when I finished. "This place gives me the creeps."

25

Karla moved me into a suite at the Hotel Commodore on Forty-second Street Manhattan, just north of Little Italy. The suite was much more expensive and further away, but also much better than the no-name rat infested boarding house where I had been staying. This new place was worth every penny.

I now had my own bathroom and shower, a comfortable bed, dining and living area, room service, and a beautiful balcony with a loveseat pointed towards a magnificent view of the city skyline. I started to feel like a million bucks with beautiful Karla with me in that suite. Me, a lobsterman from Harpswell Maine who not long ago had no plans to go anywhere or do anything else.

There was a strange sensation in the air as we aimlessly strolled around inside, checking out our new surroundings. I could tell we both sensed it.

I wandered out onto the balcony and leaned out on the railing to take in the magnificent view of the hustling, bustling streets below, and the burgeoning New York City skyline in front of me.

"This almost feels like Déjà vu," I said.

"What's that?" Karla asked, taking a place next to me.

"I just feel like I've been here before."

"Have you?" Karla inched away from me. I couldn't tell if she was serious or just being playful. "Have you been here before with another woman?"

"No, of course not. It's just a feeling I'm having. Weird, huh?"

Karla gave me one of her sideways looks, then sat down on the loveseat. I slid in next to her and the two of us sat in silence, staring ahead.

After a few minutes the silence began to get awkward, so out of the blue and without considering how I might be breaking the mood, I announced, "I need to go back to Maine."

Karla looked at me with bright eyes as if she was not expecting this surprise announcement with such huge implications. "Why? Don't you like it here?"

"I love it here. I feel like I'm falling for you, too. But I keep thinking I need to try and get back home to the shelter. They're depending on me."

"Ok, time to come clean, Popeye. What is this shelter you talk about? Are you running away from something or someone? Are you hiding from the police?"

"No, not at all. The shelter is a safe place where abused women and children can go to recover and try to work out their problems."

"Ok, I'll bite. What kind of problems?"

"I guess I need to start from the beginning. One night at our cottage a woman named Chrissy showed up. She had been severely beaten by her husband or boyfriend and needed help."

"What did she do to her husband?"

"I beg your pardon?"

"What did she do to her husband to cause him to beat her?"

"I don't know what she did, but it doesn't matter. Whatever it was, she didn't deserve a beating, especially the one she received."

"She must have done something to deserve it," Karla said.

"No, she didn't. No one deserves to be bullied like that, woman *or* child. Or man for that matter. Maybe attitudes are different here and now, but back home we try not to allow this to happen. When it does, someone needs to help the people who are unable or unwilling to help themselves."

"You don't believe in survival of the fittest?"

"I believe it's sometimes up to the fittest to step in and help the others survive. Chrissy needed medical attention, so we took her to Dr. Lynn."

"Who is Dr. Lynn?"

"A woman doctor my cousin knew. She specializes in helping those who need help but can't afford it."

"A woman doctor? Maine has women doctors?"

"Yes, Maine has women doctors. So does New York, and just about everywhere else. If you want, with a whole lot of schooling you can be one, too. You can be anything you want. Dream big and work hard to realize your dreams."

Karla looked at me as if I was crazy.

"Dr. Lynn is a wonderful woman who dedicates her time to helping those less fortunate," I continued. "She sewed Chrissy back together and now is resident at the shelter. Chrissy has stayed on as a counselor. What started out helping one person has grown into housing and counseling for dozens of victims."

I looked over at Karla. She seemed to be hanging on my every word.

"A wonderful woman lawyer also helps us by donating a lot of her time to the shelter. Peggy Sanders really is a sweetheart but is also a pit bull when it comes to tracking down both men and women abusers and bringing them to justice. Plus, she raises money for the shelter."

"A woman lawyer, too?"

"Yes, the world outside Fat Tony's Diner is full of amazing things."

"Don't call it that."

"Sorry."

"So what do you do there?" Karla asked.

"A lot less than I used to. In the beginning, I was involved in every aspect of building, staffing, and running the shelter. Now it runs fairly well without me, but I do supply most of the funding. I began to run low on money and that's why I tried to venture out to bring in more. I made a wrong turn and ended up here."

"Do you regret it?"

"Right now I regret nothing. If I hadn't shown up here, I might never have met you. The thought makes my eyes water."

"What are you, some kind of hopeless romantic?"

"Only around you," I said, and then paused to regain my composure. "Sorry, I sounded corny didn't I?"

"Shut up." Karla leaned over and opened her heart, and her lips, and positioned them as close as she dared to mine. We sat in this position, lips all but touching, for what seemed like an eternity. Each of us wondered whether to take the plunge, cross that invisible barrier of intimacy, forever changing our relationship. Should our lips touch, there was no turning back.

Although it seemed like an eternity, in reality it was a mere split second before our lips met, releasing pent-up emotions, beginning a kiss so passionate, so filled with emotion, so fabulously life-changing it now felt it would never end. It lasted longer than most first kisses, both of us lost in the moment, completely letting go of all our inhibitions, extinguishing our shyness towards each other.

The kiss continued as I picked her up and carried her into the bedroom, where the rest of the walls came crashing down.

* * * * *

When we finally finished consummating our budding love, we both were left emotionally and physically exhausted.

"Are you gay?" Karla said, breaking the silence.

"What? No, why?"

"You're not happy? I'm not making you happy?"

"Oh, gay. Yes, of course I'm happy. I thought you might be judging the way I made love."

"Why would I do that?"

"I don't know. The word means something else where I come from."

"What does it mean?"

"It's not important. I mean, it's ok to be gay where I come from, but it's just, I'm not," I said, stammering. I tried my best to lighten the moment.

"Now I'm confused. You're not happy?"

"Never mind. I'm very happy," I said. We both knew I should just shut up.

"Well, I'm not that kind of girl, you know," Karla said.

"What kind is that?"

"The kind who jumps into bed with total strangers. Not even before. It was always Margie who went with the boys and Don Antonio's men. Not me."

"I believe you." I nuzzled up close to Karla's neck, giving her a quick kiss below her ear. "I hope you don't consider me a stranger."

"I don't. Not anymore." Karla rubbed her arm to flatten the goose bumps.

"So wait, are you telling me you are, or were, a virgin before today?"

"I didn't say that," Karla said, although she considered herself to be. Taking care of the Don's men was creepy at times, but didn't mean she had to go all the way. Being forced to watch Margie didn't count.

She knew she was Don Antonio's special girl. He looked after her, protected her, and treated her like his own daughter. Karla didn't understand why, but she didn't discourage him either.

One time, one of the Don's peripheral soldiers tried to force himself on her. She managed to fight him off and when the Don found out, well, no one heard from the soldier again.

"I think we have something exceptional together. I think I'm falling in love," Karla allowed herself to say, although until today, she wouldn't have thought she would dare believe she could feel this way.

"That's remarkable. I'm feeling the same thing. What should we do about it?"

"What do you mean?"

"You're Don Antonio's girl. I haven't met the man, but from what you said, or implied, the longer I can postpone that meeting, the longer I'll live."

"If you don't do anything to cross him, you should be ok."

"As long as he doesn't find out about us, or the money I brought with me."

"Yes, the money might put you in his sights," Karla said.

"I guess we'll just have to keep it quiet."

"And don't mess with Frankie. He's just as dangerous."

"Frankie won't do us any harm. We're regular buds now. Friendly ribbing each other and all. He likes me enough not to cause us any problems."

"You're probably right. It's just—"

"Just what?"

"Everything in my life is so FUBAR," Karla said.

"FUBAR? You know what FUBAR is?"

"Of course I do silly. Why wouldn't I?"

"What does F U B A R stand for?"

"Fouled up beyond all repair. Why?"

"Ok," I said. The way I knew it, in the parlance of commercial fishermen 'fouled up' had been replaced with an expletive.

"I have an idea," I said. "We should get all my investments together and get out of here."

"Where would we go?"

"Back to Maine."

"Besides the shelter, what's in Maine?" Karla scooted down to switch places with me and rested her head on my chest.

"We have a cottage right near the beach, my house next door, and a big old house that used to be a bed and breakfast. It's over a hundred and sixty years old, built in 1855."

Karla slapped me on my bare belly. "Where did you go to school? 1855 wasn't even a hundred years ago. Boy Howdy, you *do* exaggerate."

"Sorry, I don't have enough fingers and toes to count that high."

"Don't start with your, 'I'm from the future' stuff again. No one likes a fibber."

"Why don't you go with me? You have a good heart and you'd fit right in with the people at the shelter."

"To Maine? I don't think so," Karla said, although the idea of leaving Little Italy and going to Maine did sound romantic.

"Well, give it some thought."

"You're sweet," Karla said.

26

"Let's do something fun today," I said when we woke up the next morning.

"Like what?"

"I don't know. What do you do for excitement around here?"

"We could take a train down to New Jersey. There are some beaches there. That might be fun this time of year after most of the tourists have gone home."

"Sounds great, let's do it."

"OK!"

"That gives me an idea. If I remember my history, Albert Einstein lives at Princeton University. How far away is that?"

"I don't know. Why?"

"He's become known as the greatest mind of his time. Do you know $E=MC^2$?"

"No, why would I?"

"Humor me. I remember reading about him. He said time travel is possible, but only in one direction. Towards the future."

"So?"

"So, we only want to go one direction—to the future. Maybe he can figure out a way we can get back to my time. I have lots of friends and family there. I'm sure you would love them, and they would love you. What do you say?"

Karla sighed. "Just when I thought you were beginning to seem normal, you come up with the whole time travel thing again. Can't we just enjoy a nice day at the beach together?"

"Yes, of course. I'm sorry for bringing it up." I hesitated. "But maybe we can swing by and say hello after?"

"You're insufferable."

* * * * *

Later that morning we hailed a taxi to Grand Central Station where we battled our way through the early morning crowd to buy two first class train tickets to Asbury Park.

We boarded the train without too much trouble, took our seats and settled in to what should have been a two hour trip south.

"This will be so much fun," Karla said, grabbing my arm and sliding herself over close to me.

About a half hour into the ride, the conductor approached to punch our tickets.

"What are you two lovebirds up to today?"

We looked at each other and smirked. 'How does he know?'

"We're getting out of the city to spend a couple quiet hours on the beach," Karla said.

"These tickets say Asbury Park," the conductor said. "Ah, Asbury Park, fun, games, laughter. To be young again."

He let the sentence hang for a moment. "But if you want quiet beach time, Asbury Park might not be your best choice. There are rides and vendors and all kinds of activities, and fun for sure, but many, many tourists, too. Asbury Park has its merits, but being a quiet getaway is not one of them."

I started scratching my chin again in my own weird way, which elicited an awkward look from the conductor. He turned away and looked at Karla.

"Might I suggest getting off a stop early at Long Branch? It's a quiet little town along the shoreline with miles of sandy beach. At this time of year, most of the tourists have either gone home or moved to Asbury Park, so it should be a lot quieter."

Put on the spot, neither Karla nor I could come up with a viable answer to either continue on to Asbury Park or get out at Long Branch.

"Tell you what," the conductor said when he noticed our indecision. "The train station at Long Branch is only a couple blocks from the ocean. You can see the beach from there. I'll let you know when we get close. Take the next hour to decide."

"That would be great," I said.

The conductor gave us a wink and a wry smile, nodded his head and moved on to stamp the next passengers' tickets.

"I think he works for the Long Branch Chamber of Commerce," I said.

Karla took my hand and laid her head on my shoulder. "It does sound dreamy."

"Long Branch it is, then."

We didn't speak much over the next hour, our minds wandering while our eyes kept busy taking in the sites as New York City gave way to an industrial area, which in turn faded into residential areas spotted among tidal swamps and at times lush vegetation.

Before we knew it, the conductor peaked his head through the cabin door to announce the next stop would be Long Branch. He looked at us, implying his interest in whether or not we would be disembarking. I gave him a positive nod.

He smiled broadly and closed the door behind him.

As the train creaked and squealed to a halt, we could see the conductor's description was spot on.

There in the distance, only partially blocked by occasional houses and scattered small cafes and businesses, the Atlantic Ocean dominated the horizon.

Climbing down onto the platform, we made our way down the closest street leading towards the beach. The conductor was also correct, as there were hardly any people to be seen. The ones we did see avoided eye contact. By the end of the tourist season they'd probably had their fill of city slickers taking over their quiet little hamlet.

It only took us about 10 minutes' walking to make our grand entrance onto the beach. "I can see why they call it Long Beach," I said, as the yellow sand stretched for as far as the eye could see in both directions.

"Long Branch," Karla corrected me.

"Ok, so it's a long beach in Long Branch," I said.

We found a comfy spot up against a sand dune topped by a grassy knoll, and sat for a while in silence, watching the waves crash into the shore.

"Do you miss it?" Karla said.

"Miss what?"

"Miss the ocean. Home. Your friends and family."

"Yes, I suppose I do. I admit, though, I hardly think about them with you around."

"You're sweet." Karla again laid her head on my shoulder. "You know all about me, tell me something about you?"

"I don't know, there's not much to tell."

"Come on, there must be something that stands out."

"Well, I did save a guy's life once when I was younger."

"Go on."

"I was cutting the grass for the woman I told you about. The one who willed me all that money. She had some visitors up for the week, staying at her big old house. I think the woman's name was Maggie, or something like that. The husband was Alfred, who I'm pretty sure was in the army—or maybe he was retired from the army, I don't know. Anyway, Mrs. M's house had a long dock stretching out into the cove in front. There was a ramp down to a float at the end where she kept a canoe for guests. I also kept my skiff and outboard there.

"That day, Alfred took the canoe for a paddle. I could tell right away he wasn't experienced with canoes, as he sat all the way to the stern. When you're alone in a canoe, it's a good idea to sit towards the middle to keep it level. He was in the back and the bow was tipping up into the air, so I kept an eye on him just in case.

"It was kind of breezy that day with a bit of chop due to the wind battling the tide. The combination was pushing him further away from the dock and he was having trouble controlling the canoe. Sure enough, as he tried to turn back towards home, the wind pushed the bow too high and he capsized.

"I stopped the riding mower and watched to see if he knew how to right the canoe and get back in. He didn't. To make matters worse, instead of going with the current towards shore on the other side of the cove, he was trying to push the canoe against the current towards the dock. That's when I knew he was in trouble."

"So what did you do?"

"His missus was sitting on the porch reading a book, so I figured I'd better let her know what was going on. I was still just a kid and I guess I wanted to make sure I wouldn't get in trouble by stopping work. So I rode up to her and told her, 'your husband is having trouble in the canoe and I'm going to take my boat out and get him.' To my surprise, she nonchalantly told me, 'ok' and went back to her book. I guess it must have been a good book."

"Crazy woman," Karla said. "Or maybe she didn't like her husband."

"Maybe, I don't know. I rode the mower down to the dock, jumped off and ran down to my boat, untied it and headed out to get him. By the time I got there he was exhausted and having trouble keeping his head above water. I grabbed him by the collar and spun him around so he could grab the side of my boat. Then I reached down behind him and grabbed his belt and hauled him aboard. He flopped down onto the deck, soaked and exhausted, without saying much of anything. I think he tried to say 'thanks' but was too tired.

"I watched him a minute to make sure he wasn't choking, which he wasn't, so I pulled the canoe aboard, emptied it, and pushed it back into the water right side up so I could tow it back to the dock.

"When we got there, I suggested he go back to the house and dry off, I'd take care of the boats. He was still dazed and off he went.

"After securing the boats, I went back to work mowing the lawn and when I was done I parked the mower in the barn and rode my bicycle home as usual.

"The next morning when I returned to work at the normal time, I knocked on the kitchen door, as usual, to find out what chores would need attention that day. When Mrs. M opened it, the husband and wife were waiting in the kitchen with her. Remember, I'm still a kid, so I'm thinking, 'Uh oh, what did I do wrong?'

"The wife started apologizing right away. She was telling me, 'You acted so calm when you told me what was going on, I had no idea how bad it was.' The husband had his arm over her shoulder and was smiling. I guess all was forgiven regarding her unusual reaction during his near death experience. He wanted to make sure I knew he wasn't mad at her.

"He said thank you and handed me a bank check for a hundred dollars. 'It's the least we can do,' he said, 'for saving my life.'

"It caught me completely by surprise and I tried to give it back. 'I don't deserve this,' I said. 'I was only doing what anyone would do.'

"Mrs. M. told me to keep it, as it meant a lot to them to be able to give it to me. She said I saved the man's life and they wanted to show their gratitude. So I shoved it in my back pocket and gave them my broadest grin.

"One hundred dollars back then for a twelve-year-old boy was like a king's ransom."

"What did you do with all that money?" Karla asked.

"Mrs. M gave me the rest of the day off, so I rode my bike home and talked my mother into taking me up to the bank in Brunswick to cash the check. Our family was really poor. We existed on whatever we could catch from the sea and a lot of leftovers. I think I bought a couple of sodas, then made my mom take me to Hannaford's where we had a great time filling the cart with groceries. It is one of the fondest memories of my adolescence. We ate well for a week."

"You're a real hero," Karla said.

"No, not a hero. Anyone would have done the same thing. But it did make me feel good. After being put down all the time at home, it was the first time in my young life when I felt useful."

"I think that qualifies you as a hero," Karla said.

"Ok, I may be a hero, but I'm hungry, too. Let's find something to eat."

Karla punched me softly in the fatty part of my shoulder, again. "You sure know how to spoil a romantic moment."

"Sorry, it's hard to be romantic with my stomach growling like it is."

"Typical man. All you think about is your stomach."

"That's not all I think about," I said, raising my eyebrows in my best Groucho Marx impersonation.

Karla stood up, unimpressed. "Ok, let's go find someplace to eat."

After a ten minute walk inland, we found a small diner still open. A half-dozen people sat inside, locals no doubt, and by the sounds of their banter our entrance didn't go unnoticed as we took a booth by the window.

The waitress brought over a pair of plastic coated menus. "I'm Claire, I'll be happy to take your order when you're ready." She stood for a moment looking at Karla as if she recognized her. The two looked to be about the same age, the same build, so similar, in fact, they could be mistaken for sisters.

"What'll it be sailor?" Karla said to me, ignoring Claire's stare.

I noticed it, however, and spent a moment or two looking back and forth between them. Deciding more than likely they weren't sisters, I looked over the menu and settled on a club sandwich and a Coke. "How about you?"

"The same," Karla said and handed the menus back.

"Two clubs, two Cokes, coming up," Claire said.

"Did you notice how she was looking at you?" I asked.

"Yes, I get that a lot. Even you did it when we first met. Remember?"

"I wonder why that is."

"Beats me."

"What's that big building over there?" Karla asked when Claire returned with two bottles of Coca-Cola and two glasses filled with ice. Karla pointed to a barn outside of which a crowd of people had assembled. They began filing in as soon as the doors were opened.

Claire didn't need to look where Karla pointed, as it could only be one place. "The Tack and Jib? It's our one bar and dancing joint in town. It's usually open 7 p.m. until late, but today there is an end of the tourist season party."

"What time?" Karla asked.

"It's already started."

Karla looked at me longingly and mouthed 'dancing'. As soon as Claire left to pick up the subs, she said, "I love dancing. Come on, let's go over there when we finish here."

"I have two left feet," I protested.

"Ah, come on. It'll be fun."

"For you, anything," I said. "But don't expect me to turn into Fred Astaire."

"Don't worry. I'm no Ginger Rogers. Hurry up and eat. Let's get over there."

With club sandwiches and Cokes finished, the check paid and a generous tip for Claire, we stepped outside and headed in the direction of the Tack and Jib. We could already hear the music booming through the walls as soon as we exited the diner.

Another five minute walk up the road and we stood peering in through the front door. To our surprise, the place was almost full.

A man saw us and walked over. "Five dollars, all the punch you can drink, all night," he said. "Be warned. It's spiked and can be lethal. Beers and mixed drinks are extra after your first five."

I reached into my pocket, fumbled around and pulled out a ten dollar bill.

"Here are your tickets," the doorman said. "No limit on the punch. The barkeep will mark your ticket if you order beer or mixed drinks. Have fun." He then danced his way back into the crowd.

"Shall we?" I said and stuck out my hand.

Karla grabbed it and yanked me out onto the dance floor. "I love this song."

"What is it?"

"*Solid Potato Salad* by the Ross Sisters." Karla began swinging and dipping her shoulders back and forth in rhythm with the music.

I tried to do the same and felt like a fool.

"Oy, Oy," she sang with the music. "Take a bowl, fill it up and bring it right back." She was having the time of her life.

A couple of songs later, the dance floor lined up in formation and began a swing dance. Since this was way beyond my skills, we retired to the punch bowl.

A similar scene, where we would dance a few numbers, then hit the punch bowl while the choreographers took over, repeated itself several times until late in the evening.

By closing time we'd reached the silly drunk level. We also realized we'd missed the last train and any chance to get back to the city.

"Let's just go back to the beach," Karla said. "It's a beautiful night and I can think of no beautifuller way to spend it."

"Beautifuller? That's easy for you to say."

We were the perfect young couple in love as we laughed and danced our way back to the beach. The stars were out bright on this moonless night, and the waves seemed to be alive as they splashed onto the sandy beach. Each curl was a bright, almost neon blue, releasing thousands of blue stars in the froth spread across the sand.

"Is the water full of lights? Or am I dreaming?" Karla said.

"It is. It's plankton. Lights up when you swoosh it. C'mon, I'll show you."

I led her to the water's edge and tried to pull her closer, but she resisted.

"I'm not going in there like this," she said. "We'll freeze tonight if we get our clothes wet."

"You're right. What was I thinking? Hey, if we take our shoes off and—" I turned around and nearly choked when I saw Karla had already kicked off her shoes and now was wrestling to remove her blouse.

"No," she said. "I want to see the lights in the water."

I stared in awe as she stripped the rest of the way naked.

"Are you coming, or are you going to stand there gawking?"

I couldn't get my clothes off fast enough. After tripping on my pants and falling flat on my face, I got up covered in sand and followed her into the surf. The water was surprisingly warm. Much warmer than the ocean in Maine.

We spent the next hour or so splashing around in the brilliant bioluminescence on this most magical of nights. The exertion and the refreshing water sobered us, leading to the inevitable—a romantic imitation of Burt Lancaster and Deborah Kerr's famous beach scene in the classic movie, 'From Here to Eternity'— even though the movie wouldn't be made for another nine years. James Jones or Fred Zinnemann must have been watching us from the dunes.

27

The sun rose early the next morning. We had managed to dress in the darkness and find a semi-comfortable spot to curl up and sleep last night. But now, with the rude seagulls squawking overhead, it was time to try and find the diner again for breakfast and coffee. We were counting on the food, water, and caffeine there to chase away the rest of our hangover.

It helped but wasn't a cure-all.

"You two must have had quite a night," Claire said as she poured our second cup of coffee.

Luckily we were the first in the diner, but our privacy didn't last. Local god-fearing townsfolk, regulars for morning coffee, gave us disapproving stares as they took up their favorite places.

"Yes, thanks. May we have our check now, please?" I said, feeling quite uncomfortable by their stares.

"Ok," Claire said, but she took her time adding it up. She was a little too obvious in making sure everyone in the diner could get a good look at us.

We couldn't get out of there fast enough.

"That was strange," Karla said once we managed to escape.

"Yes, I think we've gained a reputation. It would be best to put that diner behind us as soon as possible and never return."

"Good idea," Karla agreed. "I think I remember the train station is over this way."

"I have a better idea," I said when I spotted a yellow taxi idling in front of the Tack and Jib. The thing was huge. I went straight to it and asked the driver, "How much to Princeton?"

"Princeton?" Karla said.

The driver looked us over. Our clothes were dirty, wrinkled and covered in sand. We must've looked like ragged bums. "How much you got?"

"Enough." I said and pulled out a wad of bills.

The driver straightened up. "Where in Princeton?"

"The university, if you don't mind."

"Twenty dollars," he said.

"You've got a deal." I handed him a twenty, opened the back door and motioned Karla to get in. She shook her head in a mild protest, for now the secret was up.

"Einstein?"

I winked.

The car interior was big enough to host a cocktail party. The seats were furry fabric, not the 'pleather' seats of autos back home.

"Excuse me, sir. What kind of car is this?"

The driver looked at me in the rear view mirror. "1939 Dodge D11 Taxi," he said. "Why, what's wrong with it?"

"Nothing's wrong with it, I've just never seen a car like this before. It's huge, isn't it? It's like a land yacht."

The driver looked over his shoulder at me, then back at the road. "Same size as all the rest of the cabs in the fleet. Does it live up to his highness's desires?"

Karla nudged me with her elbow. She shook her head no, I guess to keep me from further conversation with him. As always, I dutifully obliged.

Two hours later without further discourse among any of us, we pulled up to Princeton University. "You two should get cleaned up," the cabbie said. "You look like bums."

"Thanks for the advice," I said and helped Karla out of the car.

"Man, that cabbie was a piece of work, wasn't he?" she said as the taxi drove away. "Now what's your plan?"

"Now we ask around."

We searched for the next couple of hours without any success. Everyone knew *who* Albert Einstein was. No one knew *where* he was. Our circuitous route eventually brought us to the front of the Institute for Advanced Study. A few minutes later, to my utter amazement, Albert Einstein appeared through the front doors. He kept his head down as he marched away from the building. Having just finished his latest lecture he was on his way home.

"Excuse me, sir," I said. "We've come a long way. May we please have a few moments of your time?" I tried my best to sound at least a little bit intellectual.

Einstein looked us over. Our clothes still showed evidence of our previous night on the beach. "Are you bums?" he said in his thick German accent. "I don't carry any money with me."

"No," I said, finally realizing the cabbie was right. I started brushing the sand off my clothes and tried to straighten them out. When I started doing the same to Karla, she slapped my hands away, which elicited a laugh from Einstein. I had to admit, at that point our actions did resemble a comedy routine.

"We came down from the city yesterday. We were having so much fun, we missed the last train back," Karla said.

"There were no hotels where you were?"

"We thought it would be more romantic to spend the night on the beach," I said. Karla smacked me in the arm.

"Ah, to be young again," Einstein said. "How can I help you?"

"That's an awkward question," I said. "I read about how you said time travel is possible, but only towards the future. With all due respect, sir, I come from the future. I'm not here to argue your theory about time travel. I'm here because I hope you can help me get back home."

"Have you eaten?" Einstein said.

The question caught me by surprise. "No, why?"

"I'm starved. Can you cook?" he asked Karla.

"I'm not a great cook, but I can get by."

"Ok, you're hired. Follow me, my housekeeper is on holiday and I could use a good home cooked meal. By the looks of it, so could you."

My eyes must have bulged. The thought of seeing Einstein was beyond belief. The thought of being invited to his home was beyond even that. I was speechless.

"We wouldn't want to put you out," Karla said.

"Nonsense," Einstein said. "It's not every day I meet a crazy young couple claiming to be from the future after a romantic night on the beach. Follow me, we can talk on the way. And for God's sake, you need to get cleaned up. You're beginning to smell."

A short way into our walk we approached an intersection with Einstein in the lead. A car came careening out of control straight for us. At the last second, I pulled him out of the way.

"Sorry for being so rough."

"Nonsense young man, you saved my life."

I suddenly felt a huge weight on my chest. It caused me to double over.

"Are you ok?" Einstein said.

"Paul, what's the matter?" Karla grabbed me to try and keep me from falling.

"I don't know, but whatever it was, I think it's passed." I was able to get up, shake my head, and once again stare at the greatest mind of his generation.

"Now, where were we?" Einstein said. "Ah, yes. Time travel." As he began to walk across the street, all three of us looked both ways before proceeding cautiously.

"You say you're from the future?"

"He said he is, not me," Karla said.

"I see," he replied. "From 'when' do you say you come?"

"2018."

Einstein smiled smugly. "Impossible. Think of the paradoxes it would create."

"I have heard a theory about that," I said and began trying to explain.

"Hold that thought young man," Einstein said as he led us up the stairs at 112 Mercer Street. His house was a relatively small, white, two-storey with black shutters, fronted by a comfortable porch, its roof held aloft by stately white wooden columns. "We're here. We can take this up after dinner."

As we entered, I felt faint. All this was way too surreal. I'd been forced to study Einstein in school; now here I am in his home. I took a close look around. I wanted to soak up every bit of this experience.

The first thing I noticed was there were many windows in the front and back, but only a couple on the sides. A sturdy wooden table covered with a lace tablecloth filled most of the dining room to one side, a music and sitting room to the other.

As Einstein led us towards the stairwell, I peeked around the corner and spied the famous physicist's study towards the rear of the house. A chalkboard dominated one wall, and his large desk looked much smaller covered in books, loose papers, a magnifying glass, shears, and a letter opener. A globe sat on a stand next to a full bookcase, near a table and two wooden chairs in front of a bay window. A painted iron radiator sat under the window, while a small throw rug with what looked like Indian symbols lay smartly on the floor.

Einstein pointed to the upstairs and downstairs bathing facilities. "I don't care who uses what, but you need to bathe," he said. "I will not be able to eat with you in your current condition."

I went up, Karla stayed down.

While we washed behind closed doors, Einstein picked up his violin in the music room and began to play.

Ten minutes of beautiful music later, Karla reemerged from the downstairs bathroom acting as if it were just another day. "Where's the kitchen?" she asked Einstein.

"Right through that doorway. Help yourself to anything."

As Karla disappeared into the kitchen, Albert Einstein resumed playing his violin.

28

I felt my hands shaking as I descended the stairs and followed the music. Not wanting to interrupt, I sat quietly in the corner, listening and watching. Einstein smiled, continuing to play for his enamored audience of one.

Karla emerged an hour later, announcing dinner would be served. She brought out plates of cooked fish, buttered rice, and fresh salad.

"I had all this in my kitchen?"

"Well, no, I snuck out to the little market up the street. I hope you like it." She set three places at the table, brought out a bottle of wine and poured three glasses, then joined us at the dining room table.

"This is exquisite," Einstein said. "You are a great cook, Karla, much better than Helen my secretary. You are a lucky man, Paul."

Karla blushed. I tried to force a smile.

We continued with small talk during the meal, after which I helped Karla clear away the dishes.

Einstein feigned protest, "Leave them alone. I can take care of them later."

"I saw how you take care of the housework in your kitchen," Karla said. "It took me ten minutes to clean enough crockery to cook."

Einstein didn't argue. Instead, he introduced me to a fine bottle of cognac, had me pour three glasses and follow him out to the back garden where we retired to take in the cool late summer evening.

"Ok, so what is this nonsense about time travel?"

"I really am from the future, and I would like nothing more than to go home. If possible, I would like to take Karla with me, too, if she will go."

Karla had just returned from the kitchen and turned several shades of red as she slid into the seat next to me.

"As romantic as this sounds," Einstein said. "It's not possible. You would need to find a way to travel at or near the speed of light, and everyone knows this is not possible."

"Why?" Karla asked, her flush disappearing.

"Because the faster you go, the more energy it would take. You would need almost an infinite amount of energy to reach the speed of light. Unless you have that in your pocket or know which little market would sell it to you, I'm afraid you won't be able to get going fast enough."

"How can I convince you I'm from the future?"

"You can't."

"I'll try anyway. I have a friend in Maine. His name is William Vrill the Fourth. He said he's a descendant of a Nazi SS officer named William Vrill, I assume the first."

"Ach," Einstein said. "I have heard of the infamous Col. Wilhelm Vrill. He's a fool. A nationalistic idiot. If you believe anything he says or does you would be just as big a fool."

I was stunned. My argument shot down before I had a chance to present it. Nonetheless, I pressed on.

"My friend, Vrill the fourth, is a genius. He built the time machine by perfecting 'the fool's' notes. He also told me he and other scientists have a theory about these paradoxes you mentioned. They say—"

"Don't say it," Einstein said.

"Don't say what?"

"Don't tell me about the Heisenberg uncertainty principle. I don't believe it. God doesn't play dice with the universe. You are here because of Newtonian determinism. The universe is a clock. It was wound up at the beginning of time and according to Newton's laws of motion has been ticking ever since. So, you being here was previously ordained. If you make it back to wherever you say you come from, it will also be because it was ordained."

"I have no idea what the Heisenberg uncertainty principle or Newtonian determinism are, but it sounds like these make the case I was about to talk about. My friend says paradoxes cannot be created by time travel to the past because whatever a time traveler does in the past is part of history. He says people who go back into the past do so not only because they can, but because they must."

"Nonsense," Einstein said. "Creating an instrument to travel back in time would be nothing more than building a gateway to paradoxes, many of them."

"My friend," I continued, "who claims to be a descendant of the German Vrill you despise, used you as an example. He told me, 'What if someone went back in time and killed Einstein, either on purpose or by accident? We might not ever have known all the great things he accomplished'."

"Yes, that would be a paradox," Einstein said. "Luckily it never happened because it couldn't. So what is the point you tried to make?"

"Today on our way over here you almost walked right out in front of a speeding car. I pulled you back. If I hadn't, you could have been killed. If you think about it, I needed to go back in time for that purpose only."

"I can think of two things straight away to debunk your theory. First, I'm old. The love of my life, my wife Elsa has passed away and I may not be far behind her.

I've already accomplished most of the 'great' things you talk about.

"Second, if you didn't delay me on my walk home today, I wouldn't have been at the precise place at the precise time the car came by and almost hit me. Thank you for saving my life, but it could be argued it was because of you, my life needed to be saved."

"Two very good points," I said. "I can't argue with either. What if I hadn't saved you? What if you had died today? If that had happened, I'm sure I would have been arrested, hung, electrocuted, lethally injected, and all those things, twice. It would also have meant you wouldn't be able to continue to work with the US military on the physics necessary to create the atomic bomb."

"How did you know that? You are a spy!"

"No, I keep telling you I come from the future. I can also tell you a large airplane called the Enola Gay drops the first ever atomic bomb on Hiroshima, Japan."

"No, they wouldn't do that without telling me."

"It doesn't happen until next year. They drop another one on Nagasaki and the Japanese surrender. This is taught in every American school in the future. It saved millions of lives by ending the war."

Albert Einstein sat in silence for a long time. Every once in a while he would almost imperceptibly shake his head no. A tear ran down his cheek.

"I'm sorry, I can't help you. It's getting late. You missed the last train again. You're welcome to spend the night in the extra room upstairs."

He then retired to his upstairs bedroom and that was the last we saw of him.

29

Our benevolent host had already left by the time we awoke early the next morning. He left a note for us to help ourselves to breakfast, but to please be gone before he returned.

We did as asked.

When we got back to the city, Karla talked me into going straight to the diner. "Someone might be worried about me."

We walked in arm in arm, giggling and laughing, reminiscing about the previous two nights. We stopped dead in our tracks when we saw Police Captain Martin Young of the New York City organized crime division, along with two of his officers waiting for us.

Frankie and a couple of his friends were there, too.

The two groups of men sat apart at each end of the counter, which was just long enough to separate them.

Margie and Friar Tuckles stood behind the counter between the two factions, keeping out of the way.

"Where have you been?" Captain Young asked Karla, all the while glaring at me. "We thought maybe he kidnapped you and did something terrible."

Karla was stunned. It took her a few moments to get her bearings. "It's not like that Martin. We're good friends. We took a trip to the Jersey Shore together."

"Good friends, eh?" Captain Young said. "It appears to be more than that to me."

Frankie smiled and nudged one of his goomba friends. He was well aware of the captain's obsession with Karla and took great pleasure seeing him cut down to size.

"It's none of your business," Karla said.

"I can see that," Captain Young said. "Let's go boys. I guess we came here for nothing."

As the officers marched out, Captain Young stopped and glared up at me. I was several inches taller and I could tell his attempt at looking fierce was a strain on his neck. A few seconds later, without saying anything, he left.

"What was that all about?"

"I think he has a crush on me," Karla said.

"Why didn't you tell me? I might have acted differently."

"Different? How?"

"I don't know. I think he believes I'm some sort of criminal now."

"He's a pushover. I'll straighten him out."

"You will?"

"No! Not like that."

"I didn't mean to imply anything. I just thought, I don't know what I thought. I guess I'm not too smucking fart today, am I."

"What?"

"Never mind."

"Bada bing," Frankie said. "I ain't never seen the uppity captain taken down like that. Come on boys. Karla's safe. Paul's the man, and we need to tell Don Antonio what's been taking place. Keep it up, stud," he said and threw a fake punch at my stomach as he walked past.

"Are you two lovebirds hungry?" Friar Tuckles asked. "You look like you could use something to eat."

"Yes, that would be great." Karla ushered me over to an open booth. "You seem dazed."

"I suppose I am. I was just warned by a police heavy who has a crush on you and congratulated by a gambling mafia hitman who owes me money. I'm miles, or worse still, years away from home. So, yes, I think any normal person would be."

"Don't forget the last couple days," Karla said. "I know I'm dazed."

"Yes, me too. Very much." I smiled, thinking myself stupid for not catching on to what she meant in the first place.

"Ok, so tell me all about it," Margie said as she brought over the food and slid into the booth next to me, facing Karla. "What have you two been up to?"

Karla began to blush. I took a long drink from my glass of water, keeping the glass pressed to my lips so I wouldn't need to speak.

"Maybe another time," Karla said. "I'll just say we went dancing and spent the night on a beach. We also met and spent the night at Albert Einstein's house."

"That Jew scientist?" Margie said. "Why him?"

"That 'Jew scientist' as you most impolitely call him, is the smartest mind in a thousand years," I said.

"Pshaw," Margie said. "So what?"

I could see my objections were futile so I let it drop and went back to the steak and eggs Friar Tuckles rustled up for me. The good Friar remembered.

We had barely finished when two squad cars pulled up in front. Six uniformed officers disembarked, led by none other than Captain Martin Young.

They stormed into the diner and roughly pulled Margie out of the way. "Hey!" she yelled at them.

They did their best to wrestle me to the floor. I didn't resist, but I was so much bigger than them, they struggled to pull my arms behind my back and lock my wrists in handcuffs.

"What are you doing?" Karla said. "He's done nothing wrong."

"Is that so?" Captain Young said. He tilted his head towards his men and towards the door. They dragged me outside and pushed me into the back seat of a squad car.

"You can't do that," Karla said. "He's done nothing wrong. If you're going to arrest him, you better arrest me, too."

"As much as I'd like to put you in handcuffs," he said, then looked at the others. He acted as if this was the first time he saw them. "I can't."

He slowly backed away and out the door.

"Don't worry, hon," Margie said. "We'll get him out."

"You're damn right we will." Karla stormed outside and tried to open the back car door where they had put me, but couldn't. She then pounded on Captain Young's window. "Let him go. He's done nothing wrong."

He stared straight ahead, refusing to acknowledge her. The car sped off, nearly knocking her over as it did.

"Try to find Frankie," Karla told Margie. "I'm going down to the precinct."

30

I was brought into the station, sat down in an interrogation room and chained to a table. A mirror took up most of one side of the room, which I rightly figured was one-way. I could only guess who was on the other side.

After about an hour alone, the door swung open with a crash. It broke the silence so abruptly I nearly jumped out of my seat. It would be a while before my heart slowed down.

Not just one interrogator, but a parade of men filed in. Captain Young was among the entourage but was unceremoniously pushed into one corner and told not to speak.

A man with dark, close-cropped and greased back hair, a well-worn black suit, white shirt and thin black tie, who emitted a strong scent of aftershave, introduced himself as Special Agent Ryker. He didn't give his first name. He went around the room to introduce everyone else, but skipped Captain Young.

I couldn't remember a single name other than Ryker, but I did note their titles included a lot of agents, colonels, and commanders. I detected what I thought might be army, navy and coast guard uniforms.

I had to wonder why they didn't stay behind the two-way mirror, out of sight. Were there even more men crowded in that little room on the other side? It was quite a show of force and if he was trying to intimidate me it worked. I was intimidated. I didn't know what was going on or why, but I felt certain I was now in deep kimchee.

"Do the words Operation Pastorius mean anything to you?" Ryker began his interrogation after he finished the introductions.

"Operation what?"

"Pastorius."

"No, should it?" I asked.

"Where are you from?" Ryker continued.

"Maine."

"Where in Maine?"

"Harpswell."

"And where is that?"

"On the coast, near Brunswick. A bit north of Portland."

A murmur spread through the room. Did I say something wrong?

"Why are you here?" Ryker asked.

At that point I knew I was in trouble as I didn't have a believable reason for being in New York.

"I inherited some money and wanted to invest it," was all I could come up with. As soon as the words left my mouth, I felt better. The truth will set me free. Certainly this must be a reasonable answer.

"How much money?"

"None of your business."

"Oh, I think it is very much our business. Have you ever been to Germany?"

I swallowed. It caused another murmur. "No."

"Are you certain?"

"Yes, why?"

"We've had someone in Tony's Diner following you since you showed up out of nowhere. He said he heard you telling the waitress you will be going to Germany to an SS base in the mountains. Why would you say that?"

"I didn't. I wouldn't. I never—"

"Our guy is dependable. He said you whispered it to her once."

"I'm telling you I didn't." I thought hard. The only time I could remember mentioning this was to Karla on our way to Wall Street. By that time we were at least a couple miles away from the diner. Could we have been bugged? I trusted Karla wouldn't have told anyone. Frankie perhaps?

Ryker brought my internal detective work to a halt. "Captain Young over here," he said and for the first time acknowledged him in the corner, "said he had a tape recorder hidden in the diner to gather intelligence on the Italian mobsters who hang out there. Would you like me to play the recording?"

"Yes, I would."

"We'll get to that. But for now, we have no records of you anywhere. It's like you suddenly appeared from thin air."

I cringed. I knew this was exactly how I arrived. I couldn't tell them that, though.

"A couple years ago, a German U-boat dropped off four spies on Long Island. They ran into Coast Guard patrolman John Cullen," Ryker pointed to a uniformed man standing tall among the brass. The man bowed his head. "He was threatened and had money forced upon him as a bribe to keep his mouth shut. He could have done just that and kept the money, but he is a true patriot and reported the incident. Are you a true patriot, Mr. Millard?"

"Yes, of course. How can I help?"

"Under intense interrogation, the spies said they were part of something called Operation Pastorius, Part One. They said there would be a Part Two. So, Mr. Millard, if that really *is* your name, are you Part Two? If you want to prove you're a patriot, you can tell the truth. You can tell us where your other spies are and give back the money the Nazis gave to your operation."

"Oh no, no, no," I said. "I'm not a spy. I don't know anything about other spies, and there is no way I am going to just give you my inheritance because you think I'm someone I'm not. That money is going to a good cause and not into government pockets."

"I see," Ryker said. "Is that your final answer?"

"Yes, that is my final answer."

"Ok, just a couple more questions. How old are you?"

"Twenty-five."

"Twenty-five? Why aren't you over there fighting with the boys, either in Europe or in the Pacific?"

I was stumped, for of course Ryker was right. If I had been born and raised here, I would be in the military with the rest of men and boys my age. "I was injured," was all I could think of.

"Injured?" Ryker looked me over as best as circumstances would allow from the other side of the desk. Even though he saw no obvious injury, he nonetheless didn't pursue the matter. "Lock him up, boys. Let him sweat for a day or two. We'll see if he'll talk then."

Until that moment I never thought being locked up would sound like a welcome relief. I was sure glad Ryker didn't follow up on my injury excuse. I wouldn't know how to answer if he had.

The entourage of counterintelligence men filed out, leaving just Captain Young behind. Before calling in officers to unlock my restraints and take me to the cells, Young sat at the edge of the table, doing his best to tower over me.

"I knew you were a criminal or a spy. You showed up out of nowhere, you hang out with mobsters, and you came waltzing in with money and charm and swept Karla off her feet. Well I'm not going to let that happen." He punched me hard in the face. When the first one didn't have an effect, he hit me again.

Captain Young might have been considered average height for men in 1944, but he had a slight build. His punches hardly caused a reaction. I wanted to tell him he hit like a girl but thought better of it. I licked the tiny drop of blood off my lip, winked at him and smiled. "Whatever you say, boss."

"I'm going to keep a sharp eye on you," Young said. He called for his men to come in and get me, but when he did, his voice squeaked. I tried hard not to laugh but couldn't help myself. I burst out in an uncontrolled chortle, albeit a short one. It ended in a hurry when the much larger uniformed officers entered, battered me around, and dragged me off to my cell.

Along the way, I could see Karla at the front desk arguing with the officers on duty. I felt a deep attraction for her at that moment, more than I had ever felt for anyone in my life.

This, too, changed quickly when Ryker showed up, started talking with her, and had the officers forcefully drag her away. She was kicking and screaming, "Let me go!"

"Atta girl. Don't make it easy for them."

31

Forty-eight hours after my arrest, I was still sitting in my cell. No one had talked with me since the first interrogation. All my attempts to speak with someone about Karla's condition were denied.

Finally, Ryker arrived with a jailor and unlocked the door.

"You're free to go," Ryker said.

"Just like that?"

"Yes."

"What happened to change your mind?"

"We searched your hotel room and interviewed everyone who had contact with you. We couldn't find any evidence to dispute your story. We couldn't find anything to corroborate it either, so you may still be visited by the military as to your claims of injury for not enlisting. But we can't keep you more than forty-eight hours without charging you."

"What about the tapes you said you had?"

"There aren't any tapes. That would be illegal."

"Your guy at the diner?"

"He said it was someone else who looked like you."

"Who is he?"

"You know I can't tell you."

"I'll look for him at the diner," I said.

"You won't recognize him."

"What about Karla? Where is she? Is she ok?"

"Yes, we asked her a few questions and decided we could eliminate her from our list of potential Nazi spies."

"So, you interrogated her, too? I'm sure that made her happy."

"She kicked up a fuss, that's for certain. We let her go after a couple of hours. Ever since, she's been hanging around the station talking to anyone who will listen, trying to get you freed. You have a good woman there, Mr. Millard."

"Yes, I know."

I was taken to the exit antechamber where a clerk inside a metal cage counted out and gave me back all my belongings, checking each one off a list. He was taking his time, I was sure on purpose. When finished, an officer led me to a door and practically pushed me through it out into the streets.

Lucky for me, Karla was waiting.

She ran up and jumped into my arms, giving me a big hug and kiss. "I knew you were innocent."

"Thank you. I'm glad you're safe, too."

"Come on, let's get out of here."

"I need a shower and a bed. I'm a different person now. Being in prison really changes a man."

"Oh come on," Karla said and laughed. "You were only in there a couple days.

"Yes, but they were brutal days," I said and smirked. "It was touch and go for a while. I was afraid they might start pulling out my fingernails. *'Vee vill make you talk.'* Some of those guys, particularly your boyfriend Captain Young, really thought I was a traitor."

"You're not a traitor. I knew they would figure it out sooner or later. Maybe after they pulled off your fingernails or wrenched out your teeth, though." Karla grabbed my index finger and gave it a twist.

"Ow! I'm beginning to think you really like hurting me."

* * * * *

Over the next couple of weeks I spent my free time between hanging out with Karla, trying to figure out how I might get to Germany, and gambling on Yankees baseball games with Frankie the Mole. My iPhone didn't let me down. It always kept me informed ahead of time not only who would win, but final scores, box scores, number of home runs, hits, doubles, everything I could use to gain a gambling advantage.

I made sure to lose as many bets as I won, just to keep the betting alive without landing myself in trouble with the mob. When I was arrested, I was on one of my upswings and the plan was to start losing on purpose to even it out again.

But something Karla said got under my skin. When she asked people to help get me out of jail, she said Frankie had told her, "Let him rot in there. I owe him two and a half G's and if they string him up I won't have to pay."

Stupidly, I let my anger get the better of me and I allowed my winnings to grow back up to twenty-five hundred dollars again. To make matters worse, the next time I ran into Frankie after it got to that level I decided to go for a sucker bet.

"Frankie, I know you're a bit behind so, since you're such a good friend, I'm going to give you a chance to get some back. But only if you give me some odds."

"What do you have in mind?"

"I don't know, how about something silly, like I'll bet you a thousand dollars that Hersh Martin will hit two home runs in tonight's game, but only if you give me five to one odds."

"That's ridiculous," Frankie said. "No bet."

"Ok, so no bet tonight. But I'll keep the offer open if you change your mind."

Frankie left without finishing his coffee, crossed the street and disappeared inside a butcher shop. He emerged a half hour later and walked with purpose straight across the road and into the diner.

"I made some calls. Martin isn't a home run hitter. He had only seven all year, and you want to bet me he will hit two tonight?"

"That's the bet," I said. "Are you interested?"

"Not for a grand," Frankie replied. "I'll bet five 'Gs. The two and a half I owe you and two and a half more."

"At what odds?"

"Straight up," Frankie said.

"Not interested. If you give me five to one odds, I'll take the bet."

Frankie stared at me a moment as he tried to figure out what I was up to. The chances Hersh Martin, a career minor league player who barely made it to the bigs with an average Yankees team would hit two home runs in one game were slim at best.

"Three to one."

I sat for a moment to think. I was experiencing a twinge of doubt. Not about whether Martin would hit two home runs, I knew it would happen thanks to the baseball almanac page on my iPhone. But because of what might happen to me when he did.

"Yeah, I thought so," Frankie said. "You're yellow. No guts."

"Since you put it that way, you're on. Let's shake on it."

Frankie was quick to grab my hand and shook it with extra vigor. I took a deep breath. It was too late to back out now.

"Shall we head over to Yankee stadium?" Frankie said.

"No thanks. I think I've had enough excitement for one day."

"Don't you go running off, you hear? I want to be able to collect my twenty-five hundred tonight. I may go out on the town to celebrate."

"Don't spend it yet. You never know what might happen."

Later that evening, Hersh Martin played the game of his career. He went three for four, hit two home runs and drove in all five of the Yankees runs in their five to four win over the Chicago White Sox.

* * * * *

With his gambling losses now at fifteen grand, Frankie was in trouble. The amount didn't seem like much to me; I recently had millions at my disposal. However, $15,000 was a lot of money to a mid-level wise guy in the 1940s.

Frankie knew he could no longer cover the bet without help, so he resigned himself to seeing his boss, Don Antonio, to bail him out.

When Frankie informed the Don of his losing streak, and how he now owed me fifteen grand, the Don's reaction was predictable.

"Who's Paul?"

"Some guy I met and have been keeping an eye on."

"Some guy you met?" Don Antonio's face turned red but his demeanor remained calm. "Go get him and bring him here. I want to meet this 'some guy you met'."

Frankie hesitated a second or two, trying to figure out how best to get himself out of this mess. "I just want to tell—"

Before he could finish the sentence, the Don yelled, "Now!" and thrust his finger towards the exit. When Frankie hesitated again, he became the beneficiary of a hard right cross to the side of his face.

Staggered, Frankie somehow managed to keep his feet, which angered the Don even more. Frankie shook his head, trying to maintain consciousness, rubbed his chin and made a hasty exit. Another punch would have knocked him out cold.

"Tommy, you go with him," Don Antonio called out to Tomase Gracini, aka Tommy Two Guns, who could have been mistaken as Frankie's twin brother. "Make sure he doesn't do a runner."

Tommy nodded and followed Frankie out the door.

It didn't take them long to find me. I was walking along the street on my way to the diner to meet up with Karla. I was only a few steps away, so close in fact I could see her standing just inside the glass door, smiling, watching me approach.

Tommy pulled up alongside in the company Packard, running it up on the curb to block my path. Before I had a chance to respond, Frankie burst out from the passenger side with his handgun at the ready. He reached up, grabbed me by the scruff of the neck and forced me towards the car. Even though I was a much bigger man, the thirty-eight special jammed into my ribs was more than an adequate equalizer.

Tommy reached over the front seat and pushed open the back door. I ducked my head and got in without a fight.

Karla looked on in horror as the Packard sped away.

"What's this?" I said. "If you wanted me to go someplace with you, all you had to do was ask. There's no need to jam a gun in my ribs."

"It's about the fifteen large I owe you. It's time for you to collect, but since it's so much you need to go get it from our boss, Don Antonio Napoli."

"Fat Tony?" I said before realizing my mistake.

Tommy Two Guns gave me a menacing glance in the mirror. Frankie re-aimed his handgun at my face, "Shut up. Don't ever call him that."

With Karla's warnings ringing in my ears about how I should never, ever cross the Don, I decided I didn't need the money. "It's ok. I don't need it. I can wait. Forever."

"A bet is a bet, and all bets are honored. If the situation were reversed and you owed him, you better believe he'd collect. It would be seen as a sign of disrespect if you don't collect. Believe me, Paul, you do not want to disrespect Don Antonio Napoli."

"No, really, it's ok. Keep it. I don't want any trouble. We can wipe the slate clean. Start over again from scratch."

"If the boss doesn't pay you, word would get out how Little Italy's top enforcer couldn't be trusted to back his bets. In this business, perhaps more than any other, a man's word is his bond. If people started to think a man couldn't be trusted, well, let's just say it wouldn't be long before some wise guy trying making his way up the ranks would come along and pop a couple shots into the back of the Don's noggin."

32

Tommy Two Guns maneuvered the Packard through the back streets and pulled up to a wide two-story warehouse.

After the three of us disembarked, Frankie slid open a wooden door just far enough to allow single file passage inside.

Our steps echoed in the hollowness as we walked across an open floor littered with crates, and headed towards a glassed-in office to one side. We didn't make it all the way there before a huge man emerged with four other smartly dressed men in tow.

I consider myself to be a bit larger than most men, but this man's arms were bigger than my legs. His upper body could be used as a poster for barrel chest, and his head sat firmly on his shoulders, with no neck in sight.

Don Antonio de Napoli, head of Little Italy's Napoli Family, had a few obvious scars. These war medals were a testament to having fought his way up through the ranks, including two almost identical round scars, one on each cheek, remnants of when he was shot in the face. He had been lucky his mouth was wide open, yelling profanities at one of his enemies while another was off to the side in an ambush. The bullet went through one cheek and out the other, piercing only skin, missing tongue and teeth on the way through.

Neither of the men survived the attempt. Tony made sure their deaths were slow and painful.

The man extended his paw, greeting me with, "So you're the man who knows so much about baseball he's put my best bookie fifteen grand in the hole."

"Pure luck, Don Antonio, sir," I bowed slightly and took the man's hand. The Don's grip was crushing and it didn't seem he would ever let go.

"Call me Tony. You've earned it. Frankie the Mole tells me you not only win, but win on strange bets, then rub it in. 'Who's the baseball expert now, Frankie?'" Only the Don could get away with calling him 'Frankie the Mole'.

"Tell me, Paul, what's your method? How do you know when a team will get three hits against a pitcher, not four, not two, but three? Or how a man who hadn't hit a home run all year manages to hit two in one game—and you predicted it?"

"Pure luck," I said. "Frankie liked to rub it in every time he won, so I was giving it back to him. I didn't mean any harm."

"That's not the question, is it? The question is, how did you know all these things before they happened?"

I shook my head. "I didn't."

"There's a nasty little story around about how you, somehow, are from the future."

I gasped.

"Yes," Tony said. "That's what I hear."

"That's ridiculous. Impossible. Easy to deny because there is no way it could be true."

"You're a liar, future Paul. Your winning streak and the odd, impossible bets say different."

"You can't be serious," I said. "The future?"

"Oh, I'm serious. Deadly serious. Tell you what I'm going to do. I could, but I won't kill you. Not yet anyway. I'm tired of losing bets to Myron Lipinski in Brooklyn, so I when I found out about you, I bet him a hundred thousand dollars I'd win an outrageous bet with him. He said he would be crazy to take such a bet without knowing what he was betting on. So I gave him ten to one odds. He still balked. So I told him, if I can't come up with a viable bet that he'd agree to by midnight tonight, I'd forfeit and he'd win. He said he'd be stupid not to take the bet, as all he would have to do is say no and he'd win. He was right, so I told him a complete outsider would need to agree the bet was viable. If the outsider said it was viable and Lipinski still don't want to bet, the wager is off. No one wins, no one loses. But if he takes the bet and I win, he gives me a hundred grand. If he takes the bet and he wins, I give him a million. If I can't come up with a viable bet, determined by the outsider by midnight tonight, he still wins. He agreed. Now it's up to you to give me an outrageous bet about tonight's game that you know will win."

"I assure you, I can't do anything of the kind." I didn't have my iPhone with me. Even if I did, I couldn't get it out now, as it would be proof of my less than honorable methods.

"Yes you can and you will."

"Believe me, I can't." I'm an idiot. How I let this happen was indisputable proof of that. I let my ego get the better of me and now I may pay with my life.

"Believe me you will," Tony said. "I'll give you a choice, silver or lead."

"Silver or lead?"

"Bring me silver winnings or take a lead bullet."

"Can you give me some time to go back to my room and study the newspaper?" It was my last attempt to find a way out of the death sentence the Don had declared upon me.

"Oh, hell no. I'm not stupid. If I let you leave you'll do a runner, sure as I'm standing here. I'm not letting you out of my sight. You're staying right here where I can watch you."

Tony turned away for a moment. "Frankie, go out and buy today's paper. Paul needs to study it for tonight's game."

"Yes sir." Frankie was gone in an instant. He didn't want to end up on the business end of another of the Don's hard right crosses.

"I can't and I won't," I said.

"You can and you will," Tony repeated.

At that moment, which turned out to be the most inopportune time, my neck began to itch. Must have been nerves. I started to scratch it in my own particular way, quite subconsciously, with head titled back, palm facing in, fingers straight and flicking the itch out from under my chin.

I continued until I realized the entire room was silent with every eye fixed on me. Including Tony, whose face was dark red. I'd never seen anyone's face as dark red as his. Was he having a stroke? I almost felt I should have been seeing smoke come out of his ears.

"Is that what you think of us?" Tony said. The veins on his no-neck seemed as though they were about to burst.

Confused, I could only stammer, "What? Why?" I hadn't yet realized I had just given them the Sicilian equivalent of the middle finger.

The next thing I heard was, "You useless douche bag."

Fat Tony swung, connecting a hard left hook to my jaw. The blow caught me off guard and I staggered, but to everyone's surprise, including mine, I didn't go down.

As I wavered between consciousness and total blackout, the sudden pain seemed to bring back a flood of childhood memories of when my stepfather beat me senseless. I had wanted to fight back but was too young, too small.

It did teach me that I could take a punch. It also taught me to never suggest impropriety or confuse hope with reality when Popeye is halfway through the night's five gallon jug of Gallo wine. Three-quarters or more is ok. By then he's too drunk to care. The mean streak comes out around the halfway mark. By the age of twelve I learned it's best to keep my mouth shut and make myself scarce.

Now, after years of hard labor, the long hours of swinging lobster traps out on the sea had hardened me. Combined with the Thai boxing training I took up last year, it gave me more strength than even I realized.

Without further thought, I deftly landed a hard kick to Tony's thigh, which buckled him, and followed this with a quick spin and a hard elbow to Tony's jaw a little below his ear. It knocked the big man to the floor.

A moment of stunned silence was broken by a chorus of clicking when the hammers on perhaps a dozen handguns locked into place. Every weapon was trained on me.

"Put them away," Tony growled. He shook his head, trying to knock out the confusion while he regained his feet—and his composure. He had not inherited his position as a mob boss, he'd fought for it. Growing up on the mean streets of New York City, Fast Anthony, as he thought he was known in his younger days, didn't back down from a fight and he never lost. It had been years since the last time anyone had dared to fight him and even longer since he'd tasted the saltiness of his own blood, felt its stickiness on his lips.

Somehow this didn't enrage him. It brought back fond memories of his struggle to the top. Instead of wanting to kill me right away, he very much wanted to feel the aliveness of being in a knockdown drag-out fight with a worthy opponent. He didn't want any of his henchmen to shoot me before he had a chance to win on his own. "So, you think you're a tough guy, eh? Let's go."

Tony brought his fists up, striking a 1940s boxer's pose, and began circling me.

I didn't want anything to do with this, so I raised my hands, palms out in surrender. It didn't take a genius to realize this was a no-win situation. Either I would be beaten to death by the strongest, toughest, meanest man I had ever had the displeasure of meeting, or if by some miracle I managed to win the fight, I'd be gunned down by a platoon of wise guys defending their boss.

Tony would have none of it. "Oh no, you *will* fight me." He turned to Tommy Two Guns. "If he doesn't put up his dukes by the count of three, put one in his knee. One—"

I balled up and raised my fists, but it was obvious I was in no position to defend myself.

Before another blow could be landed by either side, the warehouse doors slid open and dozens of New York's finest came streaming in.

The Don snarled and I thought for sure he would throw a punch before they got to us. But he held back. Dropping his fists, he turned to look at the oncoming posse to size up his odds. About half the uniformed cops were on his payroll. Still, the other half weren't, which turned the odds against him.

Police Captain Martin Young was the officer in command. He ordered his men to spread out around us, engulfing the circle the Don's armed soldiers had formed as a human boxing ring around our budding fight.

"What have we here?" Young said.

Tony's men all slid their weapons into various holsters and prearranged concealed places at the first sign of trouble.

Tony was so furious he couldn't speak, so I took the initiative. "Just a friendly meeting among friendly friends."

"Is that right?" Young said. He motioned to one of his men to retrieve me and take me outside.

Captain Young for some time had been trying to make a name for himself by breaking up organized crime in his district. After receiving an anonymous phone call about how something bad was about to go down at the warehouse, he assembled dozens of men into a posse to raid Don Antonio Napoli's lair.

What could the Don do? He did, however, notice the uniform who had been ordered to take me outside *was* on his payroll. It only took a half-second look and an almost imperceptible lift of the Don's chin for the cop to understand his role in the developing situation.

Once outside, the dirty cop told me to "run, and don't look back". At first I hesitated, but he pointed his service revolver at my head and repeated, "Run."

The Don's cop knew as long as I was on the loose, Don Antonio could chase me down and deal with me. So he let me run.

I thought for sure he would shoot me in the back and tell everyone I had tried to escape. But I also felt I had no choice. Be shot in the head where I stood, or make a zig-zag run for it.

To my surprise, no gunshots were forthcoming as I ran. When I dared a quick look back, I witnessed the cop hitting himself in the head with the butt of his revolver. It all started to make sense. I was now a marked man. I couldn't trust the police and I couldn't trust any of the local hoods I'd come to know.

A green flash caught the corner of my eye back on the other side of the warehouse. I couldn't be sure, but it looked like William Vrill IV was peeking around the corner. Whoever it was, he had a strong grip on the side of the wall and was having a difficult time standing. It also seemed like he was hiding, searching for something or someone.

33

I ran straight to Fat Tony's Diner to find Karla, the only person I could trust. "What are you doing here?" she said after I explained what had just happened. "This will be the first place they'll look. Take my keys and wait for me in my room."

"No way," I said. "If they're going to look for me here, when they don't find me they'll head straight for your place. I'm sure of it. I have to figure out something else. Someplace they won't think to look. Do they know about the Commodore Hotel?"

"I don't know, maybe. Probably. I told Margie; she might have told someone."

"Well, let's hope I can get in there to gather my things and out again before any of Fat Tony's men show up."

"Then what?"

"I don't know. I'll figure it out when the time comes."

Karla sighed, grabbed me by the face and gave me a big wet kiss. "Get out of here sailor, before someone comes looking."

"Yes mam."

I ran as fast as my legs could carry me back to my room at the Commodore and gathered up all my belongings. I didn't check out, as I was sure Don Antonio would send men there to stake out the place. If they thought I'd return, they might stay there on the lookout. It might mean at least two less men wandering around town looking for me.

I made a hasty return to the back of the diner, peeked in the back door and saw Friar Tuckles leaning against the ice box. When he saw me, he held up a finger to keep me from coming in, turned and made a quick whistle through the opening out into the diner. A couple seconds later, Karla burst into the kitchen.

"What are you doing here?"

"I came to give you these," I said, handing her the keys to the safe deposit box. "I need you to go there first thing in the morning. Empty the box and bring everything back here. Hide it somewhere safe. I'll find you as soon as I figure out what to do."

"But," she started to say. It was too late, I was already out of sight and on the run.

Back at the warehouse, Captain Young and his men couldn't find anything incriminating and had no choice but to file out of the warehouse and return to their posts. "I'll be watching you, Fat Tony," Captain Young said, infuriating the Don even more.

Once the entourage had filed out, and when calmness returned, Frankie the Mole showed up with the day's newspaper, unaware of what had taken place moments before. "Here you go, boss."

Tony was so angry he could have killed him right then and there. Instead, he calmly told him, "I want you to take Tommy Two Guns and Jimmy the Tuna and go find this grifter you call Paul."

Frankie looked around and for the first time realized I was no longer in the warehouse. He nodded his agreement, fully aware of the metaphorical red flag that had just gone straight up. Frankie was in big trouble. Other than himself, Tommy Two Guns and Jimmy the Tuna were the Don's best assassins. He knew right away the three of them would not be out looking for me.

James Garaciolla, aka Jimmy the Tuna, was a huge oaf of a man and had one purpose in life—to do the Don's wet work. His moniker was a condensed version of Jimmy the Piano Tuner, so named for the piano wire fastened at both ends to deer antler handles he used as his weapon of choice. He was strong as an ox, but too slow, both of foot and of mind, to do much of anything else other to kill on demand.

Frankie could almost feel the wire tighten around his neck. He instinctively stuck his chin upwards and to the right, twisting his neck.

"We'll find him," Frankie said, just in case he was wrong about his impending kiss of death.

Don Antonio turned and walked back to his office, followed by the rest of his men. He didn't look at any of them, instead threw his hand up over his shoulder, effectively erecting a wall between him and what he had just ordered.

Frankie had been a good earner but in the last week or so would have given a chunk of it back through bad bets and loss of face with other dons.

Now, the Don had to figure out how to handle his bet with Lipinski. He'd deal with that when his other soldiers caught up with me. As soon as Frankie, Tommy and Jimmy were out the door he ordered a search party to find me and bring me back. Alive, "But I won't mind if you have to shoot him in the knee."

Meanwhile, Tommy Two guns and Jimmy the Tuna didn't in any way acknowledge the Don's unspoken order. "This Paul shyster has turned out to be a real pain in the ass," Tommy said on the way out to the Packard.

As they approached the car, Frankie watched as Jimmy took great effort to climb into the back seat and position himself in his usual spot behind the passenger. This gave him easier access to his victim in front. Not being overly agile, he needed surprise and proximity.

Tommy Two Guns would be the driver.

In one smooth move Frankie took out his .38 revolver, unseen, and as he slid into the car he fired three shots through the passenger seat at Jimmy the Tuna behind. Whether by luck or by skill, all three shots hit center mass. The Tuna was dead before he felt the pain.

Satisfied, Frankie reached over and stuck the revolver into Tommy's ribs. "Drive".

Tommy looked in the mirror. Jimmy's eyes and mouth were wide open, but nary a muscle on his body was moving. Tommy shifted his gaze towards Frankie. "Where to, boss?"

"You know damn well where we're going," Frankie said.

Both men remained calm as if this was just another day at the office. Tommy started the Packard, pushed the clutch pedal to the floor, shifted into first gear, and popped the clutch. The car leapt forward and stalled. The jerky motion jolted everyone, slamming Jimmy the Tuna's extremely heavy dead body into the back of Frankie's seat. The momentum pinned Tommy to the steering wheel and Frankie to the dashboard.

Frankie's gun never left Tommy's ribs. Tommy heard the click when Frankie cocked the hammer back one notch.

"Nice try," Frankie said as he and Tommy pushed the seat back to its rightful place. The car bounced again when Jimmy's body flopped back to its original spot behind them, then rolled onto the floor.

As soon as the car stopped rocking, Frankie reached over and removed both of Tommy's two guns, sliding the weapons into his coat pocket.

"If it means anything," Tommy said, "I'm not happy with all this."

"It doesn't," Frankie said coldly. "Shut up and drive."

Silence pervaded the two hour trip to a deserted stretch of dunes along East Hampton on the shores of Long Island. When they reached a suitably desolate area, Tommy pulled to the side of the road and stopped.

"What now?"

"You're going to help me dispose of Jimmy and we're going to drive back into Manhattan. I'll decide what to do with you on the way back."

Relieved, but still wary, Tommy nodded his agreement.

It was a major struggle getting the massive limp body out from the back of the Packard. Dragging him across the road and into the dunes was no easy task, either. After a few yards into the marsh, both men were exhausted.

Along the way, Tommy noticed a gun Jimmy had hidden in his inner coat pocket. When he thought Frankie might be looking the other way, he went for it. Like Jimmy, he too never felt the bullet that killed him as it passed through the back of his head, a bullet from one of his own guns. Within in an instant, before his mind had even registered the sound of the gunshot, he collapsed dead on top of Jimmy the Tuna.

Frankie reached into his pocket and pulled out the pair of leather gloves he always kept with him for times like this. Putting them on, he slid his handkerchief out of his breast pocket, gave it a shake, and used it to wipe down Tommy's two guns.

Not that it mattered. Anyone who cared about the scene in front of him would already know what had happened and who was involved. There was no way anyone would share this information with the police, at least not the police who weren't on the payroll. It's doubtful other police would investigate the matter either, as to them, having two fewer wise guys to chase down was nothing more than a small blessing.

As the sun began to rise it turned the dark cloudless sky into a pale blue. The sound of the waves crashing on the shore was eerily soothing, although the morning gulls sounded hauntingly sad. Looking at the pile of bodies beside him, Frankie thought, had things gone horribly different this might have been a decent final resting place for himself. He threw the guns on top of the pile of bodies.

Snapping back to reality, he took a long look around the area to see if anyone was out here at this time of day. Convinced there were no witnesses, he climbed into the Packard, fired it up and began the trip back to Little Italy.

As he pulled away from the scene, Frankie felt a slight bit of remorse. He and Tommy had been close friends and often worked together on jobs. Given their closeness, Frankie figured killing him was Tommy's punishment for not intervening when the gambling got out of hand. Don Antonio was a brutal, unforgiving boss. Had Tommy and Jimmy killed Frankie, Tommy, due to his partnership with Frankie, might have faced the same fate once he made it back to Manhattan. Frankie was never destined to know.

His remorse didn't last. It was business, nothing personal. He'd been faced with these kinds of decisions most of his chosen life and came to know, whoever you are, when it comes down to either you or me with no other possible outcome, both you and I will choose to survive. Survival is part of our animal instinct. The answer is always better you die than me.

The long ride back alone left Frankie with plenty of time to think. By the time he entered the outskirts of the old neighborhood, he knew exactly what he needed to do.

34

A few minutes before closing, when everyone else had gone home, Frankie walked into Tony's Diner, sat down and ordered a cup of coffee. Karla could see blotches of blood on him but made herself look away and not stare. It was all she could do to keep calm, especially the way he was looking at her. He must know. Had he come here to punish her?

Frankie looked menacingly nervous and Karla thought she detected his hands shaking slightly when he lit his unfiltered Lucky Strike. He seemed awfully interested in the butcher shop across the street.

"What are you up to tonight, doll?" he asked when she approached his booth.

Does he know it was her who sent the police to the warehouse? "Nothing," she said, "I've been here working all night."

"Relax doll, this ain't no interrogation," he said, but her response sparked his interest. He spat out a fleck of tobacco, turned to look at her up and down, and settled on her powerful eyes. "I've always liked you Karla. You've got real moxie, the one bright spot in this dark and ugly world."

Karla felt a drop of sweat roll down the back of her neck. This psychopathic contract killer who'd think no more about murdering her than lighting his cigarette sounded strange. "What can I get ya, hon?" she managed to squeak out, almost in a whisper. She immediately cleared her throat. "Sorry, must be a frog in my throat. What can I get you, hon?" she repeated.

She tried her best to exude confidence. After all, she'd been serving Don Antonio's men at this diner for years.

"Don't snap your cap, kid. I'm not here to hurt you." Frankie's saying so seemed to take the air out of him, though. "Look doll, you and your boyfriend need to get out of here. Leave, as soon as you can."

"What b, b, boyfriend?" Karla stuttered.

"You know who I'm talking about," Frankie grabbed her wrist for emphasis. Karla pulled back, but his grip was firm. "Things are changing around here awful fast kid. I'm sure you know it. Mostly because of your boyfriend. And if I can make the connection, Fat Tony can too."

Karla knew something bad was happening when Frankie called him Fat Tony. None of the Don's men ever called him that, at least not in public.

"I wouldn't want to see you end up on the wrong end of a devil's piano," Frankie said. "Pour me a black cuppa joe, then get the hell out of here. It could turn nasty real quick like, and you shouldn't be around when it does."

Frankie returned his stare to the butcher shop and didn't utter another word.

Karla walked behind the counter and picked up the coffee pot as smoothly as she could. She brought it over to the table, flipped over a cup to face-up on its saucer, held her hand as steady as possible given the circumstances, and managed to pour a full cup without spilling anything.

Frankie paid no attention.

Karla backed away and returned to make a pretense of cleaning the counter and getting ready to close. She tried her best not to look at him again, but every once in a while she would steal a glance. He remained preoccupied with whatever was out the window across the street.

When he finally rose to leave, he threw a dollar on the table for a ten cent cup of coffee, gave her one last long look and headed out the door.

She ran over and locked it behind him, flipped the sign over to closed, switched off some of the lights, and collapsed behind the counter.

Once she mustered the courage to peek out the front windows, she could see a man in a trench coat on the other side of the road smoking a cigarette. When he took a drag, the red glow lit up his face. It was Frankie. He must know she had called the police. He must be waiting for her.

Once again she was overcome with fear but managed to gather her thoughts and her belongings and sneak out the back door. She raced home through the back alleys, dug out her travel bag from its hiding place, filled it with as many clothes as she could fit in, along with her toothbrush, toiletries, hairbrush, and an extra pair of shoes, then headed back out. When she reached downstairs, she peered out the front door, scanning for anything potentially threatening. She saw nothing unusual, so she hustled her way out, not knowing where to go.

* * * * *

Frankie was on a mission of his own. He came up with a plan during the bumpy ride back. He had to leave town, that was a given. Wherever he went, it would need to be far enough away so the goons wouldn't find him. Tommy Two Guns' Packard would do for his getaway car, so that was taken care of. Eventually he would need to clean Jimmy the Tuna's blood out of the back seat, but that would be something he could worry about later. Now he needed money. Lots of money, and fast. The only place he knew where he could get that much money at this time of night was the counting room behind the butcher shop across from Tony's Diner.

Don Antonio, among his other illicit activities, which included robbery, extortion, and murder for hire, ran several high-stakes poker games and gambling joints around the borough. The nightly take was brought to a counting room in the back of Paulie's Butcher shop on Mulberry Street. Frankie knew of it, and everything about it, because he had been stationed there as a guard back in the early days when he was trying to make his bones with the outfit. He also knew it was still there, being used, and full of a substantial amount of untaxed, untraceable cash. He headed straight for it.

Once Frankie arrived, he parked around the corner, reloaded his thirty-eight, tucked it in the pocket of his overcoat, and checked the time. If schedules were still being kept, and he was certain they were, a drop would happen within the next half hour. To kill time, he had stopped into Tony's Diner.

Out of the corner of his eye, he noticed the delivery truck pull up to make the drop. He watched in silence until the driver returned and drove away, then threw a dollar on the table, left the diner and walked across the street.

Frankie lit a smoke and waited outside a few moments before he performed the secret knock. Paddy was on call that night and opened the door. His face lit up when he saw Frankie.

"Hiya Frankie. What're you doin here?"

"I came to relieve the guards. It's my turn to watch tonight."

"I din't hear nuttin about that. I gotta check first—"

Within the blink of an eye, Frankie stuck a knife deep into Paddy's throat. Poor Irish kid, Frankie thought. Numb as a pounded thumb, he only worked there because he didn't know enough to do anything else. With nothing but distress in his future, the underboss had taken pity on him. Frankie didn't.

Inside there could be anywhere from two to four guards in the front room. Tonight there were two. Behind them would be the counting room with one armed guard and one or two wimpy money counters. Frankie knew the drill well. As he entered the front room, he shot the first two people he saw. Two headshots. They were dead before they hit the floor.

He knew the loud noise would alert the counting room along with Scar's double barrel shotgun guarding the loot and the counters. Frankie kicked the door hard and immediately dropped to the floor. Sure enough, Scar cut loose with both barrels, cutting the door in half.

It was what Frankie was counting on. In order to shoot again, Scar would need to reload. The time it would take was all Frankie needed to take him down with a barrage of gunfire from his trusty thirty-eight.

Scar was hard as nails and even though he was being hit with shot after shot, he was almost able to finish reloading his shotgun and shoot back before a final, fatal head shot took him down for good.

After that, it was easy pickings. The two counters were soggy-diaper banker types who weren't paid enough to get shot on the job. Their hands went skyward, backs against the wall in absolute terror, revealing an enormous amount of money on the table. Either it had been an amazingly good night around town or the money had been saved up a few days before counting. Either way, there must have been close to a million dollars. All the better for Frankie. He needed as much as he could get to escape Fat Tony's clutches.

"I'm not gonna hurt ya," Frankie told the milquetoasts, "as long as you help me gather the loot into something I can carry out the door."

Obedience was immediate. Bank bags were produced and within a few short minutes, the table's entire contents were swept into them. Frankie kept his gun pointed at them, not because he believed they would put up a fight but because he wanted to keep them scared and willing to do as he said. It didn't matter that he hadn't had time to reload. His gun was empty.

Before he left, Frankie reached into the bank bags and gave each a stack of cash. "You never saw me."

Eyes as big as saucers, they didn't respond. "I said, you never saw me," Frankie repeated, this time a little louder.

"Never saw who?"

"Me!" Frankie shot back. After a moment passed, he seemed to catch on to what they were saying. "That's right, you never seen who."

With that, Frankie was out the door, around the corner, and into the Packard. He fired it up and drove north. Checking the mirrors often, he was sure no one was following him.

Just outside the city, when he started to relax, he turned on the car radio for company. After scrolling through the static, he landed on a WLIB newscast. The main story was how an investment firm had been robbed of hundreds of thousands of dollars in cash. Frankie couldn't decipher the name, but it sounded like a woman's name. Marianne perhaps? Couldn't be, he must have heard wrong.

It dawned on him why the counting room had so much money. One of Fat Tony's men, perhaps even the Don himself had pulled off the heist to pay for his bets with Myron Lipinski. The loot was brought to the counting room to store until tomorrow.

Frankie turned off the radio, glad to be speeding away from the underworld, even though it was the only life he'd ever known. He kept driving through the night, not stopping except for gas. Much of the time he drove through near blinding darkness, the road dimly lit by his faded headlamps.

When morning's dim light began to creep back into his world, still Frankie drove, past isolated country churches, dilapidated houses settled next to leaning barns and dismembered tractors, rocky cow pastures giving way to hills and valleys. Past postcard views of mountainous streams snaking alongside the empty road, and one traffic-light towns until he was far north near the Canadian border in a sleepy little village in upstate New York called Potsdam, several hundred miles and twelve hours' drive away from the city. Only then did he feel safe. Only then did he rest.

35

The next morning, Karla managed to talk her way into emptying the safe deposit box at the bank. She introduced herself as Mrs. Paul Millard and was convincing enough to pull it off.

She didn't dare go back inside the diner, though, and instead she hid in an alleyway outside, down the street, waiting for me to arrive. She nearly had a heart attack a few hours later when I announced my presence behind her.

After hitting me hard, twice, in the soft flesh of my shoulder, she told me all about her experience with Frankie the previous night.

"You did the right thing by not going back," I said. "We're fugitives now. We need to lay low, then get out of here as fast as we can."

"Where will we go?" Except for our trip to the Jersey Shore, she had never been anywhere outside Little Italy and the few blocks in the surrounding area.

"I have a plan," I said. "We can start by heading over to Grand Central Station."

We took our time getting there in case anyone spotted us. Instead of walking a straight path, we walked a meandering track down side streets, stopping at an occasional storefront, market or bakery, making sure no one was following.

By the time we arrived it was already beginning to get dark. We did our best to blend in with the hundreds, maybe thousands of people who scurried about inside, some waiting to begin passage to somewhere far away, others waiting for friends or family arriving from distant lands.

Dozens of soldiers milled about, too. It wasn't difficult to tell who were on their way to the theater of war, and those who were coming home. The former wore clean, pressed uniforms and seemed to have boundless energy, walking around, talking with each other, playing practical jokes.

The soldiers returning home from the front lines in Europe remained quiet and sullen. Most had blank stares and refused to engage in conversation with the new boys. Many showed signs of injuries, with bandaged wounds, a missing limb or leaning on crutches.

I found a bank of lockers for rent, paid for one and stuffed my knapsack, stock certificates, cash and bonds inside. I then gave Karla the key.

"You wait here. I'm going to have a look around and see what I can find."

Karla bit her lower lip when I didn't give her a chance to protest. As I walked away, she took a seat on one of the benches near the locker.

Out through the back, I followed the smell of the sea on a thirty-minute walk down side streets and alleyways from Grand Central to the shipyard along the Hudson River. Making my way to the docks, I spied two huge container ships. Outside one, a dim light hovered over the end of a gangplank, breaking the darkness where two men stood. An occasional tiny red glow gave away their roll-ups. I sauntered over and as casually as possible asked, "Where are you headed?"

"Why do you care?" the taller of the two answered with a British accent.

"I'm looking to hitch a ride across the Atlantic," I said. "Do you need an extra deckhand?"

Both strangers remained silent for a long time, eyeing me, no doubt trying to figure out what I was up to. After this long, pregnant pause, the first man broke the silence. "Are you aware there's a war on?"

"Yes, I'm aware of that," I replied.

"Crossing the Atlantic is a dangerous proposition on a good day. Today ain't a good day," the Brit said. "The sea is infested with U-boats trying to make sure no one makes it across."

I considered what the man said and while doing so looked up at the ship. There weren't any big guns, at least none I could see. No heavy armament and nothing obvious to make the ship resemble a wartime threat to anyone. I thought the vessel looked more like a cargo ship. "What are you shipping?"

"Food." The smaller man joined the conversation, revealing a gap in his front teeth.

"I can't imagine a container ship full of food would be a very high priority target for a German U-boat," I said.

"That's where you're wrong, mate. You Yanks send thousands of tons of food to London every day and Jerry makes sure about half never arrives."

"The Germans sink humanitarian food shipments? Why would they do that?" I said.

"Believe it Yank. Jerry wants to break the will of every decent human being who doesn't kiss the Führer's arse. How better to do this than to bomb them into insanity and starve them to death."

I had been in this time zone for a while and during my stay I knew major war campaigns were being waged around the world. But I spent most of my time with Karla, Frankie and more recently Don Antonio and his crew, trying to seek my fortune and make it back home. For the first time since I arrived, the realities of war became overwhelmingly obvious. My sheltered life here was about to end.

"I've worked on boats almost all my life. Granted, none as big as this one. Can you use an extra hand or not?"

"Why are you so hell bent on risking your life to cross the Atlantic?" the first Brit said, rubbing out his cigarette on the gangplank handrail.

"That's the question, isn't it?" I pondered for a moment, wondering how to proceed. "I guess the truth will set you free."

Both Brits looked at me as if I might be an idiot. Perhaps I was.

"Ok, here goes," I began. "I'm on a mission. I met someone who is a relative of a Nazi SS officer. I have it on good information this branch of the SS has set up a secret base in southern Poland where they are working on unusual weaponry. I intend to go there."

I left out the bit about how I wanted to help SS Vrill build a time machine so I could find my way home. No doubt revealing this might put a strain on our budding relationship.

Listening to me explain my alleged mission attracted their attention. "I'm Albert, this is Mcdougall," the taller man said, extending his hand to shake mine. "So you plan to infiltrate this base? Where's your crew?"

"I don't have a crew."

"Brave man," Albert said. "What kind of weaponry will you be taking with you?"

I started to feel uneasy. "I'm unarmed."

"Ah, so you speak German then? You kind of do look a bit like a Jerry."

"Uh, no, I don't speak any German."

"Let me get this straight," Mcdougall said. "You want to cross the Atlantic on our ship, make your way across hundreds of miles behind enemy lines to a secret Nazi SS base somewhere in the south of Poland, unarmed, and you don't speak the language?"

"That about sums it up," I said.

"This bloody Yank thinks he's Superman," Mcdougall said. "What's in it for us?"

I had to think hard about this. Since I had no believable, honest answer, I had to make one up. "What if my mission could end the war? You two would, of course, remain anonymous, but would go to your grave knowing you saved thousands of lives, perhaps millions."

The British deckhands exchanged looks. I could tell both men were having trouble deciding whether or not to believe me, this crazy Yank who suddenly appeared out of the darkness.

"You're full of shite," Mcdougall said.

"Maybe, maybe not," I replied. "Do you want to live out your lives knowing you could've ended the war, but didn't take the chance?"

Neither seemed to budge, and I realized I might be taking the wrong approach. "Ok, so it's not like you would be inconvenienced in any way. All you have to do is hire me to do the garbage work. In fact, my coming aboard could make your lives easier. You know, new guy and all."

Albert and Mcdougall stood in silence for a bit. Now I was talking their language. Enough of this 'ending the war' nonsense, having a new guy on board to do the grunt work was all I needed to say.

"Ok Yank, I'd be more than happy to help you fulfill your death wish. The captain and first mate are always looking for more able bodies to come aboard and earn their keep while we make these treacherous crossings. We don't even need to ask, just introduce you later. Welcome aboard," Albert said, once again extending his hand.

"When do we set sail?" I asked.

"Set sail," Mcdougall said, "the bloody Yank thinks we're in the middle ages."

"We'll be leaving in a couple hours, but we can board the ship now so you can settle into your new position, if it pleases the honorable Yank," Albert said, ignoring Mcdougall. He began to enjoy his newfound role.

"Yeah, well, I can't go right now," I said.

"What?" both Brits responded in unity.

"There's a woman nearby waiting for me. I need to tell her what I'm doing. It shouldn't take very long."

"A girl," Mcdougall said, prancing around, pretending to pull on an imaginary skirt.

"I'll go with you," Albert said. "We wouldn't want you to lose your way back."

"Yes, thanks," I said. "Let's go."

We made our way back through the alleyways to and through the back door at Grand Central. Karla sat in the same place I left her. She smiled when she saw me approach, but looked curiously at the strange man following me.

I knew this would be difficult. I had truly hoped to spend the rest of my life with Karla, but I knew all too well my chance of survival while navigating through Europe at the height of World War Two would be slim at best. My heart wouldn't allow me to risk Karla's life this way.

I also believed if I could make it back home, Vrill would figure out how to return me to the precise time and place to pick her up and take her back to Harpswell. Of course, that would also depend on my ability to convince Vrill.

Since my plan involved Karla staying put at Grand Central, I had to try and convince her to trust me, in spite of what it might look like.

"I found a ship," I said. "They're going to take me across."

"Across?" Karla asked, sitting back down.

"To Europe." I knew full well it was time to reveal my plan and how Karla might be hard to convince.

"Ok, let's go," Karla said.

"I wish you could go, Karla, I really do. But this is going to be too dangerous. Besides, if everything goes to plan, and I am able to find Vrill and—" I stopped myself to determine if Albert was listening.

He was. "Can you give us a minute, Albert?"

"Sure mate, no worries. I'll be standing under the center clock whenever you're ready."

"Thanks Albert," I said and turned back to Karla once he was out of hearing range. "If everything works to plan, I'll be back in few minutes, right through the door over there." I pointed towards the entrance. "If this works, you will hardly even notice I was gone."

"You're not talking about the time machine again, are you?" It started to sink in how my plan didn't include her. "Why don't you just stay here with me instead of running off?"

"I want to, I really do. But Fat Tony and his men are after me—after us, for my stupid gambling. Captain Young and the police are trying to find any reason to put me away because of my dealings with Fat Tony, Frankie and the crew. The FBI thinks I must be a spy because they can't find any record of my existence. Special Agent Ryker said he will be contacting the military about me, and if he did, they will certainly be showing up soon, full of questions. They may even arrest me thinking I'm a deserter for not being over in Europe or the Pacific fighting the Axis.

"So, if I stay here with you, we will always be on the run, constantly looking over our shoulders for any number of people who mean to do us harm. I'd much rather find a way to get back home to my time, then come back here to get you and take you back with me. If we can just get through this challenge, I have to believe it'll be much safer for the both of us."

"I don't know," Karla said. "I have a bad feeling about this."

"I have to do what I have to do," I said, trying to sound convincing. "If everything goes right, I should be back here to pick you up within ten minutes of your time. I know this is hard to understand, but you need to trust me, ok?"

By now her fists were clenched, she was biting her lower lip so hard it was turning white, and the rest of her face was turning a darker shade of red. She stopped biting just long enough to wrinkle her nose and say through pursed lips and clenched teeth, "This is a fine time to dump me."

I guess I wasn't convincing enough.

"I have no intention of abandoning you. If I can do this part alone, it will be so much easier for me to take care of you once this is all over."

"What if something goes wrong and you don't come back in ten minutes?"

"I will," I said. I took my pack and some cash out of the locker, leaving the bulk of the cash and all the stocks and bonds inside. "But if I don't, take whatever's left in the locker and run. Fat Tony is still looking for me and by now he realizes the best way to find me is through you. That means you're in danger too, now maybe more than me. So take everything and get out of here. Find somewhere you like far away from here. Settle down and start a new life."

"I don't want to run alone."

"Please Karla, if I'm not back in ten minutes, don't wait. Just go. I will find you again, no matter where you go. Just run, ok?"

"You better go kill that nasty Hitler and be back here in the next ten minutes or I'll never speak to you again."

Albert had made his way back over to us and smiled when he overheard this last demand from Karla. Maybe this Yank was ok after all.

"That's my girl," I said. I leaned down and gave her a long kiss on the lips, then rose, staring at her beautiful eyes. "How could I not come back and be mesmerized by you again?"

She snarled back at me.

"Now I know you're a complete lunatic," Albert told me as we headed outside. "You must be if you're leaving behind a beautiful dame like her."

36

Once the USS Shelly threw off her lines and the tugboats began guiding her through the tangled mess of New York Harbor, down the Hudson River toward the Atlantic Ocean, the crew was assembled on deck.

After a few minutes of jostling for position, we all looked up in unison when the stern door of the bridge flew open with a flourish, banging against the opposite wall. Out stepped a tall, well-built man in dress whites. A white captain's hat sat comfortably askew on his head. Gold bars lay across his shoulders while hard-earned medals pinned over his heart covered a wide swath of his uniform.

Captain Steve Kirkpatrick, a man large in stature and even larger in reputation, was known for being someone unafraid to tackle perilous adventures, but all the while keeping a calm head; someone who would push the limits but always keep the crew's safety first. He had made the Atlantic crossing dozens of times, and despite it being full of enemy warships and submarines, so far he and his crew remained unscathed.

"Gentlemen, you are undoubtedly some of the bravest men alive. For this crossing, we have on board over a thousand tons of non-perishable food. If we are successful at crossing the Atlantic during this time of war, we will deliver this food to the near-starving citizens of London and beyond. They don't deserve to suffer as they now do at the hands of the Nazis. Your sacrifice, your willingness to brave rough autumn seas filled with German U-boats is nothing short of heroic. I can guarantee you a spot in heaven shall we not be successful, or a place in history if we are. May God be with you—with us—and may our gunnels soon kiss the shores of England."

"Hip, hip hooray!" the men cheered thrice, although I could tell they were less than enthusiastic. I guessed, perhaps rightly so, the men didn't choose to be here; perhaps risking their lives on this ship might have been the only way they could provide for their families.

Albert and Mcdougall both gave me a shake of their head and led me below to the crew's quarters.

"You realize you will be starting as the lowest man in the ranks," Albert told me.

"I wouldn't expect anything else," I replied.

"This means scraping rust and applying primer to about half the ship," Mcdougall chimed in while suppressing a grin.

"It won't be the first time," I said, although it would be the first time on a vessel this size.

"After you finish," Albert continued, "you'll be sent off to the galley to help Chief by scrubbing his pots and pans."

I could see how hard they were trying to rattle my nerves and I wasn't about to give in. I smiled. "Anything else?"

"We'll see how you manage after you deal with rough waters tossing us about for the entire journey. Have you ever experienced thirty-five degree rolls?" Albert asked, not waiting for the answer. "But for now, there isn't much we can do except hunker down for the night."

With those being the most appealing words I had heard in days. Despite the looming danger ahead, my thoughts drifted to the beautiful green-eyed girl waiting for me back in New York. I felt safe for the first time in a long while.

* * * * *

At times my experience at sea tended to be rather uneventful. If anyone had bothered to ask, I might have chosen the word 'boring' as a more accurate description. Scraping rust, slapping on primer coating, repeat. I did this a dozen times in a dozen rusty places, always remaining resolute, not showing any kind of contempt while my new companions hung about watching my every move, not once offering to help.

One afternoon, however, the monotony turned bizarre. Under a gray autumn sky, wind whistling across the deck, I was stubbornly wire-brushing rust off a tenacious metal cleat. As Albert paced the deck and Mcdougall leaned against a rail, both watching me 'to make sure I did it right', I felt the onslaught of another migraine.

This time was different. Out of nowhere, an aircraft appeared, the likes of which I'd never seen. It fired a strange weapon on my position, creating blinding flashes as explosions erupted on the ground all around. Yes, the ground. No longer on the SS Shelly, I found myself behind a large rock in the middle of a field, fighting for my life.

Banking into a wide turn, the aircraft circled back for another pass, firing not bombs, but some kind of laser weapons. I began firing back—where did I get this weapon? I managed a direct hit on one of its wings, but caused little damage. This time it didn't circle back. Instead it kept going into the distance and over the horizon.

I slumped to the ground. Where am I? More flashing lights blinded me and when my vision returned, I was back aboard the ship, wire brush in hand, other deckhands staring at me.

My arms and legs felt like lead and I gasped for air. "Did you see that?"

"We saw you have a seizure," Albert said.

"No, no, no," Mcdougall said, his Scottish accent suddenly appearing. "That was no seizure. He changed back and forth between how he is now, and a strange person, dirty, with a beard, crazed eyes and terrified. Hell no, that was no seizure."

"I mean the aircraft shooting at us. You didn't see them?" I asked.

"I didn't see any airplanes," Albert said. "Only you having a seizure."

I sat back against the railing and stopped talking. What was happening to me?

The commotion over, the deckhands dispersed. Albert and Mcdougall, however, kept their stares on me as they backed away. Could it turn out to be a mistake to have brought me on board? I was either crazy, or sick, or both. Most of all, they didn't want to be responsible if something worse happened.

* * * * *

Lucky for me this didn't happen again aboard the SS Shelly. The next day, outside work was put to rest when it became too dangerous as the North Atlantic bared her fangs, sending strong winds and monster waves crashing over the bow.

Sleep was intermittent at best and not until I managed to appropriate a length of rope and use it to tie myself into my bunk did I manage some shuteye, disturbed as it was.

Once in a while the SS Shelly would hit a calmer patch enabling the constant hum of a ship underway at sea to take over from the sounds of rushing wind, thumping waves and seawater washing along the sides.

When not out working on deck I kept busy in the galley. I struck up a friendship with the gregarious cook everybody called Chief. If I ever learned his real name I've forgotten it, as no one called him anything other than Chief. Even the ship's captain.

Way back when Chief came aboard several crossings ago, the chief engineer had taken exception. After all, there is only one chief aboard any seagoing vessel. He had worked hard to earn his title and wasn't about to give it up. But given how our cook was the descendant of an Apache warrior chief, the engineer finally acquiesced. On this ship, there could be two Chiefs.

The best description anyone could come up with for him was that he was a character. He did look like the descendant of an Apache warrior, with his broad shoulders, hawk nose and darkened skin. Coupled with his thick Scouse accent, he certainly turned heads.

A solid man who kept his long hair tied back in a braid, he wore a white t-shirt, navy jeans and a stained white apron at all times, even when not in the galley. No matter what the weather, or what the circumstances might have been, he remained the happiest, most devil-may-care person on board.

He also claimed to be a member of the Golden Knights of Mysticism, a society whose members believed in magic, the occult, metaphysics, and paranormal activities. Members dedicated their lives to discovering the unknown and the unknowable. Formed at the turn of the century, they evolved during World War Two into an anti-Nazi force. Knowing of Hitler's fascination with the paranormal and his orders to find ways to use it to win the war, they used their collective knowledge and power to try to keep this from happening.

After Chief learned who I claimed to be, 'when' I came from and what my intended mission was, he couldn't help himself; he had to get to know me. We became best buds.

"So, you're telling me you're on this ship to gain passage to Europe in order to find a way through enemy lines to a secret Nazi base where they are working on alien technology, and, wait—you're from the future and you think you can talk them into building a time machine so you can find a way home? Did I leave anything out?"

"No, that pretty much sums it up, although when you put it that way, it sounds rather incredible."

"Not at all. I think I can help. My colleagues in England and I have been waiting for someone like you for a long, long time. If you think you can make this happen, we can find a way to get you there.

"Our order is hidden away in London. So far, our block has managed to dodge Luftwaffe bombs, at least it had when I left. Who knows who will be there to greet us, but there should be enough members around to devise a plan. When I tell them who you are, word will spread and more will come. Together, we'll think of something, I'm sure."

37

Some thought of Sir James M. Little as privileged. Those who did obviously didn't know him. True, he didn't enlist in the armed forces. He didn't need to survive basic training and he never donned a uniform or helmet. He had never been issued a standard military rifle and he wasn't given the chance to 'enjoy' the right of passage of being trucked off to the front lines to face the enemy head-on.

It was also true he came from a wealthy, highly decorated family. His father, Sir Malcolm Little, fought in World War One, distinguishing himself at Megiddo in 1918 during one of the greatest battles in British history.

Under the command of General Edmund Allenby, whose skillful tactics and use of air support, artillery, and ground forces in what some historians consider to be the forerunner of the German 'Blitzkrieg' of WWII, Colonel Malcolm Little led his infantry and cavalry units to take Damascus and Aleppo in what is today Israel, Jordan and Syria, forcing the Turks to sue for peace.

Col. Little's decisive leadership and bravery earned him a chest full of medals, making his father proud.

Malcolm's father, Sir James T. Little, after whom James M. was named, earned the Victoria Cross in the battle of Rorke's Drift in 1879 during the Zulu War in South Africa. Following the overwhelming defeat of the

British at Isandlwana, and in one of the most remarkable defenses in British military history, Sir James T. Little had been one of 150 British and colonial troops who defended their garrison on the Buffalo River against an intense assault by 4,000 Zulu warriors.

Both Sir James T. and Sir Malcolm Little retired as generals, something Sir James M. Little would never achieve, no matter how long he lived.

Between hostilities in the late 1800s and early 1900s, Sir James T. Little the elder parlayed his global connections into considerable wealth in imports. When his son, Sir Malcolm gained control of the business upon his retirement at the end of World War One, he became one of the wealthiest men in Great Britain. This, in part, was through being involved in the British financial industry, which at that time enjoyed its position atop the financial world, the largest on earth, and in part by making investments in railroads and shipping across the Atlantic in the up and coming industrial powerhouse, the USA.

So, yes, it could be argued that Sir James M. Little did grow up in a wealthy family and might be mistaken as having a privileged upbringing. However, Sir Malcolm made sure young James knew from whence he came, was schooled in his family's history, and knew what it took to achieve the wealth his forefathers had accumulated in the family name. He also made sure young James was aware he would not enjoy any part of this wealth if he didn't distinguish himself in some way palatable to his father and grandfather.

At first, it did not please them when young James opted not to join His Majesty's Army and not to follow in their footsteps. Sir Malcolm tried to convince him to continue his family's military legacy, but at the urging of Sir James T. the elder, in the end he respected his son's choices.

Young James rewarded their decisions when he became a war historian, an expert if you will, studying all the books he could lay his hands on. When World War Two, the war to end all wars broke out, he was too old to change his mind and become a recruit to work his way up from the bottom as his father and grandfather had done. So instead he parlayed his knowledge to join His Majesty's Secret Service, earning his mettle in intelligence, saving millions of lives, often working behind enemy lines gathering intelligence, helping His Majesty's armed forces' war efforts without ever firing a shot. All without publically taking credit for his achievements.

During the 1941-1942 tug of war for North Africa, the British benefited from radio intercept information, due in no small part to a concentrated effort by the then still James M. Little (not yet with the Sir) and his underground intelligence team. They found a leak and broke what the legendary 'Desert Fox' Field Marshal Erwin Rommel called *die gute Quelle* (the good source); information leaked from the U.S. military in Cairo by the unwitting provider, Brevet Colonel Bonner Frank Fellers, the U.S. military attaché in the Egyptian capital.

James Little and his crew discovered the Italians and Germans had both broken the Black Code coming out of the US Embassy in Cairo, which therefore gave them the ability to find out just about everything being planned by the Allies. Little knew that, although Feller didn't like the British, he needed their help, so he began feeding Feller false information to report. Once this began, the war in northern Africa began to turn, leading to the British achieving another one of their greatest battle victories in history—the Battle of El Alamein.

After the battle was won, it became too dangerous for Little and his men to remain in Africa, so they were brought back to England. Upon his return, HM King

George VI knighted James M. Little and gave him the option to retire in glory.

Not wanting to quit His Majesty's services, at least not until the end of the war, Sir James rejoined the effort in Europe, commanding small scouting missions to gather intelligence against the Nazis on the western front. His achievements had become legendary, and by 1944 he was given complete autonomy.

During the later stages of the war he dedicated much of his time to working with the Belgian underground resistance, which also included helping minorities escape persecution and death camps. He had admired the spirit and results achieved by a short, barrel-chested Belgian member of the resistance named Patrice Van de Velde, affectionately nicknamed Frenchie. The two became close friends and worked together on missions, many that were quite dangerous.

38

"I heard you had a bit of an adventure out on deck today," Chief said when I entered the galley to clean up from dinner.

"It was no big deal; just another migraine," I said as I tied on my apron to begin washing dishes.

"Hmm, a migraine. According to your friends, whatever happened was more than just a headache."

"Yes, well, weird things happen when I suffer these headaches. I had one before in New York and someone's pet hamster appeared out of nowhere."

"Hamster?" Chief dumped his famed spaghetti meat sauce into a steel container to be used for sloppy joes at tomorrow's lunch.

"Yes, I know. It was someone's pet and not all that unusual, but we couldn't figure out where it came from," I said, taking the empty pot from Chief and bringing to the sink.

"What about today?" Chief said, pausing from his prep work to give me his full attention.

"Today was strange. I felt like I had been beamed to another place, in the middle of a battle with strange aircraft shooting at me."

"Yes, I heard. I think I might know what happened," Chief said. "I believe what you experienced wasn't just another migraine. In the ancient past, members of the Golden Knights of Mysticism knew how to time travel. However, their written knowledge of this was destroyed during the great witch hunts of the dark ages, and so far, none of the ancients have returned yet to teach us.

"But bits and pieces of the literature survived. One of our elders devoted great effort to deciphering the remaining texts, including the side effects of jumping through time. His descriptions are eerily similar to what you say is happening to you."

"What kind of side effects?"

"According to the ancient writings, time travelers would sometimes have trouble remaining in the time period to which they had traveled, and would experience brief moments in another dimension where they had either already been, or would be at some point in the future. 'Flashes', they called them. They wrote how, by definition, time travelers would be living in two or more time dimensions at the same time. During the flashes, their future or past self would replace them in the current time period."

"Sounds confusing," I said, still trying to scrub the burnt spaghetti sauce from the bottom of the saucepan.

"Yes, well, what it means is, when you had your flash today you went to another time period, a time you have either already been in, or will at some point go. While you were there, you from the other time transferred here to take your place, which is what the deckhands saw. It sounds to me a lot like astral projection, which is something we do know how to do," Chief said, as he wrapped leftovers in wax paper to put in the icebox.

"Well, whatever it was, I wish it would stop. The headaches almost knock me unconscious."

"I've been thinking," Chief said, taking my mind off scrubbing the particularly stubborn pot. "Instead of risking your life by traveling so far behind enemy lines, why don't you use astral projection to go there and find out if the person you're looking for can help you?"

"Astral projection?"

"It means you would leave your physical body here and travel your spirit self through the fifth classical element, the aether, to visit him," Chief said.

My eyes glazed over.

"If you concentrate enough, you can present yourself in his dreams. You both will be lucid and you will be able to ask him anything. If he knows the answers, he will tell you—and in a language you will understand. He may or may not remember when he wakes. Most dreams are lost within the first few seconds after waking up. Even if he did, your spirit would be back here with answers, and never be in danger of getting caught. I can teach you how if you want."

"It sounds like a great idea," I said. I tried to humor him, although I couldn't quite grasp what the hell he was talking about. "But if Vrill can help me, I'd rather be there, you know, physically, so I can help him finish his version of a time machine and go home. If he can't help me, I will try to find someone else there who can. His name is the only one I know, so if he tells me he can't help me in his dreams I will be going there blind without the name of a person to search for."

"I see," Chief said. "Well, it was just a thought. Don't worry, we have a well-connected underground able to get you there without too much of a fuss. The Golden Knights have many members, including German members who are on our side during this nasty war, and who will be excited to meet you—the time traveler."

I could tell Chief's comments hinted of sarcasm. *Touché*. If I can be from the future having traveled here through space and time, it would be hypocritical for me to doubt the realities of astral projection.

On what was a relatively calm, scenic day with flat seas, an autumn rarity in the North Atlantic, a sudden jolt nearly knocked me off my feet and brought my conversation with Chief to an end. This was followed by a loud screeching sound, metal on metal.

The ship must have hit something or run aground.

Since a ship that big takes miles to stop when at full steam, the SS Shelly continued forward, although listing considerably to one side. Whatever it was she'd hit, she was dragging it with her, sending her erratically off course.

39

Captain Kirkpatrick and the helmsmen in the wheelhouse tried to disengage from whatever it was we'd hit by steering hard to port, then hard to starboard, then reversing hard to stern, engaging the craft and crew in a bizarre open water ballet with the submerged object. Whatever it was, it wasn't about to give up without a fight. It must have been huge.

After a lengthy battle, the SS Shelly came to rest in the middle of the ocean with no land in sight. Only then did they discover what they had hit.

"Prepare the depth charges!" Captain Kirkpatrick commanded over the ship-wide intercom. "We've hit a U-boat!"

Chief and I dropped what we were doing and raced to the site of the accident.

The collision caused the ship to ride up on the sub as the U-boat surfaced to look around, no doubt trying to locate the exact whereabouts of the SS Shelly so they could zero in their torpedoes. When neither captain saw the other's vessel, the two collided, leaving the sub somehow stuck under the SS Shelly's starboard side aft.

Jerry's U-boat was unable to fire off a torpedo without sinking his own vessel, and the SS Shelly couldn't roll a barrel-sized depth charge over the side without putting a hole in her own hull.

The standoff led to one of the most bizarre incidents of the war at sea. Both captains tried unsuccessfully to free their respective boats from the other until it became apparent they needed cooperation to complete the task.

Dead in the water, Captain Kirkpatrick looked out at U-boat 666 and saw the top hatch open, followed by its captain climbing up and out onto the conning tower.

"Ahoy," Captain Jerry said, "we seem to be in a spot of bother." He spoke near perfect English with a British accent.

"Aye," Captain Kirkpatrick answered back. "What do you propose we do about this predicament?"

After some intense discussion, the two sworn enemy captains came up with a plan where the SS Shelly would turn hard to starboard and U-boat 666 would do its best to do reverse hard to port. The maneuver worked, freeing the U-boat from the SS Shelly's underbelly, sending both vessels in opposite directions. But when Captain Kirkpatrick saw Jerry making a steady turn to a heading which would put the SS Shelly in the line of fire, he realized the pleasantries were over. Without hesitation, he ordered the crew to release a depth charge.

Almost as soon as the charge hit the water and began to sink, it exploded, creating a much bigger explosion than what was expected. By some strange coincidence, the depth charge reached the perfect depth at the exact moment the U-boat's torpedo arrived, igniting both.

The explosion's wave caused the SS Shelly to roll forty degrees to port, but our luck held and no damage was done.

The underwater shockwave hit U-boat 666 hard, cracking its weak shell and nearly sending her to the bottom. Captain Jerry decided perhaps he'd pushed his luck enough and guided U-boat 666 away from the SS Shelly, back towards more friendly waters.

The encounter turned out to be the only one the SS Shelly had with Jerry for the rest of the trip. Despite the incident, the rough seas and high winds to follow, captain and crew made it to London in one piece.

* * * * *

Once we docked in London, the crew disembarked for some well-deserved shore leave. For the first time ever, I had trouble finding my land legs on my initial foray onto the docks. During the last few days of our approach we experienced thirty degree rolls and although I had grown up on the ocean, I had never been out to sea for so long, especially aboard such a large vessel or in such violent storms.

I wobbled and staggered like a drunken sailor until I finally gained my land legs. For his part, Chief had no such trouble as he led me through a maze of back alleys and rubble-strewn streets.

The devastation throughout London was heart-breaking. Some of the buildings had been destroyed by Nazi bombs, many others had at least partial damage. Bricks, stones, furniture and people's belongings were left in piles. Everywhere I looked, people wandered around in in shock. Some searched through the debris for lost items, others scavenged through garbage for food. Still more called out names of people who had disappeared, a ghostly reminder of the cruelty of war.

Less than half an hour into our walk, sirens began blaring, sending people scurrying about, looking for cover. A minute or two later I could hear a whistle, followed by a ground rumbling boom. I looked down the street, between the buildings left standing, and could see a plume of black smoke rising high into the air off in the distance. Seconds later, people emerged from their hiding places to calmly resume whatever it was they had been doing before the sirens sounded.

Chief led me to an iron door in an otherwise nondescript building. It had somehow managed to avoid bomb damage, just as Chief predicted.

He performed a rhythmic knock, which I guessed to be a secret known only to members. An older gentleman slid open the peep slot cover and peered outside. Seeing Chief brought a wide smile. This disappeared when he saw me. "Who is he?"

"Someone you've been waiting your entire life to meet," Chief said.

"How so?"

"Let me in, you old geezer and I'll show you."

The gatekeeper scowled, but complied and opened the door.

The three of us climbed a set of stairs leading into a hallway with several doors. Each door was decorated with painted symbols resembling Egyptian hieroglyphs. The gatekeeper stopped at a door with a colorful cross filled with strange symbols and ushered us inside.

Four men and one woman sat at a small round table, their attention devoted to a shortwave radio from which emanated the dulcet tones of BBC presenter Alvar Liddell as he announced the day's war news.

Judy Yanok, I later learned, was the highest ranking person in the room. An *Adeptus Exempta*, her rank was as high as she could achieve in the Second Order of the Golden Knights of Mysticism. With her tenure in the order, her wide-ranging achievements in all things mystic, and her advanced study of the knighthood, she had earned the right to enter the Third Order. Her promotion would be granted in the coming days.

None of the five seemed to notice our arrival until Judy said, without looking away from her radio, "Come in, we've been expecting you."

I looked at Chief who by now sported a wry grin. "They knew you were coming."

Chief's words prompted all five people to turn and look. "He doesn't look much like a traveler," Judy said. "Has he had any flashes?"

"Yes, he has. But that's not the best part," Chief said, turning to me. "Show them what you have."

"What?"

"Go ahead, don't be shy. The white thing you carry in your pocket."

"The iPhone?" I said. "How did you know about my iPhone?"

"Never mind how, show them."

I pulled it out of my pocket, clicked the on button, and to my amazement it still worked. After scrolling through a few apps and showing them what it could do, they seemed much more convinced I truly was a 'traveler' as they had put it. The quality of the color photos I could show them on the tiny smartphone screen seemed to impress them the most, compared with the grainy black and white images they were accustomed to seeing on photo paper.

"Is this your time traveling invention?" Judy asked.

"No, well," I struggled to decide how to describe it. "It's a communication device which doubles as a computer."

"Computer?"

"Ok, it's a telephone I can fit in my pocket. I can also use it to see maps, add and subtract numbers, write letters to my friends. It has many uses."

"A telephone? So, telephone someone," Judy said, challenging me.

"I don't know if I can. It might be a telephone in the future, but I haven't tried calling anyone here."

"Try CEN 8385," Judy said. She turned to her friends and whispered, "This is where I buy my fish for dinner."

I duly typed in the number, pressed the call button and waited. Dead air. I hung up and tried again. Still nothing. "Maybe they're closed?" I said.

"They were open this morning," Judy said. "Maybe your telephone only works in the future."

"Sorry, but this is the best I can do."

"So, if you're from the future and you can do lots of other things with that, can you tell us when the war ends?"

"Good question." I clicked open Google, typed in WWII end, and to my amazement it worked. "On 8 May 1945, the Allies accepted Germany's surrender, about a week after Adolf Hitler had committed suicide. VE Day—Victory in Europe celebrates the end of the Second World War on 8 May 1945."

The room fell silent.

"Hitler commits suicide?" Judy said.

I looked up from the smartphone screen and saw every eye in the room was staring at me. "Maybe I shouldn't have told you."

It occurred to me the information might be a bit much for anyone to handle, especially in the middle of the war. They looked as if they were unsure whether or not to believe me. It might have been good news that the end of the war was in sight, but even if true, it was still months away. The bombing and all the death that goes with it will continue at least until May.

"Never mind, let's move on to the matter at hand," Judy said.

Chief and I took turns explaining my situation, the goals I harbored for this trip, and thus my presence in their order. This, of course, took some time, during which a few others straggled in, at times causing us to start over from the beginning.

When we managed to tell the entire story without interruption, a consensus was reached—getting across the English Channel would be the first challenge, but one they thought they could manage using an old fishing boat. With only two or three people on board, chances are it would pass an inspection should a U-boat spot us.

The quickest crossing would be from Dover to Calais, but it was deemed too risky. I had to admit I was a bit disappointed, as the thought of seeing the White Cliffs of Dover was appealing. However, Paris had only just been liberated in August, so perhaps landing in France might not be our best option. A better plan would be to leave from Ramsgate or Broadstairs and travel a longer route to Blankenberge or De Haan in Belgium.

The British and Canadians had retaken Brussels last month, and there might still be pockets of Nazi resistance, but the probability of attracting U-boat attention would be less crossing to Belgium rather than to France.

"Where in Poland do you want to go?" Judy asked.

No sooner had the words left her lips when air raid sirens blared again, bringing the meeting to a halt. The room went dark and silent.

No one, including me, knew if this would be our last moment on earth.

40

A few minutes after the sirens began, a devastating explosion could be heard coming from a few blocks away. So strong, it rattled the meeting room walls. Concrete dust, shaken loose from the ceiling, cascaded down over our heads. It felt a bit like a spider web had covered us in the darkness.

About a half hour later, the sirens went silent and the lights came back on. To my amazement, the meeting returned to normal as if nothing had happened. People simply brushed away the gray dust from their hair and clothes. Those who had taken further shelter under tables and chairs regained their composure and retook their places in the room.

'These poor people,' I thought. 'All this death and destruction happening all around them and they've somehow become inured to it. Just another event in a series of event-filled days while living inside a warzone.'

"Where in Poland do you want to go?" Judy asked again once the dust had settled.

"Southwest Poland near the Czech border," I said, trying my best to shake off what had just taken place. My heart was still pounding, my hands shaking. "Do the 'Owl Mountains' sound familiar?"

A lone figure emerged from the shadows. A thickset man, well built with a shock of white hair told us, "I know where he's on about. I've been there. It's a Nazi

SS base. Most of it is built underground in tunnels. Up top, though, they're working on something called 'Die Glocke', aka 'The Bell'. It looks like Stonehenge, but much smaller. It's not in Poland. It used to be Poland, but it's now part of the Third Reich."

My eyes lit up. "Yes, that's it. Die Glocke. Have you seen it?"

"Yes, but to get there won't be easy. From here, it's on the other side of Germany. We'd have to go straight through the heart of Nazi territory."

"We?" I said. "Will you take me there?"

"It would be up to the others," he said, looking around the room.

"Wait," Judy said. "Who are you? Why do you know about this place? And why would you have been there?"

"My name is Sir James Little. My details are irrelevant. Churchill received reports of this secret Nazi SS base and thought it might be a good idea to send someone to find it, have a look, and take coordinates so we could bomb it into the Stone Age. They sent me and my colleague. Problem is, it was already in the Stone Age, deeply underground in fortified bunkers. Top brass decided it wouldn't be worth the time and resources, as it's doubtful bombing would have done anything other than kill a few krauts loitering above ground."

"How safe is it?" Chief asked.

"Safe?" Sir James scowled. "Of course it won't be safe. Chances of success are slim at best. Hitler is mercilessly bombing Antwerp and Liege with his V2 rockets, so we would need to steer well clear of those areas. Fighting on the Western Front is vicious, and if we make it through alive, we'd still need to traverse hundreds of miles through the middle of Nazi Germany. We can hope the Nazis would be too busy fighting the Allies on all fronts to be watching the interior. If that turns out to be the case, it might give us a fighting chance to make it through to Poland."

Sir James paused to assemble his thoughts. "Even if we get this Yank to Poland, chances are minimal he'd be able to succeed in what he's trying to do. SS officers aren't exactly welcoming to Americans." He let the sentence drop.

The room went quiet for several minutes as the stranger's words sunk in.

"I speak German," Sir James began again. "I have a contact in Belgium whom I plan to meet in Blankenberge in a couple days. If the price is right, we'll do what we can to make sure your boy arrives there alive."

"What price are you looking for?" Judy asked. "Remember, there is a war on. Money is tight."

"I'm not looking for money, although what I'm asking won't be cheap. The reason I'm meeting my contact is to bring two Jewish families across the channel to England to try and provide them with passage to America. If you can accomplish this, I will bring the Yank to the Owl Mountains in Southern Poland so he can fulfill his death wish. I'll get him there; after that he's on his own."

"How did you find out about this meeting?"

"You told me," Sir James said to Judy. "I am a member, although on the fringe."

"We didn't tell any fringe members," Judy said.

"No, but you put out word there would be an exceptional meeting today, which I heard about, and I sensed it would have to do with something like this."

"All settled then," Chief broke the tension. "We're going to Blankenberge, Belgium. I know a fisherman in Ramsgate named Stephen Beard who I know would be willing to make the crossing and bring back a family escaping persecution."

"Two Jewish families," Sir James corrected him.

"Two Jewish families," Chief agreed.

* * * * *

Chief handled contact with Stephen Beard in Ramsgate, and as he said, Stephen was more than willing to do his moral duty by providing his fishing vessel as a means of transportation. A departure time was established and met, with the secret voyage underway right on time.

There was a constant swell as a rushing tide battled a roaring wind, whitecaps and plenty of 'refreshing' autumn ocean spray along the way. Other than that, the crossing was uneventful.

Coming ashore in Blankenberge turned out to be a tad more challenging. In order to arrive undetected, we decided to avoid any commercial piers and land on a beach. With our running lights off, we idled the engine forward until the water became too shallow to continue.

Sir James jumped ashore alone and pushed Stephen's boat back out, where Stephen and I would wait for a signal. From there, Sir James scrambled up the embankment and walked to the nearest town where he found the local pub. Sure enough, Frenchie was enjoying a pint of stout with two other men. All three were talking German.

Frenchie stood a full head shorter than Sir James and had an angry face, the kind of face that looked angry at all times, even when he wasn't. When he saw Sir James arrive, he gave him an exuberant welcome before introducing the two men at the table—the heads of household for the two Jewish families. They had been waiting for him for a little over a week, wondering if he would ever show up, hoping he didn't abandon them, or worse yet, get into some kind of trouble.

They had passed their days trying to blend in unnoticed and their nights consuming Belgian ale in this little pub, the predetermined rendezvous point.

Daniel M. Dorothy

The women and children had already gone to bed, but they were woken as soon as James arrived. After gathering their belongings, the men brought the two families back to the shore where James signaled for Stephen to guide his vessel back in.

Once the families were safely aboard and on their way to England, and I safely on land, James, Frenchie and I returned to the pub and drank a few more pints.

* * * * *

In the morning, strong Belgian coffee, along with farm fresh eggs, fresh ham and Belgian fries struggled to fight off the residual effects of the previous night's beer, which only now, with this massive hangover, became obvious to me to have been much more potent than anything I'd ever experienced in America.

"You're up," Frenchie said with a hint of sarcasm.

"Yes. What was in that beer?" My head was hanging low.

"You sure took a liking to the waitress last night," Sir James said, adding to Frenchie's morning amusement. "She doesn't speak English and looked terrified until she realized what a pushover you are. You put on quite a show."

"Really? Gawd, I don't even remember," I said. "I think someone slipped me a mickey last night."

"No one slipped you a mickey," James said. "You Yanks drink Belgian beer like you do the watered down American beer. You aren't the first Septic to succumb to the higher alcohol content."

"After you passed out in the corner," Frenchie said, changing the subject and becoming more serious, "James explained what it is you want to do. I think you're crazy, but if that's what you want, I think we can find a way."

218

By this time in the morning, my hangover made everything I was planning to accomplish seem crazy. And why was he talking so loud?

41

"We should travel by train to Welkenraedt near the German border," Frenchie said, explaining his plan more to James than to me. "The Jerrys have been all but driven completely out of Belgium so we don't need to try and hide. The Krauts are still bombing towns along the way and we don't know for sure if the tracks are still in working order all the way there, but we can at least try to come as close as we can."

"There are plenty of Americans in Belgium now," James added. "It will be up to Paul to handle any situations we might encounter involving the Yanks."

"Once we make it to the German border, we need to commandeer a vehicle. It shouldn't be too difficult," Frenchie said. "There is a path into Germany that both Allies and Jerrys ignore, keeping it open so spies from both sides can come and go. They don't want just anybody using it so it shows up on the map as a no-go area, too dangerous to cross.

"Once inside Germany we should wear German uniforms but try to avoid contact with other Germans. This morning I found someone to forge official paperwork ordering us to report to the Eastern Front. We can use it as a last resort in case we run into any trouble we can't handle.

"As long as Paul leaves the German-speaking to us we shouldn't encounter too many problems, for surely we must have done something wrong to be singled out and sent to the Russian front. This might get us there. Poland isn't on the Eastern front but it is almost on the way. We can claim we got lost."

James added, "The path will take us a long way across Germany and we will have plenty of time to teach Paul as much of the German language and behavior as we can. It might help him once he arrives in the Owl Mountains."

Frenchie handed me a handgun. "Hang on to this in case you need it. If by some miracle you make it inside the base and can figure out how to use this time traveler thing to go home, it would be a great service to your friends and the Allies if you would shoot as many SS officers as you can before making the trip."

"Ok," I said with some trepidation, as I'd never killed anyone before. I thought for a minute before continuing. "I have to ask a favor of you."

"What?" Frenchie said. "Risking our lives isn't enough of a favor?"

"Of course it is, but I told a beautiful woman in New York I'd return for her. If by some miracle she's still waiting for me back at Grand Central Station, and if something happens to me and you survive, please try to get word to her what happened."

"I thought you were crazy before," James said. "Now I know it. What the hell are you doing here if you have a beautiful dame waiting for you back in America?"

"You wouldn't understand."

* * * * *

There was no problem catching a train as I could pay in cash with American dollars. It helped how dollars had become coveted in Belgium after the Allies kicked out the Nazis.

Once underway, the first few miles passed without much excitement. With my hangover diminishing, I tried to strike up a conversation with my new traveling friends. "James is British Intelligence, but what about you Frenchie? How are you involved in all this?"

"I joined Luc back in the beginning before it changed to Marc."

I had no idea what he was talking about. Was this something good to be congratulated? Or something tragic to offer condolences? Frenchie didn't offer any clarification.

James broke the impasse, "Luc, and later Marc, are Belgian underground resistance groups. The network Frenchie and his mates run, supplies the Allies with around 80 percent of all intelligence they receive from resistance groups in Europe."

"That's impressive," I said. "Why are you bothering with me then?"

"We want to take another look at the Owl Mountains to find out if anything has changed," Frenchie said.

"So, would you have been going there anyway, whether or not I wanted to go there?"

"Sooner or later," James said. "But you provided us with a good excuse to go sooner."

"Why is that? You might have a lot less trouble without me tagging along."

"Yes, definitely," Frenchie said without hesitation.

"We shall see," James said. "You might be an asset. Look at how your American dollars made it so much easier to board this train."

I shook my head in silence. Perhaps conversing was not the right thing to do right now. After an uncomfortable moment, Frenchie folded his arms, laid back and closed his eyes.

James became preoccupied with the route ahead, so I returned to watching the scenery. At first, most of the surroundings looked untouched. But before long the once beautiful countryside began giving way to occasional bomb craters and destroyed troop carriers. The further along the route we traveled, the more damage could be seen. Bombed farmhouses still smoldered in little towns, while dead livestock rotted in fields.

I spied my first casualty of war—a disfigured body in a gully; then another, and still more. 'Isn't anyone around to bury these poor souls?' I thought as the horrors of war continued to play out along the rails through Belgium.

Hours later the train came to a stop. The conductor walked down the aisle making announcements in Belgian, German and French, none of which I could understand. Passengers rose, gathered their belongings and began exiting.

Frenchie became involved in a heated discussion with him, to no avail. Breaking away, he told James, in English so I could hear, that the tracks ahead had been bombed and were no longer passable. We had gone as far as we could via train and would now need to find other means of getting to the border.

I grabbed my LL Beans knapsack and followed my comrades toward the door. Disembarking, we discovered we had stopped in a little town just outside Welkenraedt. As luck would have it, we were very close to the new German border.

We kept a close watch around us as we walked through the little town, past vacant eyes staring out shophouse windows, two-storey buildings pockmarked with bullet holes, some of them missing all or part of their walls, and surprisingly, some areas untouched by the mayhem.

We stopped when Frenchie spied something and broke off. He approached a young boy, perhaps no more than nine or ten years old, who sat alone near a pile of rubble.

"Watch this," James said. "Frenchie has a knack for finding the right person with the right information at the right time."

"But he's just a boy," I said. "How can he help us?"

"Just watch."

Frenchie sat down next to the boy on the rubble, talked with him, patted him on the shoulder, shook his head yes and no at the right moments, and eventually gained the boy's confidence. When he did, the young lad became animated.

I had yet to see this side of Frenchie. Out from underneath the war hardened exterior, a kind and gentle person emerged. Even his ubiquitous frown had disappeared.

Frenchie motioned for him to stay put, got up and walked back to James and me. The boy watched every step.

"I told him we have an American spy who wants to go into Germany to destroy a Nazi base, and we need his help. As soon as I said 'American' I couldn't get him to shut up. He says he knows where there is an abandoned Nazi officers' car. They left it there, keys and all when they ran away from the Allies. He also said the local laundry has German uniforms left behind during Jerry's retreat."

Frenchie turned to me. "I told him you would give him some American dollars if he shows us where."

"Yes, of course," I said. "Whatever he needs."

Frenchie returned to addressing James, "He also said he can tell us where the new crossing point is. Jerry paid him to keep it quiet, but he hates the Germans. The Nazis killed his entire family. He's the sole survivor."

"Ouch," I said almost inaudibly. "His whole family?"

"Welcome to Belgium," Frenchie said.

"So, what do we do now?" I asked.

"It's up to you," Frenchie said.

"The stakes are life and death," James added. "Chances are, the Germans would execute the boy if they found out he helped us."

"What are the chances they'll find out?"

"Does it matter?" Frenchie said. "Besides, now it's too late. He already helped us. It's up to you how much money you want to give him to survive once we leave."

"I hope we can somehow ensure his safety."

Frenchie shook his head in disgust. The kind and gentle person was back in hiding. The war hardened exterior and the frown reappeared.

I was beginning to think Frenchie didn't like me very much.

42

Our new little friend led the three of us through town, past bombed-out businesses, piles of rubble several meters high, and a handful of near-starving people. I thought the term probably had not been invented yet, but the empty eyes I saw must be symptoms of post-traumatic stress disorder, the worst I'd ever seen. Worse even than some of the battered women who made their way into the shelter back in Maine.

The walk led to an alleyway, also filled with cement rubble, where an old car sat partly covered in bricks and soot.

James' face lit up. "Ah, yes, a Horch Type 930. This is not just any car. Germans use it to tote their generals around. It'll be perfect."

The boy started running towards it, but Frenchie grabbed him. "Hold back. It might be booby-trapped."

The boy struggled in his grip and ran off once he got free.

We walked cautiously towards the car and carefully began removing rubble, keeping our eyes out for tripwires or anything threatening.

We were just about to finish when a clump of cement fell out of a large hole on the second floor of the building above us. It caused a loud bang and sent everyone diving for cover.

Everyone except Frenchie. He pulled out his sidearm and crouched down on one knee, keeping the weapon pointed outward, aimed at any possible enemy in the area. He even aimed his steely gaze at me and for a second I thought he might pull the trigger. After seeing nothing immediately threatening, he let out a string of French expletives.

"That scared the shite out of me," James said. "What the hell happened?"

"Someone is in the room above. Stay here, I'll go investigate," Frenchie said.

He swung into action, staying low to enter the building undetected. James and I crouched down behind the car, watching Frenchie at his best. A few moments later he appeared in the opening where an apartment wall once stood. He had the young boy by the scruff of the neck.

"Here's our rat," he said. "He says he wanted to get a better look at what we were doing."

Frenchie dragged the boy inside and gave him a right tongue lashing in German and French. I didn't understand what he was saying, but he sounded mad.

"Now that the excitement is over let's see if we can get this thing started," James said. He slid into the driver's seat, turned the ignition and the beast turned over, but didn't start. He tried again and again, but nothing.

"The battery is good," Frenchie said after reappearing next to us, dragging the kid by the back of his coat. It occurred to me I still didn't know the kid's name and I can't remember if anyone had asked him. Frenchie pushed him aside and pointed a strict finger at his face, I assume telling him to stay put.

"It sounds like it's out of petrol," Frenchie said. He started swearing again when the kid ran off, again.

"Where are we going to get gas around here?" I asked.

"Look around for dark green or grey metal cans," James said. "The Krauts might have left some petrol here when they retreated."

After about a half an hour of futile searching, we were about to give up when the little guy showed up dragging a gas can. It was heavier than he was and took all his strength to get it as far as he did.

Frenchie's eyes lit up like a proud father. *"Tres bien,"* he said as he relieved the proud young man of his burden.

"Viens avec moi, viens avec moi," (Come with me, come with me) the little guy told Frenchie. He was so excited he could barely get the words out fast enough.

Frenchie handed me the gas can and as I began pouring the fuel into the Horch, Frenchie and the little guy walked away, disappearing into what was left of the shell shocked town.

After emptying the can into the Horch's gas tank, James slid behind the wheel again, and turned it over a few more times. Still nothing.

"Let's look under the hood," I said. "These old engines are not so difficult to understand. My guess it might be the spark plugs."

James popped the latch and as we raised the hood there was a strong smell of gas.

"I flooded it," James said.

"Yes, it appears you did. Give it a few minutes and we'll try again. Too bad we don't have any ether."

"No ether, but we do have gun powder," James said.

I couldn't tell if his wry smirk meant he was joking or just being devilish. "Let's try starting it again first, before we blow it up."

James's smirk turned to a look of disappointment. Nonetheless, he climbed back in, turned the key and voila, the old beast sputtered to life.

He tucked it into gear and coaxed it forward over the rubble, bumping his way into the street. "Get in. Let's go for a ride."

We'd only turned one corner before we saw Frenchie and his new sidekick walking towards us.

"Over here. There's a laundry just over there," he said. "The little rascal took me inside and showed me a shelf full of abandoned uniforms Jerry's boys left behind. They sure must have been in a hurry."

James and Frenchie picked out enlisted men's uniforms for themselves and a colonel's uniform for me.

"Since you can't speak German, you should sit in the back and keep quiet," James said. "Frenchie and I will do the talking if we run into problems. If anyone tries to talk to you, just yell '*Was ist das! Schnell, schnell!*' like an angry German officer. Whoever is driving, me or Frenchie, we will take off in a hurry as if under orders."

By this time it was getting late so we decided to take our uniforms and hunker down for the night in an abandoned shophouse. We debated the pros and cons of crossing the border at night but decided a day crossing in a Nazi flagged car while dressed in our Nazi uniforms might give us better luck when passing through any German checkpoints. A night crossing might raise too many suspicions.

Once settled in, Frenchie said something to the boy, who left without question. He returned a short while later with a small bag of potatoes, a half dozen eggs, and some dried jerky.

"Word has been spreading around town about who we are and what we're doing," Frenchie said after talking with the boy. "Everyone wants to help."

"That's not exactly good news," James said. "The more people who know about us, the bigger the chance the wrong people will find out. We need to stay alert. This means a night watch tonight.

"Paul, you should take first watch. Don't fall asleep. I'll relieve you around midnight," James said after dinner was finished. "I'm going to try and get some shuteye. You should, too Frenchie."

James climbed into the back of the Horch and disappeared from sight, spread out on the bench seat.

Frenchie disregarded the suggestion, opting instead to watch over me.

"I take it you're not impressed with my sentry skills," I said.

His expression didn't change.

"Well, if you're going to stay awake for a while, maybe you can do me a favor. I'd like to talk with the boy. Can you translate?"

His expression still didn't change.

"Ok, what's his name?"

Frenchie turned to the boy and translated. The boy proudly proclaimed, "Matthias Peeters".

"How old is he?"

Frenchie said, "Ten".

I was all smiles, excited to be able to communicate with this young hero. "Where are your parents?"

Frenchie translated. The boy shook his head no.

"Family?"

Same response.

Frenchie began a long conversation with Matthias, who I could tell was quite uncomfortable with the direction the conversation was going.

After some time, Frenchie turned away from the boy, and with watery eyes told me, "Matthias said the Germans were entrenched here for a long time. His parents were killed by Nazi Storm Troopers when they first arrived. They put him and his brothers to work, and abused his sisters. Eventually they managed to hide but during one of the Nazi retreats they bombed the town from across the border. Being the youngest, his older siblings hid him under them, forming a protective human shield. When one of the bombs hit their hiding spot it killed everyone but him.

"When they found Matthias, the SS grabbed him and turned him into an informant. He hated them, but they fed him and it was the only way he could survive.

They grew to trust him and even told him about the new crossing point. Luckily, he managed to run away before the Allies pushed them back across the border."

I reached into my pack and handed the boy a handful of US dollars, telling him how sorry I was and how I hoped Matthias would never again have to endure anything like it.

When Frenchie translated, Matthias didn't acknowledge the money. Instead, he brushed right past to give me an emotional hug.

After several moments, I came to realize the boy didn't want to let go.

43

It felt like I had just fallen asleep when Frenchie kicked me hard in the bottom of my foot. "Wake up princess, it's time to go." Dawn's early light had only just begun creeping into the streets. I could almost make out the concrete supports barely holding up the ceiling above us in the shelled out little shop we'd settled into for the night.

Frenchie threw a bundle of clothes in my face, "Put these on, it's time to go." He had already changed into a Nazi corporal's uniform and it was time for me to assume my role as colonel.

James was busy loading up the trunk of the car with whatever he thought we might need to help get us across the border.

I looked around for Matthias but the little guy was nowhere to be found. "He must have run off like he did before the Nazis retreated," James said.

I felt a certain bond and would have liked to say goodbye, but I hoped the boy would take the money I gave him and run as fast and as far away from this awful place as he could get. "Ah well, good luck to him wherever he went."

As Frenchie took the wheel began to maneuver the Horch on a bumpy ride down the narrow streets past empty oxcarts and bombed out buildings, doing his best to dodge the rubble, we heard a significant bump behind us.

"I must not have left the trunk latched," James said. He got out and tried to pull it open without the key and when it didn't give, he surmised, "That last bump must have slammed it shut."

A few minutes later we left the relative safety of town and headed towards the secret crossing point Matthias had shown Frenchie. The road out of town cut through the middle of an open field and led toward a small gulley protected by hedges.

"This is not good," Frenchie said as he began to speed up. "We're way too exposed."

As we approached this invisible border, James turned to me, "The first few minutes, even the first hour or so will be the toughest. Anything can happen on our way through and behind German lines."

Sure enough, we were barely inside Germany when we began to take heavy fire—not from the Germans; from the Allies who saw a German officer being whisked across the border from Belgium into Germany.

Tracer rounds whizzed past all around us. Some hit the car. One knocked off the driver's side mirror. Another went straight through the back window, mere inches from my ear. It passed over the top of the front seat between James and Frenchie and into the dash.

The barrage might have continued had it not been for a small Panzer division appearing out of nowhere, lighting up the other side. I couldn't decide which was scarier, the Allied bullets flying past or the Nazi tank shells flying over our heads ironically meant to protect us.

I crouched down, protected by the metal plate installed behind the back seat meant to shield German officers. In this position, though, I began to have another one of my flashes, fading in and out.

For brief moments I was in a desert on a hot day with people in robes following me. Or was I following them? There were no bullets flying by but I did see flashes of light. My head was pounding.

Frenchie had the old Horch's pedal to the metal, deftly dodging deadly rounds from both sides of the border. He blasted the car through hedges, barricades, and a handful of soldiers here and there advancing past the fight until the fury began to fade away behind us.

James looked over into the back and saw me slumped over. "Are you hit?"

No answer.

Again, "Are you hit?"

Still no answer. What James saw, though, was not a man riddled with bullets but a man in a swirl of light, sometimes in robes, sometimes back in his German officer's uniform.

My flashes were getting stronger.

Frenchie looked in the review mirror but couldn't see me or what was going on in back. He did see flashes of light, though. "What the hell's going on back there?"

Still no answer.

James kept his distance from me until the lights slowed to a stop. "I don't know either," he finally said.

After another twenty minutes speeding away from the border, Frenchie spied a dirt path off to the left. It was muddy and rutted but he took it anyway. He drove another few minutes to the top of a hill in the forest where he stopped to make sure everything was ok.

"Was anyone hit?" Frenchie said, more of an announcement than a question.

I couldn't seem to get out of my funk.

Frenchie turned to look, "He doesn't look like he's been hit. I don't see any blood."

James reached back and shook me by the shoulder. He received a vacant stare in return.

"Battle trauma," Frenchie said. "I've seen it before. Poor guy is scared out of his wits. This must be his first time."

"Maybe so," James said. "But something weird was going on back there during the firefight. I don't know, but I think a tracer round started bouncing around in the back seat. If that happened to me, I'd be traumatized too."

At last, I began to come around. "That was close."

"Are you hit?"

"No, I don't think so. How about you?"

"Me either," James said, relieved there was nothing serious. "We better check the car to make sure the gas tank, brakes, or anything else we need wasn't damaged.

All three of us disembarked and began looking under and around the car. There might have been a glut of bullet holes, but luckily, none had hit any of us.

Frenchie circled to the back of the car to see how much more damage was done. "We took a number in the bonnet," he said. He opened the trunk to see what the damage was, gasped and slammed it shut.

44

I was busy trying to find a way to reattach the driver's side mirror as James and Frenchie checked out the trunk. I could tell something was wrong, but I had no idea. My first clue that it was something really bad was when they both stopped looking at each other and turned to look at me.

"What is it?" I asked and began walking around to join them at the back. "Did they puncture the gas tank?"

Frenchie shook his head no, took a deep breath, and slowly lifted the lid.

Matthias had somehow managed to hide in the trunk before we left. He now lay dead, riddled with Allied bullets. Bullets meant for us. Blood was everywhere.

I dropped to my knees and couldn't move. I couldn't breathe. I felt like I had been drained of life itself.

A lone crow broke the silence, its call echoing throughout the valley.

"We shouldn't be here. We need to go back," I said.

"We can't," James said. "There is only one way to go now, forward."

"I never meant for this to happen. This is all my fault."

"Wake up," Frenchie said. "This is war, people die. Children die. Women die. Old folks die. It happens. It's not good, but it happens and it's not your fault. We didn't know he was in there."

"He didn't climb in there because of you," James said with a bit more diplomacy. "He hid in there because he was trying to escape his terrible life. And he did. As tragic as it is, he's better off now than he would have been trying to survive, alone, in a war zone."

When his words didn't seem to register with me, he continued. "He died a hero, fighting against the monsters that killed his family. If you think of it, we did him a favor, and you were a big part of that. We helped him feel important. We made him feel like he was finally on the side of the good guys. He died with hope in his heart. We gave that to him. We let him help us and gave him dignity. If we didn't come along, he might have died of starvation or died helping the bastards that killed his family, all the while dying inside. You helped release him from all that."

"Now get a hold of yourself," Frenchie said. "We have a long way to go."

I clenched my teeth and glared at Frenchie. I never hated anyone as much as I hated him right at that instant. But I knew he was right. Reluctantly, I stood, straightened my uniform, and got back into the car.

Frenchie and James stayed behind to talk, but I couldn't make out what they were saying. Eventually they shut the trunk, climbed back in and began to drive.

* * * * *

I remained quiet as we traveled back to the main road and continued further along, passing yellowing cow pastures and hillsides filled with autumn foliage scattered among the evergreens. Near one of the hills, Frenchie pulled off the road onto another soggy cow path leading up a hill. A half hour or so later, bouncing along the barely passable trail, we reached a plateau.

A mile or two below, a small river wound its way through the valley. Wooden cabins with wisps of smoke rising from their chimneys dotted its banks. A new, untouched evergreen forest led partway up the hill towards us, giving way to smaller brush. The view was breathtaking, straight out of a German postcard.

We buried Matthias on the crest of the hill. It didn't matter this was German soil; the war wouldn't last forever. Wounds would heal. Over time Germans and Belgians would once again be friends.

Frenchie took the time to lash together a wooden cross, carving the boy's name into it so the words 'Matthias Peeters' wouldn't forever be lost in the wind. He also carved 'Young Hero' in French and German.

There couldn't possibly have been a more scenic place anywhere in the world for the young Matthias to spend the rest of eternity.

45

Back on the road, I kept quiet in the back seat, dressed in my stolen Nazi colonel uniform, disgusted with myself, ashamed at what I was doing. I began to wish I'd never left Harpswell.

I was lost in these unhealthy thoughts when Frenchie declared, "We've got trouble."

A Nazi roadblock had been set up around a corner, popping up too quickly for Frenchie to avoid.

James told me not to say anything unless asked and to remember my lines in case the guards were persistent.

"What is your business here?" one of the armed guards leaned into Frenchie's window and asked me behind him.

"We've been ordered to report to the Eastern Front," Frenchie broke in, shuffling through the papers on the front seat between him and James.

"No one asked you," the guard said. He turned to me and repeated, "What is your business here, sir?"

Again Frenchie tried to answer for me, "We've been ordered to report to the Eastern Front." This time he held up the forged paperwork he'd obtained back in Welkenraedt.

The guard slapped them out of his hand. "No one asked you," he repeated and turned to me. "Will you let your juniors answer for you?"

Since, of course all this was in the German language and beyond my comprehension, I had no idea what was going on, only that it wasn't pleasantries they were exchanging.

Frenchie started to burst out of the car and tear him apart, but James caught him by the arm. "Our colonel is not happy at being held up here. We have important things to do. Now, will you let us through?"

The guard stared me down.

James turned to me and his expression announced it was time for me to play my role.

"*Was ist das!*" I called out in my best German. "*Schnell! Schnell!*"

The guards nodded their heads in agreement, glad I finally said something, but didn't budge, even though Frenchie kept inching the car forward.

The situation escalated when a real Nazi colonel emerged from the guard shack and approached the car. I tried to help the situation by raising my hands in mock contempt, and I did elicit a knowing smile and nod from the colonel.

"Sorry for the inconvenience, but it's not often we see someone of your rank traveling through these parts. What might be your reason for being here, so far away from either front?"

Frenchie produced his forged papers, telling him "We were ordered out of the west and told to report to the Eastern Front."

Frenchie tried to hand the documents to the colonel, but he pushed them aside, keeping his focus on me. "Do you always let your subordinates answer for you?"

When I didn't answer, he stared at me for a few seconds. When I still didn't answer, he turned to his men, "Arrest them at once!"

The two guards who had already been arguing with us cocked their weapons and tried to push them through the windows into our car. More guards from the roadblock came running towards us with their weapons raised.

Frenchie had had enough and instead of inching forward, he floored the accelerator. Bodies bounced off the side of the Horch as we plowed ahead, breaking through the wooden barrier.

The colonel fell on his keister and slid down a small embankment, splashing into a mud filled gully. About half his men jumped in to help him, the others began firing their weapons at us.

"*Rous, rous,*" the colonel yelled at them. "Get the traitors immediately!"

I continued to try and play my role, frantically waving my hands in the back window as if I were being kidnapped, although, in reality, it didn't help matters.

It took a while for the guards to regain their wits, but they did manage to get off a few shots at us, missing, before they boarded their vehicles to give chase. By then we had too much of a head start. It would be impossible for the German troop carriers to catch the Horch 930's powerful V8.

Once we were well out of range, Frenchie yelled back at me, "What the hell was that all about, waving your hands like that!"

"I thought maybe if they believed there was a real officer in the car they wouldn't shoot at us. I guess I was wrong."

James smiled and nodded at Frenchie. "He has a point, my friend."

Frenchie grudgingly conceded it could have worked in our favor. "Thanks for letting us know what you were doing."

"I hope there won't be a next time, but if there is, I'll let you know about any more crazy ideas I might have."

"That's all we can ask," James said, more to Frenchie than to me.

* * * * *

We took turns driving and sleeping in the car to keep the quest moving, but as we trudged along through the sometimes bombed out, other times beautiful scenery through north-central Germany, we occasionally needed to stop to eat. In order to keep the situation as safe as possible, James and Frenchie would reconnoiter the local restaurants and pubs along the way. They'd go in first, and if they thought it was safe, bring me in and sit me in a dark corner.

Most of the time this worked perfectly, until one day when we had settled into a little eatery a couple hundred miles from our destination. No sooner had our meals arrived when two Gestapo officers walked in.

Seeing Colonel Me, they laughed and joked their greeting as they took up seats at our table. "Ah, it's a beautiful day to be German," the older of the two said to me. Instinct told me to smile and laugh with them.

"You are a long way from anywhere," he said. "What brings you here to our part of the country?"

Frenchie answered, "We're being sent to the Eastern Front. Are we close?"

The younger Gestapo agent remained silent, the elder gave Frenchie an odd look. He then turned to me, "You must have done something really bad to be sent there, ja?"

I half nodded yes, half shook no to return the troubled look he gave me. Staring him down, I knew right then we were in trouble.

"Why does he answer me and you do not?" he said.

Receiving no answer, sidearms came bursting out from their holsters on both sides. Frenchie and James on one side, the Gestapo on the other, each pointing at their enemies' faces.

Tense moments passed when finally I remembered my lines. "*Was ist das! Schnell! Schnell!*" I tipped over the table, knocking both Gestapo officers to the floor. In the confusion, James grabbed me by the arm and pulled me towards the door.

"This way," Frenchie yelled.

The Gestapo, still scrambling to regain their balance and extricate themselves from the entanglement of broken chairs and table legs, fired at us. They missed wildly.

Waitresses and bartenders deftly dove behind the heavy oak bar to escape the gunfire. It wasn't the first time the Gestapo shot up their eatery when they suspected foul play among the customers.

Making it unharmed to the car, we piled in as fast as we could. Frenchie fired it up, slammed it into gear, and we sped away.

"That certainly went well," I said.

James looked at me as if I were an idiot.

I turned to keep an eye out behind us, but the officers weren't close behind. Our Horch must be too fast for them to catch up.

It didn't matter. We were now marked men. The Gestapo would use radios and telegraph to mobilize troops to hunt us down.

46

"We need to avoid all Germans now, army and otherwise," Frenchie said as we careened around another corner at high speed.

"Agreed," James said.

I nodded, holding onto the armrest in the backseat. I no longer feared the Gestapo—the more immediate danger was how Frenchie was driving way too fast along this rural road.

About thirty minutes later when we crested a hill, Frenchie slammed on the brakes, bringing the powerful Horch to a screeching halt. "*Scheisse!* Roadblock."

Frenchie reversed, spun around, and headed back in the opposite direction.

"There was a small road off to the side about a half mile back," James said. "I don't see it on the map, so maybe it will lead us around the barricade and back on the right trail."

Another fifteen minutes further along, we could see a small platoon of soldiers walking in our direction, so Frenchie pulled into still another side road.

This time the road led us through forest and past unkempt farmland. There were no people that we could see.

"Look over there, in the field," James said, pointing to an old dilapidated barn. "We should hide in there until things cool down."

Frenchie spun off the rural road and made a beeline towards the barn. The doors were open—a condition we changed as soon as we were inside.

The barn had fallen into disrepair, unused for quite some time. Spider webs hung from the rafters, broken down machinery littered the floor. Bales of hay had turned black and smelled of rot. But it was big enough to hide the Horch and far enough off the beaten path to allow us a small amount of security. It would be a perfect hideout for the night.

We had only been settled in for a few minutes, however, when the door burst open and a farmer barged in brandishing a double-barrel twelve-gauge shotgun. "I will not allow German soldiers to commandeer my farm," he said in heavily accented German.

All three of us put our hands up in surprise.

"*Gehe 'raus! 'Raus jetzt!*" (Get out! Get out now!)

Frenchie, who had a knack for reading people, picked up something in his accent. "We're not German soldiers," he replied in German. "I'm Belgian, he's British, and he's American. We're hiding from the Nazis and trying to make it to Poland."

After a few cautious moments, the farmer began to lower his weapon. "I'm Polish," he said, still in the German language. "My wife is German. This is my farm, and I don't want to lose it to the Nazi filth."

Frenchie smiled. James remained wary. I didn't have a clue what was going on.

"Vee da Nazis's's hate," the farmer said to me in broken English.

After figuring out what he said, I replied, perhaps a bit too eagerly, "Yes. We do too."

The farmer nodded once in the affirmative. Returning to speaking German, he told Frenchie, "My family is hiding in our house a little way up the road. You can stay here if you want, I will go get you some food."

Having thus spoken, he left.

"Can we trust him?" I asked.

"I believe so," James replied. "His hate of the Nazis seemed genuine to me."

"Yes," Frenchie added. "But we cannot trust anyone fully. We still must be careful."

A short while later, the farmer returned with some bread, cheese, and a bottle of wine. Without saying a word, he gave it to us and left again.

* * * * *

After an uncomfortable night where each of us took turns on guard duty, we were woken at dawn by the sound of a tractor. The farmer had returned with several cans of rationed petrol he had saved up for his farm equipment. He dropped them off inside the barn door, and again without saying a word, mounted his tractor and left.

Frenchie and James called out their thank you, one in German and the other in English, but their words were lost to the sputtering of the tractor engine and the clacking and clanging of the cart as it bounced along behind.

"He really came through for us," I said.

"Yes, yes," Frenchie replied. "We have work to do."

James looked over at me with raised eyebrows.

Refueling the Horch should have been the last preparation needed to make the final leg of our journey, as long as we didn't confront any more troubles along the way.

But when we dared look out the door to determine if the coast was clear, the early morning light revealed the farmer's house about a quarter mile away. To our horror, the two Gestapo officers stood out front. One of them pointed his sidearm at the farmer's head. The rest of the family watched in horror as he pulled the trigger. The farmer collapsed in an ungodly heap. A few seconds later a loud pop echoed across the farmland.

The farmer's wife and two daughters began crying hysterically, so the Gestapo fired their weapons on the women, too.

It was all I could handle and I snapped. Grabbing my pistol I began running and screaming at the ghastly sight unfolding in front of me, firing shot after shot when I got close enough to make a difference.

My traveling companions had no choice but to follow, also firing away at the Gestapo officers until both lay dead, their bodies riddled with our bullets.

As the dust settled, Frenchie ran back to get the car. I stood transfixed at the horror in front of me, frozen and unable to move. "Should we bury these people?"

"No," James said forcefully. "Remember, it's war." He grabbed me and pulled me away from the carnage, and when Frenchie raced the car up beside us, James shoved me into the back seat. We sped away, leaving the gruesome scene behind.

47

The rest of the trip through Germany passed in relative silence. Somehow we managed to skirt all remaining roadblocks and didn't need to interact with anyone again.

Crossing into what formerly was Southern Poland, the air became cooler higher in the mountains. Driving through tiny hamlets along the way, the reactions we received from the locals changed from warm and welcoming in Germany, to dark, often hateful stares inside the occupied territory.

People turned and hurried away from us, vacating the streets, closing their doors and window shutters. Small shops slammed their doors shut, leaving no doubt they didn't want our business. After all, we were disguised as German officers heading towards an SS base.

This continued until we arrived in a little town nestled at the foot of the Owl Mountains called Gluszyca. Pulling around back behind a small pub, we changed back into civilian clothes so as not to attract attention.

"Try to blend in," James said. "Don't look anyone in the eye. Don't act like a tourist, either. We want to give the impression we belong here."

Frenchie agreed. "Keep an eye out for vacant alleyways and places we might hide if we need to. If there is any sign of trouble, meet back at the car."

It only took a few minutes reconnoitering the village before we heard a commotion. In an attempt to find out what was going on, Sir James and Frenchie went one way, and by mistake I went the other.

Without noticing I was alone I arrived at the corner of a building. Peering down the street to my left, I could see a sizable group of people had gathered. A dozen Nazi soldiers, war weapons at the ready, were keeping a close eye on them.

Not wanting to risk being discovered I decided to turn the corner in the other direction. As serendipity would have it, I turned straight into an official entourage of high-ranking officers and came face to face with none other than the Führer himself.

We both stopped in our tracks. I couldn't breathe. I thought my heart might have stopped until I felt it pounding out my chest. It became so loud in my ears I was sure everyone else could hear it, even more so when Hitler began talking to me.

"*Wo ist deine Uniform?*" He demanded.

I stood speechless. I shook my head no. I quickly extinguished the thought of the loaded gun in my backpack when I saw how many armed officers and guards stood in front of me, watching my every move. A few already had their sidearms pulled and at the ready. If I went for it, I would be dead before I could get the backpack open.

Hitler studied me, wondering why I didn't answer. "*Sie sind ein Jude?*"

I again shook my head no, this time thinking 'Jude' sounded like Jew. "*Nein,*" I managed to say. I desperately tried to remember my German lessons. *Die Sonne scheint* (the sun shines), *Axel schwimmt im Wasser* (Axel swims in water) and *üppige busen* (lush breasts) was all I could remember. (We had a fun German teacher.) So I burst out, "*Die Sonne scheint,*" raising my arm to try and signal the Nazi salute. Absentmindedly, I pointed straight at the sun.

Hitler stared at me. Probably the only thing saving me from certain death was my six foot five inch frame, by now weighing 210 pounds, with blond hair and blue eyes. I was a veritable poster boy for the Master Race Hitler was trying to create. Since many commoners in Germany would also freeze when seeing their supreme leader this close up, he was accustomed to my reaction. This didn't hurt my chances either.

Hitler turned and looked to the area where I pointed. A broad smile crossed his face. *"Ja, die Sonne scheint auf das Vaterland,"* (the sun shines on the Fatherland) he said, posturing and moving his head, shoulders and body, thrusting his *'Sieg Heil'* arm into the air towards the sun just as I did. He turned to smile at his men, pointing to the sky with a shaky hand, convinced I had heard his propaganda speech the previous night about how everything looked brighter and how the sun did indeed shine down upon the Third Reich. He nodded his approval and led his entourage away.

The high-ranking Nazi regulars and SS officers didn't give me the same approving expression.

I swear if the meeting lasted two seconds longer I would've soiled my pants.

Sir James and Frenchie observed the entire exchange from a hiding place across the street. They recognized one of the officers as Jakob Sporrenberg, aka the Butcher, the SS and police leader of occupied Poland. This was a dangerous man, reputed to have ordered the execution of 43,000 Jews during the infamous Operation Harvest Festival.

As soon as the retinue of colorful ribbons and shiny medals had passed from sight, James and Frenchie rushed over. "It's time to end this," James said. "Hitler is in town and the man who was escorting the pack was none other than the Butcher, the most ruthless SS General in the Third Reich. You were lucky this time, but they've seen you and will hunt you down if you don't leave now."

"Nonsense." My adrenaline was running at an all-time high. "I agree it was a close call but I passed. If they were going to kill me, they would have done it right then and there. And believe me, I almost crapped my pants thinking they would.

"Besides, I can't quit now. We made it this far. If I turn around now everything that has happened so far will be for nothing."

Frenchie shook his head in disgust. "We can't help you anymore. This is now too dangerous and way beyond what we can do for you."

"You're right, of course," I said. "I can't ask you to do anything more. Just point me in the right direction. From here on, I need to do this on my own. I can't thank you enough for all you have done, getting me this far and saving me so many times. There is a place for both of you in heaven when you die—of old age."

The two guides looked at each other in disbelief. Sir James pointed to where Hitler's entourage had emerged moments before. "This street turns into a winding road up the hill leading to the tunnels in the mountains. Follow it until it ends. It will be heavily guarded so it would be best to stay off it. Follow it from the woods."

"Thank you James," I said and shook his hand. "And thank you, too, Frenchie. I know you don't like me but I have a lot of respect for you."

"Good luck," Frenchie said. "You're one crazy American."

We shook hands and as I slung my trusty pack over my shoulder, we headed in opposite directions.

Sir James and Frenchie stayed in town a couple days in case I changed my mind. On the second night, however, rumors began circulating about how an SS officer named Vrill was caught with an American spy.

The scuttlebutt was, any and all spies caught by the SS were destined to be put in front of a firing squad.

Sir James and Frenchie tried to hide their disappointment. Both realized it was time to move on.

Just minutes after they had they left the pub a dozen heavily armed soldiers invaded it, looking for accomplices.

* * * * *

I walked in the direction James had pointed and only made it about half way up the hill when I started having second thoughts. Now completely alone, I started to think, what the hell am I doing here? I must be an idiot. I should have thought this through better, listened to James and Frenchie and waited until things calmed down. But no, stubborn Paul had to keep pushing on. I guessed since I'd come this far I might as well keep going.

The woods were thick with armed soldiers on patrol, and as I progressed closer to the stronghold where I hoped to find Vrill, the patrols intensified. I kept well off the traveled road, trying to keep it in sight to guide me.

When a guard approached from my front left, I ducked down inside the roots of a toppled tree. Peering over the top, I suddenly felt a cold steel gun barrel pressing against the back of my neck.

I slowly raised my arms, not daring to turn around and look my executioner in the face. The guard yelled in German, words I could not decipher, knowing only that my fate was now sealed, my mission failed.

All I could do was ignore their questions, as I don't speak the language. Instead I began repeating Vrill's name. Over and over.

The soldiers knew Colonel Wilhelm Vrill. He was one of the handful of SS scientists working on advanced technology, one of many officers these soldiers were ordered to guard, with their lives if necessary.

If this prisoner refused to answer and instead repeatedly uttered Colonel Vrill's name, they felt it was not their duty to execute me. Anyone found crawling around these woods who knew Colonel Vrill had at least earned the right to be put in a prison cell until such time Colonel Vrill could either determine who I was, or execute me with his own weapon.

48

As Karla waited for my return to Grand Central Station, time seemed to slow to a crawl. Two minutes passed and no Paul. Five minutes, still no sign of him. Ok, he did say ten minutes. But ten minutes passed, then half an hour turned into an hour, then two, three, then five hours. No Paul. Maybe he was delayed.

Karla would wait overnight, and by one or two in the morning much of the crowd had thinned out. She had just walked over to sit with a group of people when two of Don Antonio's men walked in. One of them looked right at her. At that moment a warm feeling washed over her. It felt like someone or something was protecting her.

Don Antonio's men either didn't see her or didn't recognize her, and when at long last they left, the warm feeling went away. Scared again, she started shaking uncontrollably.

The adrenaline kept her awake the entire night and well into the next day.

After another long day of waiting, when the second night approached, she realized she couldn't risk another close call. She also needed sleep, so she dug around in her purse and found a scrap of paper. Borrowing a pencil from the ticket counter, she wrote Paul a note telling him where she'd return the next day. She slid it into a crack in the locker opening.

She awoke the next morning with renewed optimism, returning to the station prepared for another wait—hoping it wouldn't be much longer.

After the second *week* with no results, one day her walk to the station was delayed by nerves. She awakened that morning feeling terrified. So scared, in fact, it turned her stomach inside out, causing her to vomit several times before she could leave her rented room.

This turned into her morning routine over the following fortnight.

After waiting week after week with no word, a strange man approached her wearing a white apron, his long hair tied in a ponytail. Speaking softly while constantly surveilling the surroundings, he first made sure she was Karla, then told her in a thick Scouse accent how he was a member of the Second Order of the Golden Knights of Mysticism. He needed to repeat this several times and gave up when Karla kept telling him she had no idea what he was talking about.

"Never mind, I have a message for you about Paul."

Karla's eyes lit up, but she soon realized he said 'about Paul' not 'from Paul'. "Is he ok? Will he be coming back to get me soon?"

"I'm sorry, lassie. Two of our agents helped him get inside Poland all the way to a Nazi base. Only our agents came back."

Chief paused, unsure of how to continue. He decided the truth would be best and to get it over with. "They fear Paul and the man he was looking for were caught and executed by firing squad. I wish I had better news. My sincere condolences."

No sooner had he finished when he walked away, disappearing into the crowd.

Karla sat in stunned silence. Unable to think of questions in time, she was left wondering about the details. He said 'they fear' he was caught. But do they know? How could she find out? After all, if what he told her was true, she shouldn't expect him to return via the normal passage.

With this new information it became apparent it would be useless for her to remain here and wait. Perhaps Paul made it back but couldn't find her and returned to Maine.

Karla borrowed another pencil from one of the clerks and wrote another note. At first, she wrote she would go to Harpswell Maine to look for him, but she tore it up in case Tony's men discovered it and would know where to look. She then wrote a second note, "If you see this, please find me in your hometown," hoping no one in the Napoli family's reach would know where it was.

She emptied the locker, leaving just the note, and boarded the first train she could find bound for Portland, Maine.

49

People in his old life called him Frankie "The Mole", not because they suspected he worked undercover with law enforcement—he wouldn't be caught dead fraternizing with coppers, much less providing them with information—but because he liked to bury his valuables somewhere only he would know where to look.

He surreptitiously buried his guns, his cash, anything he thought might be cause for concern if the constabulary started snooping around.

He'd been like this since everything nice he'd ever had while growing up on Mulberry Street in the Little Italy section of Manhattan was stolen by bigger boys. The only way to save anything he cherished was to keep it hidden away; and the only place he could be certain to keep his worldly possessions hidden was underground, clandestinely marked with a symbol or sign only he would know how to decipher. It was a strange habit, but effective.

After escaping Don Antonio's wrath and recovering his stash, Frankie settled down in a little college town called Potsdam in upstate New York. It was nestled alongside the St Lawrence waterway separating the USA from Canada.

He had grown to like his new town with its institutions of higher learning, its great game hunting, and its cheap land. He changed his name, bought a twenty four-acre plot on Sweeney Road a short drive from the village center, and built a house there, paid for in cash. He settled into an incognito life he hoped would keep him far away from the death and destruction he had left behind.

He didn't change his habit of burying his valuables in his new surroundings and split up the cash he stole from Don Antonio Napoli's counting room into two smaller bundles, burying them in different places out behind his house. One was a short way back where he could easily access it; the other much further away, near the stone wall that formed the demarcation of his property.

For Frankie the Mole, it was an ideal place to bury his wealth. If somehow they found him up here, he wouldn't have a lot of cash on hand and could try to deny who he once was. He grew a beard, cut himself on the forehead to create a noticeable scar, and dyed his hair gray to look much older.

One day he opened his front door to pick up the morning paper and was met with a shotgun blast to the face.

As it turned out, Frankie's disguise didn't fool the goombas; they'd never met Frankie—wouldn't have known what he looked like anyway. But due to his reputation as a cold blooded killer, one of the two men panicked as soon as the door opened and he came face to face with the infamous Frankie the Mole. His trigger fingers twitched on the double barrel twelve-gauge shotgun and he accidentally blew most of Frankie's head right off.

His partner was furious. Don Antonio gave them strict orders to make sure they found his loot and brought it back to Manhattan. Don't return without it, he had said. The only way they could find it would be to interrogate Frankie until he gave up the location. This was no longer an option.

Now what could they do? They did the only thing they could—tear the house apart, plank by plank, brick by brick. Unlucky for them, weeks later they still hadn't found anything.

All the while, Frankie's body lay inside the front door bleeding out. When the stench became so rancid they feared it would attract passersby, they gave up their search and headed back into the city, knowing full well Don Antonio was going to tear them apart.

As it turned out, they need not have worried. Upon reaching little Italy and entering Don Antonio's warehouse, they were met with somber faces and tales of tragedy.

The previous night, the Don had visited his favorite massage parlor. Evidently his regular masseuse had called in sick, and had it not been for the beautiful, buxom blonde woman sent as a replacement, standing naked in the room and promising a happy ending, the normally cautious Don would have left in a heartbeat.

He stripped bare and laid face down on the massage table, sliding into heavenly bliss as the woman worked her fingers into his fleshy back.

Mary Jo Freedman came from a tiny farming town outside of Topeka, Kansas. She'd come to the big city at the urging of a friend who waxed lyrical about the riches she could earn in the massage business. Sure, she might have to sell her body sometimes, but the money she'd make would be enough to buy a house back home and allow her to retire in comfort. Jobs were scarce, especially in Kansas. She completely fell for her friend's sales pitch.

She created Buxom Betsy for her trade name and sure enough, even though she was new to the business, having only worked in New York City for a couple weeks, the money came flowing in. She should have known something unusual was about to happen when the previous night Jack Levy, a lieutenant in the Lipinski family, had paid her five hundred dollars in cash for a massage, happy ending, and instructions to show up at this particular massage parlor at the instructed time to provide the same treatment to a highly valued customer. The money was too good to pass up.

She had no idea who the customer would be, but what was the worst that could happen?

It didn't take long to find out. She became scared out of her wits when she learned the highly valued customer turned out to be Don Antonio Napoli.

Now that she was massaging the most feared mafia boss in America, she began to feel sick. As her hands kneaded his fatty back, she was disgusted with herself for getting into this situation, no matter how much money was at stake.

She began to realize she might be bait. Whatever was about to happen would happen because she had lured Don Antonio Napoli into this massage room. As scary as it was, the best possible outcome would be for her to go through with the entire massage and provide the happy ending she was being paid for, and go home. Despite her profession, she had managed to stay away from Italian gangsters, feared by all of her friends. Would Don Antonio decide to keep her on as his regular masseuse?

She was still trying to figure out what else might be going on when the door was kicked open and a lone assassin pointed his Colt 1911A1 semi-automatic .45 caliber pistol directly at the Don's face.

Fat Tony started to let out a string of expletives, but didn't get far into his rave. Buxom Betsy froze. A single shot rang out.

Buxom Betsy began screaming as Don Antonio bucked up off the massage table, sending her tumbling to the floor.

The Don was dead, although it took a while for his muscles to realize it. They continued to spasm for a few more seconds as the assassin watched to make sure.

Mary Jo Freedman, no longer Buxom Betsy, whimpered in the corner, her naked body folded into a fetal position.

The assassin slowly walked over to her. This was the part of the job he disliked most. What had this poor girl done to deserve this? Nothing he could think of. Every bone in his body wanted to spare her life. Every bone except the one in his trigger finger. 'Another quick shot to the head, pop, and it was over.

The job he was hired to do meant being quick, complete, and leave no witnesses. He walked out the door, over to the window leading to the fire escape, took a look around to be sure, and left the same way he came in.

Quick. Job complete. He left no witnesses.

50

There was a chill in the Southern Poland air in October 1944. My prison cell was a cement block barely six feet square, its blood splattered walls were a testament to how it wasn't built for long term use. It had no heating, a bucket for a toilet, and a pail of putrid water sat idly on the floor, presumably for washing off the blood. A cement bunk adorned with only a slab of wood for a mattress implied it wasn't meant for sleeping. This would be a dismal place to live out the last few hours of my life.

I was the only prisoner, and my only visitor was someone I thought was probably an interrogator. All questions, always harsh, were in German. I refused to acknowledge any of them, instead continuously repeating, "Vrill ... Vrill ... Vrill..."

When the interrogator finally gave up, I thought for sure that was it. I began making peace with my life, wishing I could have made it back to Karla Gingerich, the love of my life, who I had selfishly left waiting for me at Grand Central Station. Albert was right, I was indeed insane for leaving behind such a beautiful "dame", as he had called her, and going on this, what was certain to become a suicide mission.

If I had it to do over, I most certainly would have stayed with her in New York. We could have had a beautiful life together. I missed her punches to my shoulder. If only...

* * * * *

An hour later a high ranking officer accompanied by heavily armed soldiers was brought to my cell. A comfortable chair was brought in for him to sit on, followed by a number of lesser ranked uniforms "*Sieg Heiling*" several times before the officer shooed them back.

The officer settled into the chair and sat looking at me without saying anything for what seemed like forever. I stared back.

Finally, the officer broke the silence, "*Ich bin Oberst Wilhelm Vrill. Sie haben für mich gefragt?*"

I didn't know what the officer was saying but I did recognize one of the words. "You're Vrill?" I asked, for the first time speaking a word in English.

"You're American?" Col. Vrill answered. He reached for his sidearm.

"You're British?" I answered, immediately taken by Col. Vrill's perfect command of the language, spoken with what I thought to be a British accent.

"I graduated from Oxford," Col. Vrill said as he removed his Luger and jacked a cartridge into the chamber.

"Before you shoot me," I said, of course hoping he wouldn't, "please hear what I have to say. I know your great-grandson and I might be able to help you finish your time travel project. I believe you call it dee glockah?"

"*Die Glocke?* How did you know about that? It's top secret—it would be, if it existed."

"It exists," I said. "Your great-grandson William the Fourth used your impeccable notes, updated them with modern technology—"

"My notes?" Col. Vrill cut me off.

"Your wife brought them with her to America when she escaped with your son."

"My wife and son are at home in Munich," Col. Vrill said, lowering his Luger. "How did you know about my family?"

"Your son is William Vrill the Fourth's grandfather. Your great-grandson told me all about you, and how you were shot dead by firing squad. He said before this happened you bundled up your work, put it in a trunk, and sent it off to your wife with a note instructing her to take it with her when she escaped to America."

"You're crazy," Col. Vrill said, tapping his finger on his sidearm, which now rested on his leg, pointed at me. "I would take great pleasure shooting you right now and getting it over with."

"You could," I said, staring back at him. "But you would be sealing your own fate. I can help you finish building your time machine."

"You're an American, our enemy. Why would you do that?"

"Because I want something in return."

"Ah, here comes the catch. You don't want me to shoot you because you believe that if I don't shoot you, you will find a way to escape and tell all your Allied friends you found our secret base, and give them the coordinates so they know where to aim their bombs."

"They already know about this base and its coordinates. How do you think I found it? Since so much of it is underground, they determined it would be a waste of their time and resources to bomb it. They don't believe you have anything here of importance anyway."

Col. Vrill shifted in his seat. The news wasn't totally unexpected, but it was surprising to hear it from an American.

"What I want in return is: before you go off into the future to do whatever it is you plan to do with a functioning time machine, take me home. I want to go back, sleep in my own bed and hang out with my friends in Harpswell."

"I don't believe you. Why would you come all the way here just to go home? Where is home?"

"It's not where," I said, which by now seemed like the hundredth time over the past couple months, "but when. I want to go back to 2018 and you are my only hope. Promise to take me there and I will help you finish your 'Die Glocke' project. As a side benefit, you could even say hello to your great-grandson William Vrill the Fourth. I'm sure he'd be thrilled to meet you."

Col. Vrill sat silently in front of my cell. Mostly he stared at me while tapping on his Luger. I could see the man was having trouble deciding whether or not to kill me. It would only take a few seconds and he could get back to whatever it was he was doing when the guards rudely interrupted him.

Should he disregard this crazy American who talked and dressed in a way stranger than anyone he'd ever seen? Should he put a bullet between his eyes and get it over with? The guards would certainly have more respect for him if he did.

Or was there something to what I was trying to tell him?

The war was coming to a close; he felt certain. And the Fatherland was on the losing end, which was just as certain. Was there a chance I was telling the truth, and he, Colonel Wilhelm Vrill, might be able to finish *Die Glocke* and fulfill his destiny? Could he go to the future and bring back the secret weapon the Nazis would need to turn the tide in their favor?

Could he live with himself if he killed this crazy American, right now, without seeing proof whether I was telling the truth, one way or the other? Was it possible I held the key to finish what they'd been working so hard to achieve here in Southern Poland? Did he have the right to extinguish this hope without even trying to find out?

On the other hand, what if I was lying? What if I was an American spy and had made up this incredible story? What if I somehow got loose, told the Allies about this base, and brought Allied bombers here to destroy everything they had been working on?

"Scheisse," he finally said. "Wait here," as if I had anywhere else to go. He abruptly stood up and began to leave.

It was worth a try, I thought. The end was certainly upon me now. When I once again returned to making peace with the decisions I'd made in my life, I was hit with another painful headache, blurred vision and bright lights. I let out a yelp of pain.

I was experiencing another flash, going back and forth between this prison and a strange place where I was lying on a table. It could have been an operating table. I was in great pain. Huge creatures who looked human but somehow different stood in the background watching as a woman doctor and a beautiful nurse tended to my wounds.

The commotion caught Col. Vrill's attention. When he turned to look, he gasped at the sight before him—the entire cell was changing colors with streaking lights. He stared, mesmerized as I faded in and out of existence, a heavily wounded man intermittently taking my place, split seconds of appearing and disappearing right before his eyes.

51

Upon arrival at the train station in Portland, Maine, Karla hired a car and driver to take her to Harpswell. She found the Jersey Lodge without much trouble, but no one at the busy bed and breakfast had ever heard of Paul or anyone fitting his description.

Undeterred, Karla thought it best if she used a fake name in case Fat Tony's men came looking for her, so she signed in as Karla Christianson. She then settled into a small but comfortable room on the upper floor, determined to wait.

She spent her days either in small talk with proprietors Betsy and Bob Alexander, or taking long walks through the woods behind the Jersey Lodge, along a path leading to the rocky shores lining the eastern side of Middle Bay.

"This morning I heard her vomiting in the upstairs bathroom," Betsy told her neighbor Caroline one morning while Karla was out.

"You don't suppose she's pregnant, do you?" Caroline asked. With the morning dishes cleaned and put away, the two older women sat at the kitchen table and settled into their daily routine of sipping tea and gossiping.

"I don't rightly know Caroline. Do you suppose so?"

"Where's her husband? Is the child illegitimate?"

Betsy took a deep, loud breath. "You don't suppose?"

"My lord Betsy, we better find out straight away."

"Find out what?" Karla asked as she walked in the door.

"Nothing," Caroline said too quickly.

Betsy scowled at her. Turning to Karla she said, "I thought I heard you crying this morning. It also sounded like you were having trouble keeping your breakfast down. Are you ill? Should we send someone for Dr. Radcliffe?"

"It's becoming obvious, isn't it," Karla said. "I knew you'd find out sooner or later, so it might as well be now." Karla paused. "I'm pretty sure I'm pregnant."

Caroline gasped.

Betsy scowled at her again. "I'm so sorry, my dear. Dare as I ask what happened to the father?"

"I didn't want to say anything until I was sure," Karla started.

Both Betsy and Caroline leaned forward. This would be the juiciest gossip they'd heard in this small town in years.

"My husband Paul was on a secret mission to infiltrate a Nazi base in Europe. I was supposed to meet him here when he returned. But before I got on the train one of his colleagues found me in Grand Central and told me Paul had been caught and put in front of a firing squad. I didn't know what else to do, so I came here just in case the colleague was wrong."

Both older women sat back in their chairs, and if they were to be honest with themselves, they would have to admit they were a slight bit disappointed. This wasn't gossip at all. The poor woman lost her husband in the war and needed their help.

"I'm so sorry," Caroline said.

"I'll send for the doctor," Betsy said.

"No, but thank you. It's too early for the doctor."

"Nonsense. You're pregnant and all alone. It's never too early for the doctor. You need help and we intend to give it to you, don't we Caroline?"

Caroline's mouth was still wide open, so Betsy reached over and gently pushed up her chin to shut it. The gesture brought her around, "Yes, yes, of course."

All Karla could think of now that her secret was out, and since she told them Paul had died, the conversation effectively erased any thoughts she entertained of going over to Europe to try and find him.

Within hours the story spread all the way from the tip of Basin Point to Schofield's farm how a young pregnant war widow whose husband, Paul 'Christianson', had died a heroic death while infiltrating a secret Nazi SS stronghold somewhere in Poland, was now staying at the Jersey Lodge. All this was true, Karla reasoned, except the part about his name and their marriage.

Her sad tale earned her a place in the community. The townsfolk in Harpswell have always seen themselves as having kind hearts and a willingness to help those in need.

It didn't hurt that Karla was wealthy and didn't need financial assistance. Her benevolence towards others in need and her donations to the Elijah Kellogg Church also earned her the townsfolks' respect.

During the ensuing weeks, Betsy had been inviting her nephew Nelson to the Jersey Lodge to do chores around the bed and breakfast.

Nelson Merriman was a handsome young man only a year older than Karla. A hard working, law abiding, god fearing man, Nelson was also a member of the Harpswell Volunteer Fire Department. He adored Karla almost from the moment they met and Betsy was most definitely doing her best to play Cupid.

Karla, on the other hand, remained tepid to the idea of his courtship.

When it came time for the birth of her child, Caroline and Betsy roped their husbands into fetching Dr. Radcliffe while they stayed behind to comfort her.

Along the way, the men managed to spread the word the fatherless war baby was about to enter the world.

The event turned into a monumental event as people filled every available space in the hallway outside Karla's room. Each person spoke of how they wanted to help her get through this ordeal without her deceased husband there to hold her hand. None knew how. None except one. The area became so crowded, Dr. Radcliffe had push and shove his way through them just to get to Karla's room. He immediately kicked them out.

Undeterred, they all congregated on the ground floor. Tea and biscuits were served. The women congregated in the kitchen to gossip, the men remained outside talking of boat prices and how they couldn't keep up with bait and fuel prices. If it remained like this, lobstering would no longer be a viable way to earn a living. No doubt the industry would fade away into nonexistence at some point in their lifetime.

During the birth, Nelson declined to join the men outside and instead sat by Karla, holding her hand and giving her encouragement.

The birth was not without complications. As the newborn struggled to get out, it was clear all was not well. The child had a slightly elongated head and a crooked arm, perhaps the result of the months of stress Karla had been under.

"Congratulations Mrs. Christianson. It's a boy," Dr. Radcliffe said. He picked up the child by the feet and gave him a strong whack on the bottom. No response, so he did it again, this time even a little harder. Within seconds newborn screams filled the air, much to the good doctor's relief.

He tried to straighten the arm, but with no success. He didn't want to break it so soon in its life. Maybe after a few years he might discuss the possibilities of radical procedures to fix it. But for now he'd let it go.

He also cringed when he noticed a hint of Down syndrome in the child's face and did his best to smile when he handed the deformed infant to his mother.

The sight caught her off guard but without hesitation she took him in, held him to her breast and kissed the top of his head. "My baby, my child, I'm going to name you Paul after your father. I will love you forever."

52

Col. Vrill returned to my prison cell with a small posse of armed guards. "I'll give you twenty-four hours to convince me how you can help with my *Die Glocke* project. You will give me complete, intricate details and hold nothing back. If at any point I feel you are not being honest, or if you are being economical with the truth, I will put you in front of a firing squad. Do you understand?"

By now nearly frozen, famished, and fearing for my life, I agreed.

"Unlock the door," he ordered the guards. "Bind his hands and feet. Keep your weapons trained on him in case he should be foolish enough to attempt an escape."

One of the guards entered the cell and chained my wrists and ankles before roughly pulling me to my feet and pushing me towards the door. I nearly fell face first to the ground. I only managed to catch my balance by leaning my shoulder into the doorway at the last possible moment.

"Nein!" Col. Vrill shouted.

The soldier snarled back at the colonel, but pulled me back up and half carried me out of the dungeon.

"Follow me," The colonel said. He led our armed entourage along a gravel path through the woods for about a quarter mile to a compound surrounded by a high wall. A guard shack with perhaps a half dozen armed soldiers protected the main gate. The soldiers snapped to attention as soon as they saw us, thrusting their right hands into the air at the colonel.

Col. Vrill waved his hand at them, prompting two soldiers to scurry out of the shack to unlock and swing open the gate. Their timing was precise. We entered without breaking our stride.

The colonel's house was a stately rock structure built with bay windows, barred, and a heavy wooden front door. I imagined a bomb could go off in front without doing any significant damage. The gardens were immaculately maintained, featuring evergreens and coifed hedges. They remained green despite the late autumn weather in this southwestern Polish mountain range.

I was brought inside and sat at a large wooden table. The colonel once again jacked a shell into his Luger and gave orders for two armed men to stand guard at the front of the house. He sent another six to guard the perimeter.

Once the posse had taken their positions outside, the colonel softened. "My apologies for the rough treatment. The men are highly skilled, trained to shoot the enemy on sight. You're lucky you weren't assassinated when they first found you."

I sat in silence. How does one react when learning he is lucky to be alive and could be murdered at any moment by highly skilled killing machines at the whim of a Nazi SS Colonel who is now trying to act friendly?

If I somehow make it through this, and if I live to be a hundred, I will never forget the feeling the past couple hours have instilled in me. It's been a mixture of sheer terror, self-pity, self-hate for allowing myself to get into this situation, and now total confusion as to what lies ahead in my dark, unknown future.

"You must be hungry," Col. Vrill said. "I'll have my staff cook something for you."

The colonel's house staff snapped to at his command, disappearing into the kitchen. He took a seat on the opposite side of the table and put his Luger down in front of him. It made a noticeable clunk when metal hit the wood. I'm sure he did that on purpose.

The colonel sat in silence, staring at me while the food was being prepared. I stared back. Neither of us blinked.

Once the food arrived, I was still unsure how to react, so I didn't move a muscle.

"Dig in cowboy," the colonel said in his best American accent.

Despite strict war time rationing for regular soldiers, the staff presented me with a meal fit for a general. However, somewhere in the back of my mind a little voice was telling me the bratwurst, boiled potatoes, cabbage, asparagus and red bell peppers, served with a glass of red wine sitting on the table in front of me could be my last meal, ever. I did as told, declining to stand on etiquette and engorged myself like a starving animal.

It was the first I'd eaten since before leaving my friends in the town square. It also was the first time in a while I had thought about Sir James and Frenchie. I wondered if they had managed to make it out of the area alive.

The meal finished, Col. Vrill began by telling me why he thought I might be able to help. "When I was a boy—how can I put this, some rather strange people visited me. They said they were from the future and told me I held a key to their existence. The man looked a little like me. He even shared my last name. He said his name was William, but if he ever told me we were related, I've long forgotten."

I perked up at the mention of William Vrill.

"The woman was beautiful. She had very long hair, almost to the ground. I remember her hair clearly.

There were others around at times, too, but only the man and woman stand out in my memory.

"They said they were from the Vril Society, said it was like my last name but spelt with only one L, not two. They visited daily for a week and imparted incredible and hard to believe information about time travel.

"One day, the strange people left as they normally did, but didn't return the following day. Or the day after, or after that. I waited, but they never came back. As I grew older, their memories gradually faded away. My image of their faces disappeared over time. Now, except for the woman's long hair, I don't think I'd recognize either one of them if they were standing next to me."

He paused for a moment, reaching deep into his memories to bring up his childhood. "As a child, every now and again I'd see a woman with very long hair, but it always turned out to be someone else. I was quite young. To this day, though, I can remember still some of what they taught me—and it was from these memories I was eventually able to start working on *Die Glocke*."

I watched, wondering where all this was leading.

"Imagine my surprise when you told me you knew my great-grandson, William Vrill the Fourth, with the same name as the man I met as a child. You said he built a time machine in the future, leading to you being here now.

"Was this all just a coincidence? Or are the events connected? I don't know, and perhaps I never will. I honestly don't know what to make of it. But if you can help me finish *Die Glocke*, and if we can figure out how to aim it, I would indeed like to take you home and visit my great-grandson, if for no other reason than to see if he had somehow travelled back in time to visit me as a child and provide me with enough information to begin this project."

I didn't know what to say, so I said the first thing that popped into my head. "I'm sure your great-grandson has given me enough clues to help you and you are enough of a genius to figure them out. The two of us can build the time machine, take me home, and then you can use it in whatever way you see fit. Take your scientist friends to the future, or the past, or whenever you want to go. Certainly visit William too. I'm sure he'd want to meet you."

"If he was my great-grandson as you say, why didn't he come here, instead of you?"

"I didn't give him the chance. I left without telling him. There were some extenuating circumstances that prompted my hasty exit. I found an opportunity to go, and I went."

"Tell me about these extenuating circumstances," Col. Vrill said.

"Well," I hesitated. "US Government officials thought I might have come into possession of some stolen cash."

"Did you?" He said calmly. Perhaps, if it were true, he thought I might have a reason to avoid telling the Allies about the whereabouts of *Die Glocke*.

"Yes and no. I didn't know it was stolen. Actually, I kind of suspected it was, but I thought I needed it, and it seemed rather harmless at the time. I acted on impulse and right about now I'm regretting my decision."

"It makes no difference to me what trouble you might be in with Allied officials. I'm more interested in what you can tell me about the time machine you said my great grandson created."

I thought for a minute. "The problem is, I'm not a genius like your great-grandson or you, and I didn't know what I was doing. I may have broken the machine when I used it. But if we can build one here, you can go back with me and see for yourself. What do you say?"

"I say you're crazy. But you did make it this far. Maybe there is something in what you're trying to tell me. You understand, however, I must be certain."

"I don't know what else to tell you," I said.

"I see," Col. Vrill said slowly. He stared at me for another few minutes, I suppose to see if he could detect whether or not I was lying. Apparently he didn't come to a conclusion for he summoned his house staff and ordered them to take a mattress down into the cellar.

He pointed his Luger at me and waved it towards the cellar door, motioning me to follow them. My hands and feet were still bound in shackles, which made it a challenge to get down the stairs, but I did manage to accomplish the feat without falling.

As the staff set the mattress on the floor next to a suitably strong water pipe, Col. Vrill kept his Lugar trained on me. He reached into his pocket, took out a set of keys and handed them to Albrecht, his butler.

"Chain him to the pipe."

Albrecht unlocked the shackle on my left arm, pulled me towards the pipe, wrapped the short chain around the pipe and refastened it on my left wrist, making sure it was tight enough so I wouldn't be able to escape during the night.

"I'll let you know what I decide tomorrow," Col. Vrill said before he ascended the stairs with his staff, leaving me alone in the dark cellar for the night.

I tried to settle into an uncomfortable sleep. It was quite difficult in the dark, damp, smelly basement. I could hear Col. Vrill's heavy boots on the floor above me as he paced back and forth, no doubt trying to figure out what to do with me.

I knew most likely I'd be shot dead in the morning.

53

It had become obvious Karla and Paul Jr. needed a bigger place to stay than the one room at the Jersey Lodge, so Karla once again contacted her trusted money manager, Marianne Estes.

After their first meeting on Wall Street, Marianne had stuck with her over the years. Karla always marveled how M. Estes, Money Manager never seemed to age.

Karla was her only client and over time Marianne proved she had connections in the right places to turn the money Paul had left her into a fortune.

She was always very precise in what she advised and insisted Karla follow her advice. More than once Karla thought to disagree, and every time she relented, she was rewarded with sizable gains in her portfolio.

Now that she needed a bigger place to stay, Marianne talked her into buying an old ship captain's estate off Ash Cove Road. The house had been built during the last century on the shoreline facing the rising sun over Basin Point, with Harpswell Sound and Bailey Island off in the distance. To Karla it seemed extravagant, but Marianne was persuasive and she relented.

After she moved in, Karla hardly ever saw Marianne, as she only made herself available when it was time to reevaluate her portfolio. She charged minuscule fees compared to other brokers, and sometimes nothing at all. Other than these visits, the only contact she had with her was when she received checks in the mail, sometimes weekly, sometimes monthly, providing her with more than enough income to live on and raise her child.

Karla whiled away the days taking care of Paul Jr., who, due to Karla's love and care, was leading a happy life in spite of his disabilities. Children can be cruel, though, and in the early years before special schools were created, filled with teachers properly trained to take care of children with Down syndrome, the other students in the one-room Harpswell Elementary School made fun of his crooked arm, elongated head and slow mentality. Eventually Karla felt it necessary to take him out of the public school and home school him, long before it became a fad.

She taught him how to help her with the gardening, how to read and to swim with her in the cold Ash Cove waters. Occasionally they would entertain guests, but they spent most of their time entertaining each other.

During this time, she often talked to Paul Jr. about his father, and how she hoped someday he would return and meet his son. She also felt all along the riches they were living off weren't truly hers. They belonged to Paul.

As they waited patiently for Paul's return, over time the dashing young Nelson Merriman became a bigger part of their lives. He was always there when she needed him, doing carpentry and painting work, keeping the grounds in tiptop shape, fetching the doctor when Paul Jr. took ill, and holding her hand until the doctor was through tending to him.

He'd wait by her side until Paul Jr. recovered, take them to church on Sundays, and enjoy Sunday dinners together after church. He acted as her chauffer to and from grange meetings, bean hole suppers to raise funds for the Harpswell Boy and Girl

Scout troops, and chicken dinners to raise funds for the church.

After two years of waiting for Paul, Karla came to the conclusion he was never to return. When Nelson proposed, she accepted.

The wedding turned out to be a glorious affair. Held at the Elijah Kellogg Church in Harpswell Center, with the reception catered at the Merriconeag Grange in North Harpswell, everyone who was anyone in 1946 Harpswell attended the event.

For many years after, Nelson and Karla lived happily together. Never wanting for money, Nelson nonetheless insisted on working full time and being the breadwinner of the family. He treated Paul Jr. as if his own, despite his disabilities.

When their daughter Alice was born, Nelson and Karla were ecstatic. She was healthy, happy and had no afflictions. The same proved true for Jeffry, their second child born two years later.

* * * * *

The years flew past with amazing speed. Alice and Jeffry grew up, went off to school, moved away and became successful. They both married and each started a family of their own with healthy, happy children.

After many years of happiness, Father Time caught up with Nelson. He passed away quietly in his sleep one cold winter night, once again leaving Karla alone with Paul Jr.

The older Karla grew, the faster time seemed to go. Then one day she answered a knock on her door. A bright young man who looked vaguely familiar told her he wanted to save up money to buy a new bicycle. Could she use someone to mow her lawn and do a little handy work around her house?

He introduced himself as Paul and although he couldn't have been more than eleven years old, there was something about his entrepreneurial spirit that drew her to him.

"I used to know someone named Paul," she said.

"Same as me?"

"Yes, same as you. In fact, my son's name is Paul Jr., named after his father."

She set him to work for the entire summer. Right away, Paul the lawnmower and Paul Jr. became best of friends. They were like two peas in a pod; an instant brotherhood.

Then one day when he arrived for work, Karla sat her young gardener down in the kitchen. He could tell right away something was wrong.

"Paul, I don't know how to tell you this," she began. "You have grown into such a strong young man. You will find out soon enough, so I want to tell you myself. You know Paul Jr. has been sick all his life. Doctors predicted he wouldn't live past his twenties."

Paul shook his head no, his face taut. A tear formed in his eye and ran down his cheek. Deep inside he knew what Mrs. M was about to say, but somehow he hoped otherwise. Most of all, he really didn't want to hear it.

"Late last night he began coughing and couldn't stop. He coughed for hours, and when he finally stopped, he went to sleep. A very deep sleep. He will not wake up again, ever."

"He's dead, isn't he Mrs. M?"

"Yes Paul, he passed away last night. He loved you so much. I'm so glad you two had the chance to meet and play together."

Paul ran out of the house and mounted his bicycle. Pounding the pedals as hard as his feet would allow, he raced back towards home. He didn't make it all the way before the tears in his eyes blinded his vision and wouldn't allow him to continue.

Going to work would never be the same.

Karla was even more devastated. She fell into a deep depression, some days not even opening the door when Paul arrived to go to work. Paul tried to busy himself on those days, but without Mrs. M. instructing him what job needed to be done, he had no choice but to return home.

As fall arrived with its explosion of colors, the young boy returned to school, once again leaving Karla alone to face the oncoming winter.

At the end of a long and brutal winter, and after late spring temperatures dried up mud season in Maine, young Paul returned, asking if he could work for her during the summer again this year, in spite of what happened the year before. If she wished, he was willing to accept the same or less pay and the same working hours as the year before.

She agreed, glad to have him back, her heart melting with happiness that maybe he forgave her for the way she treated him after her loss last summer.

He was good at helping around the house, but perhaps more importantly, just having him around for company made her happy. Meanwhile, the longer she knew him, the more she experienced feelings of déjà vu as if she had met him somewhere before.

Towards the middle of the summer, when it came time to pay his wages for the week, she was short on cash and asked if it would be ok for her to write him a bank check.

"No problem," he said, "I can cash it at Bailey's Store."

"I will need your full name to put on the check," she said. Her heart nearly stopped when he told her.

"Paul Daniel Millard," he said, puffing out his chest. Her reaction frightened him, for her eyes widened and her breath grew short. "Are you ok, Ms. M?"

Every summer from then on, Karla Merriman hired him back, watched as he mowed her lawn, did her gardening and handiwork, and sure enough, he began to grow into the man she remembered. The stories Paul used to tell her back in 1944 about coming from the future came to life.

Many times she stifled her urge to tell him their story, how they had fallen in love so long ago, how he had left her waiting on a bench in Grand Central Station, how Paul Jr. was his son, and how happy she was the two Pauls were able to spend quality time together, even if they didn't know the significance of their bond. And how her fortune was really his.

54

Back in Potsdam, New York, Frankie's body remained where it had been left in the foyer until the smell became so strong even people driving by would cringe. An investigation ensued, but it turned up nothing even though locals gave vivid descriptions of the mysterious men who resided there for a month after Frankie's disappearance. No mention was made of the windfalls the constabulary found in their pockets.

The house remained vacant and eventually the town tax collectors foreclosed. Even then no one dared come forward to purchase it at the low price of paying the back taxes, until years later when Mark Whitten bought it. He decided one day to install a pool in the back garden for his kids and while digging a hole for the swimming pool, the hired workers found Frankie the Mole's loot.

The Whitten family certainly enjoyed their new found treasure. But what should they do now? Should they try to sell it? Donate it to a museum? Turn it over to the police?

While trying to decide, they left it unguarded, out in the open on their dining room table. It never occurred to them anyone would try to steal it, especially given all the publicity it attracted.

One night after the family had gone to bed, the decision was taken away from them when a pair of alleged drug addicts walked into the unlocked house, picked up the tin box and walked out with it. They didn't even need to bring weapons. This was, after all, Potsdam NY. Everyone knew everyone. Doors need not be locked.

Once they got away with the old money, they also had no idea what to do with it. They couldn't use it to buy things, it was too old. They didn't know any collectors who might be interested, and even if they did, the stolen money was now famous.

Finally, they decided to contact the one person they thought might know what to do with old money, a French Canadian fence across the border in Ottawa who called himself I.M. King.

Being no stranger to all things street-worthy, King played hard to get and finally offered them little more than enough to buy a big bag of weed and an unhealthy amount of cocaine. They took the money and ran.

I.M. King soon realized all he had done was inherit the dilemma of how to profit from it. By now the story had made international news.

The Feds were brought in from Albany to get to the bottom of the whole affair in upstate New York, and given the proximity to the U.S. - Canadian border, they had already contacted the Canadian Mounties.

There was little chance King could pawn it off on anyone without raising unwanted publicity, so he locked it up in his safe hidden behind cluttered shelves in the back room of his shop.

One day while surfing the net, he happened upon a classified ad from some guy in Maine who was looking to buy old money. As the local police and Treasury Department started to close in on him, suspecting he would be the most likely candidate to fence the stolen money, I.M. King loaded up his van with spare clothes and made the trip over the Appalachian Mountains, across Lake Champlain, through Vermont and New

Hampshire, and into Maine, on a trip which led him to the coast, to a man named Paul Millard in Harpswell.

The U.S. Treasury was onto him. Special agents Carpenter and Catlin stayed hot on his trail the entire way. They managed to catch up with him in Brunswick, Maine, but only after he had unloaded the loot in Harpswell.

* * * * *

King didn't betray his buyer. The Treasury boys had no proof I had ever been involved, despite also finding my online classified ad. It was enough for them to make me their number one suspect, but they would need to catch me with the money, as all other evidence was circumstantial.

55

Col. William Vrill was awakened early the next morning by his man-servant, Albrecht. The poor fellow was shaking. "It's *der Führer*. He is very angry, yelling into the phone. You must talk with him now. He said it is urgent."

"What time is it?"

"Half six," Albrecht replied.

"It must be urgent if he's calling at this time of day." Col. Vrill slid out of bed and was helped into his bathrobe by Albrecht. Shaking the sleep out of his brain, he sauntered over to the phone and picked up the receiver.

"*Mein Führer*, what is it?"

"Why do you have an American spy in your house?!"

"How do you know about this?"

"Sporrenberg the Butcher informed me. He said you're harboring an American fugitive. He is on his way to you right now with a thirst for blood. Your blood. The American's blood. You better have a good reason or I will not stop him from assassinating you, which would be most unfortunate since you are my top scientist."

"The American is not a spy, he is a time traveler."

"And you believe him?"

"He knows about *Die Glocke*."

"Impossible," Hitler said. "How?"

"He said in the future it is common knowledge," Col. Vrill lied. "I saw him fade in and out of our time to some other place when we had him locked in our holding cell. He must be some kind of interdimensional traveler. I saw it with my own eyes."

There was a long pause, during which Col. Vrill could hear a commotion from his guard house about a quarter mile away. His personal guards were arguing with someone, and the sound was traveling all the way down the path to his house, echoing through the quiet morning forest.

This couldn't be good. Col. Vrill began speaking faster, "He said he wants to help me build *Die Glocke* so he can go home to his own time. If he's telling the truth, I will go to the future and get a super weapon. One more powerful than we have now. This surely would win the war for the Fatherland."

Hitler remained silent.

"If he cannot help me, I will kill him myself. I am loyal to you and no others. But it would be foolish not to at least give him a chance."

After another long pause, Hitler said, "Can I trust you, Wilhelm?"

"I don't believe we have a choice," Col. Vrill answered.

"Continue on, then, but beware of Sporrenberg. Don't speak with him until I've had the chance to talk to him first."

No sooner had the words come through the receiver when the door burst open and in stepped General Jakob Sporrenberg, the SS and police leader of occupied Poland, aka the Butcher, the most feared man in Europe, perhaps even the world. He had several nasty looking armed guards with him. Just as Hitler said, they all were thirsty for blood.

"Arrest him!" the Butcher said, pointing at Col. Vrill. "Where is the prisoner?!"

Col. Vrill didn't say a word. He pushed his phone in front of the Butcher's face, returning his steely stare.

The Butcher grabbed the phone and yelled into the receiver, "What!" All color drained from his face when he realized it was Hitler on the other end. He began trying to stutter out an apology but was cut off by Hitler's screaming at him.

A few minutes later, the Butcher cradled the phone and told Col. Vrill, "You have two weeks. I will be watching you. If the project works, kill the American as soon as you can, no later than when you get to wherever you're going. No one must know of this. No one. Any mistakes and I will be right here to finish you and the project. If you're not done in two weeks, I will shoot you both myself. Do you understand?"

Col. Vrill continued to stare him down, not saying a word.

"*Sieg Heil,*" the Butcher said, clicking his heels. He turned and marched purposely back out the door.

Albrecht and Col. Vrill looked at each other and took a deep breath, exhaling slowly. "Let's go see how our guest is doing downstairs, shall we?" Col. Vrill said, trying to break the tension.

Albrecht nodded and began to follow, but Col. Vrill stopped him. "Best you go make some breakfast for us. I have a feeling this is going to be a long day, and the beginning of a stressful two weeks."

* * * * *

I was awake and heard all the furious talk during the incident above me. I couldn't decipher what was said, only that it sounded tense. I wasn't entirely sure what to expect when the cellar door opened and Col. Vrill descended the stairs. He turned on a light, but it was dim and I couldn't get a read on his expression as he approached and kneeled down beside me. Was this it? Was he about to put a bullet between my eyes?

"I need to be sure," Col. Vrill said. "If I remove these chains, will you behave? If you try to escape, the men outside have been instructed to shoot to kill."

"I don't have much of a choice, do I?" I replied, trying to sound brave but compliant. "Even if they weren't there, I wouldn't try to run. I have no place to go and what I want most is to go home. The only way I can get there is if I help you build your glockah thing and earn your trust enough to take me there."

Col. Vrill produced a ring of keys from his vest pocket and unlocked the chains binding my hands and feet. He backed away with his hand in his coat pocket.

I didn't try to attack him, and instead sat trying to rub the pain out of my wrists and ankles. Seeing this, Col. Vrill clicked his Luger's safety on and removed his hand from his pocket, extending it to help me rise from the floor. We climbed the stairs together in silence, into the dining room where a full breakfast was waiting.

Col. Vrill started to give his apologies as we ate, but caught himself. I took it as another sign he wasn't quite sure how to handle me and the situation I presented. We both ate in silence, trying to size each other up.

With his loaded Luger nearby at all times, Col. Vrill was demonstrably in control, but he needed something from me and seemed unsure how to get it.

As we finished breakfast, the colonel had Albrecht bring me my backpack. "They found nothing incriminating inside except the empty handgun, which they confiscated," he said.

I took this as an offer of peace and sincerity. "Thank you."

"So, how can you help me?" Col. Vrill asked without preamble or prompting.

As best I was able, I tried to explain everything I could remember about the time machine William IV built at the Jersey Lodge back in 2018 Maine. I had trouble explaining some of the things that hadn't been invented yet, like computers and lasers, but I managed to explain the spinning mirrored wheels and the spinning laser lights pointed at them, which in turn created a vortex.

Col. Vrill picked up on the spinning part and the lights, because it sounded a lot like what he'd been working on. "I think it's time for you to see the project," he said.

"I would very much like that. I've been waiting a long time and have come a long way for this."

"Follow me," Col. Vrill said and led us outside where a small battalion of armed soldiers stood guard. "I see the Butcher has increased security."

It was a short walk to the entrance of a nondescript building, which was equally nondescript inside. Col. Vrill led me down a corridor past a number of windowed doors, behind which I could see men, some in uniform with their sleeves rolled up, others in lab coats working on things I didn't recognize.

We continued out a back door into a courtyard surrounded by other buildings. I thought it might resemble the interior of the Pentagon in the USA, and I wondered if the Pentagon had been built yet.

The center was dominated by a structure that to me resembled a small Stonehenge. In fact they called it 'The Henge'. In the center, a bell shaped object hung, its top tethered to the outside of the henge by three opposing chains. Several large, heavy cables, some half a foot in diameter, led from the building and into the henge.

Col. Vrill once again studied me, trying to gauge my response.

"What does it do?" I said as I looked on in amazement.

Col. Vrill turned and spoke German to someone I noticed had been walking behind us, watching us since we'd entered the building. The lab-coated man clicked his heels, then scurried off through the nearest door. He reappeared a bit further along behind a barred window facing the courtyard. I watched as he pulled down a large switch.

The bell shaped object started spinning, building up speed, bouncing and pulling at its chains as if it were a crazed animal trying to escape, until it seemed as if it would break loose and bound uncontrolled into the surrounding buildings.

When it became almost certain it would break away, Col. Vrill signaled to the man on the switch and he shut it down.

"That's where we are now," Col. Vrill said. "What do you think?"

"The first thing I see is you need to control it. How about chaining the bottom as well?"

"We thought of that, but we don't want to restrict its movements. We've purposely left it loose so that it could break free and travel, hopefully through time."

"So you think it's some kind of vessel? Do you want to try and get inside it and somehow ride it?"

"That's the main idea. Why? Don't you think that's what it's supposed to do?"

"Well, maybe. I don't know. You're the genius, but the contraption William IV built wasn't meant to take anyone through time. It was too big. It was more like a tool, a way to create a way to go someplace. I think the best way to describe it would be it was a door builder. A traveler would walk through the door it built and travel to another place or time."

"How would he get back?" Col. Vrill asked.

"William IV built a return gizmo he said would reverse the vortex to get time travelers back home," I answered, failing miserably in my attempt to sound knowledgeable.

"Where is this 'gizmo'?"

"I forgot to bring it."

"What?"

"I thought I grabbed it but it turned out I grabbed my," I stopped myself, realizing it would start an entire new conversation if I needed to try and describe what an iPhone was. "I grabbed something I thought was it, but turns out it wasn't. That, in a nutshell, is why I am here today. If I had remembered to bring the gizmo with me I would have used it a long time ago and you and I would never have met."

"So, if we build *Die Glocke*, and it works, and we travel somewhere to find a super weapon—" Col. Vrill said.

"Super weapon?" I interrupted. "You never said anything about a super weapon."

"It's not your concern. If we get somewhere, how will we get back?"

"If this works, we can only hope wherever, whenever we land in the future, they will have figured that out."

56

One afternoon shortly after her ninety-second birthday, Karla lay in her bed, propped up on pillows so she could look out over Ash Cove to Estes Lobster House on the far shore and across Harpswell Sound to Bailey's Island in the distance. She had suffered a stroke and despite the doctors recommending she remain in the hospital, she chose instead to die at home.

Her children were notified and on their way, but on this day a young looking Marianne Estes was her only companion. She sat on the edge of the bed holding Karla's hand and listening to her talk about the wonderful life she'd lived.

"I have absolutely no regrets," Karla told her. "If I had it all to do over again, I wouldn't change a thing."

"Funny you should say that," Marianne said. "I know you remember Paul Millard and the stories he told you."

"Yes, he was the love of my life until Nelson came along. But I will always remember my first love. Maybe I will reunite with him in heaven."

"What if I were to tell you," Marianne said, "you will reunite with him, but here on earth, not in heaven, and you'd both be alive?"

"Thank you, you have such kind words. You've always been so good to me. But I know I will never see him again."

"You always tell me you wonder how, after all these years, I never aged."

"Yes, how is that possible?"

"It's possible because Paul told you the truth about being a time traveler."

"Yes, I came to grips with that when he came to work for me. It was so precious for me knowing he was able to meet his son, even if he didn't know it."

"You did the right thing by not telling him."

"I hope so. And thank you for helping me change my will to include him."

"Yes, you did the right thing then, too."

"I had to. I knew my time was short and I could never tell him, so this was the best I could do. All this you see around you started with what he left me when he ran off and got himself killed in the war in Europe."

"Well," Marianne gripped Karla's hand a little tighter. "I hope what I'm about to tell you will make sense. It's important to me that you understand this is not intended to hurt you. In fact, just the opposite, but before jumping to any conclusions, please hear me out until the end."

Marianne hesitated for a moment to gauge Karla's reaction. She looked puzzled, but agreed not to get upset until she heard all Marianne had to say.

"First, Paul didn't die in Europe."

"He wasn't killed by firing squad?"

"No, he still lives, but in another time."

"Why didn't he come back for me?"

"He tried to, and will keep trying, but it's impossible. In his mind he did the next best thing. He left his entire fortune with you and gave you a good life even if he couldn't share it with you."

"Wait, how do you know this?"

"I'm what you might call a special kind of person. I wasn't born like you. I was manufactured by someone important a very long way into the future."

"Manufactured? How is that possible? Did Paul make you?"

"No, he didn't. Other than our meeting on Wall Street, Paul doesn't know I exist. I doubt he would remember me, but someday we will meet again. I was created by another important person, someone who is very interested in making sure you were taken care of, given a good, happy life. I hope I succeeded. Almost as important, I wanted to make sure one day you understood how Paul told you the truth."

"I always knew he did," Karla said.

"Yes, and by leaving him part of your fortune you have ensured the two of you will meet again."

"What do you mean?"

"You're about to complete what is called a temporal causality loop. By leaving Paul part of your fortune, you enabled him to finance someone to build a time machine which, a few years from now, will take him back to the time in 1944 when he met you. If you didn't leave him the money to build a time portal, he wouldn't have been able to go back and meet you. This is also why he can't see you now. If he does, or did, he would have broken the loop and made all this impossible."

"How so?"

"It would've created a paradox. If your life didn't play out as it did without him, you wouldn't have wanted or needed to list him in your will. Without that money, he wouldn't have been able to build a time machine. No time machine means he wouldn't have been able to go back in time to when you two met. And if he didn't go back in time to meet you, you would never have known him, he would never have known you, and he wouldn't have left you with the money you used to build your fortune. The same money you left him in your will which enabled him to build a time machine to go back and meet you. Around and around it goes. Therefore, none of this would've happened and I wouldn't be sitting here talking to you right now."

"I'm still confused. How is it I will see Paul again?"

"When you pass away, and I'm not trying to hurry you along—but when you do, you will begin your life again. The same life with the same people. No changes, no memory of anything other than what you experience as you grow up, become a woman, meet Paul again."

"Does everything stop when I die?"

"Only for you. Everyone else will continue on outside the loop. They will always be in your life during the loop, but once you pass away, they will continue on into their unknown future."

"How many times have you done this?" Karla asked.

"I don't understand the question," Marianne said.

"If this is a loop like you say, and my life will happen again, all of it, leading back to this point, has this happened before or is this the first time?"

"Every time is the first time," Marianne said.

"Oh." Karla took a moment to think about her words. "How about Nelson? Will I meet him again, too? And my children?"

"Yes, you will meet Nelson again, and your lovely children, too."

"That doesn't sound too bad. Not too bad at all." Karla laid back and smiled, holding tightly to Marianne's hand, quietly slipping away.

57

"Explain how you think William's invention built doors and how we might be able to fine tune *Die Glocke* to do the same," Col. Vrill said.

"Well, to start with, I see there is some kind of reflection coming out of the bottom of your bell. That's a good thing, but William IV's invention had much stronger lights and used the lights to create the door."

"In what way."

"Well, I think you need two of them," I said. "With lights and mirrors. That's what William IV did. Sort of."

"Sort of?"

"Yes, William IV had two spinning wheels, and each had hundreds of little mirrors on them. He also had different colored lasers—strong lights, pointed at the mirrors. The light reflected off the mirrors to a point nearby. That's what created the circular thing which acted like a door. I walked down the tunnel it created and out the 'door', and it brought me to this year."

"Two of them? With mirrors and lights? No smoke?" Col. Vrill said facetiously.

"Smoke? No. Oh, I see what you're saying. 'Smoke and mirrors.' Ha, ha. No, I'm not trying to teach you a magic trick."

"I suppose we have the blueprints for this one," Col. Vrill said, "so it might not be too difficult to modify it. But we need to hurry. I don't think the Butcher is going to give us much time."

* * * * *

A small army was put to work creating another ring at the bottom of the bell, decorated with mirrors and set to rotate in the opposite direction. Lights were installed nearby, pointed at the mirrors. The operation took over a week. When completed, Col. Vrill and I were brought in to inspect it.

Immediately upon arrival, I could see it still needed work, but I didn't feel I was yet in a position to say so.

Once again Col. Vrill signaled the lab-coated man to pull the switch. This time the bell and both rings started spinning, gaining speed until it looked like the contraption would break loose and kill everyone in the vicinity.

It still didn't work as intended.

"Ok, what now?" Col. Vrill asked.

"I can see a few things," I said. "First, the lights aren't strong enough. Second, the lights coming off the mirrors need to be directed to come together at a single point. I don't know if it makes a difference, but the lights William used were different colors."

"Ok, anything else?" Col. Vrill asked.

"William used lasers for this part, but I don't suppose you have any of those around," I said.

"What are lasers?"

"It's an acronym, L A S E R ... lasers are really, really strong lights. If I can think of what it means, maybe you could make some."

"Ok, what does it mean?"

"L = light ... A, I think means amplified, or something like that. S? Stimulation? E? I forget, but I'm pretty sure R means radiation. Do you have any way to amplify light with radiation?"

"Nein, we have no L A S E R around here—"

"I guess we'll have to make do but we need the strongest lights you have."

Col. Vrill had several strong airplane landing strip lights brought in, installed colored filters on them, which dimmed them somewhat but did create the different colors I suggested. He also added cones to funnel the lights and direct the beams towards the bells.

Once completed, another test was run. It still didn't work.

I suggested it was because one set of lights was being directed at one set of mirrors, and the other set of lights being directed at the other. "All lights should be pointed at both sets of mirrors," I said.

Col. Vrill said he had a solution, and a prism was added so that both sets of lights could be directed at the prism, with the light split and directed at the bell's twin mirrors simultaneously.

"Now we're getting somewhere," I said. "But we're still not quite there. William's mirrors were pointed at, I don't know, maybe a sixty degree angle, or thereabouts, and not pointed straight at the ground."

"Why didn't you say so in the first place?" Col. Vrill snarled.

The crew was brought in to angle the mirrors so that their directed light hit a spot at a seventy degree angle away from them on the ground.

Yes, more progress, but still not quite there. "William's lights were strobe lights. They flashed on and off at a rapid pace."

"I know what strobe lights are," Col. Vrill said.

I could tell he was exasperated for me not telling him this in the beginning.

Col. Vrill's engineers fastened electronic on/off switches to the runway lights, turning them into strobes.

It seemed to be working now, as a defined vortex was being created. At first we gently tossed an old kettle into the vortex and it disappeared. We had no idea where it went, but it was no longer there.

No one on the project was totally convinced it was now a true time machine, but no one was convinced it wasn't, either.

By now I realized what we had built might actually be workable, but it was too primitive to pick a spot in time and go there. We could only crank it up and hope for the best. Using it as a direct route back to 2018 was probably out of the question, but maybe it would eventually lead to a return trip home.

But was all this too late? It had been a month since we'd started, and although Hitler continued to give us extensions, word came back how the Butcher had reached the end of his patience.

After the attempt on Hitler's life in July at his Wolf's Lair field headquarters near Rastenburg, East Prussia, the remaining Nazis were much more fervent. Higher ups in the chain of command who were not involved in the plot were given more trust. And more responsibility.

Traveling between the concentration camps in Auschwitz and Terezin, it was only a small detour for the Butcher to make inspection visits to *Die Reisse* where Col. Vrill and I worked on *Die Glocke*. It was his habit to check in with Hitler upon arrival, and each time Hitler told him to let the men continue. But the Butcher could tell each time Hitler's resolution was fading.

One day at dawn, the Butcher burst into the colonel's house intent on ending what he considered a fiasco and a complete waste of time. He was determined to kill the American spy and his German collaborator.

This time the colonel was not talking to Hitler on the phone, and this time he was unable to convince the Butcher to call him.

With the end of the war coming near, along with Hitler's downward slide mentally and physically, the Butcher was taking it upon himself to tie up loose ends. He didn't want to leave any of the secret work they had been doing here for anyone else to see or use. He already had been secretly murdering some of the lesser known scientists to make sure they didn't escape with any of this knowledge.

Col. Vrill barely managed to keep him from shooting us dead on the spot. "Please, not in the house. I'm sure I've earned at least that much consideration."

The Butcher reluctantly agreed. He had his men drag us out and lined us up against the wall. No blindfolds and no binding of the hands or feet. This was going to be done quick and easy before anyone had a chance to interfere.

"Ready," the Butcher called out. "Aim."

Barely a millisecond before the order was given to fire, a loud explosion rocked the entire area, sending up smoke and dust.

Sporrenberg the Butcher, convinced the Allies had found him, ordered his firing squad and all other armed troops to meet the enemy head on. "Fight until you have no more ammunition, then fight with your hands. Don't quit until you're dead or victorious. I will personally shoot dead anyone I see retreating."

Col. Vrill and I slipped away in the confusion.

The battle squad stormed out, looking for the Allied menace, but could find none. As it turned out, the explosion was one of the other experiments conveniently gone wrong.

Now fuming, the Butcher went searching for us, first at Col. Vrill's home, then at the project site. When he couldn't find us there, he headed back towards Col. Vrill's house.

We were able to stay one step ahead, hiding when the Butcher searched the project site, then surreptitiously starting the bell when he left. I had been storing my backpack at the site and made sure to grab it.

The noise *Die Glocke* made, however, did not go unnoticed. The Butcher immediately turned around and headed back to the project site, arriving just in time to see us standing next to *Die Glocke*, which was almost fully warmed up. Seeing the terrifying display of flashing lights, showering of sparks and gusting winds it created, he darted towards the protective pillbox on the edge of the compound built for our protection should the allies begin bombing from above.

"Halt!" He commanded as he slipped inside.

"If this is the end, then let's make it a good end," I said to Col. Vrill. "What do you say?"

"You might be American scum, but you're ok. Ja, let's do it!"

We charged the tornado of light, not knowing if it would work, and if it did, where, or more precisely, when we would end up.

The Butcher aimed his Luger out through the pillbox rifle window and began firing his Luger at us. Just as he did, the two of us disappeared into the vortex causing a huge shock wave, flattening everything and killing almost everyone in a one km perimeter.

Somehow, miraculously, hideously, from inside the pillbox the Butcher survived.

*****

The Adventure Continues with
Paul Millard's Time Travel Chronicles II:
The Chosen
In a future Dystopian/Utopia, depending on whether
viewed by the drugged elite or the rebellious
underground, earth's human population has been
reduced and maintained by A.I. at less than 1 billion.
All sides believe in a prophecy where a time traveler,
The Chosen, arrives to save them.

To be followed by:

Paul Millard's
Time Travel Chronicles III:
Chased through Time
The Chosen is forced to race through time to keep one
step ahead of enemy assassins intent on keeping him
from disrupting their plans to eliminate all remaining
humans and take over earth.

Also by Daniel M. Dorothy:

Mango Rains

The epic story of a mother's lifelong
search for her abducted daughter

ABOUT THE AUTHOR

Daniel M. Dorothy is a writer, newspaper editor and author. He has been a Sci-Fi fan since the 1960s when, as a young lad at his grandparents' house he and his sister would sneak out of bed to watch Star Trek from the stairwell. We would peer through the railings as the elders stayed mesmerized by their brand new RCA color console television below, allegedly unaware their young offspring were looking over their shoulders. Maybe they were just pretending not to notice.

Dan has never time travelled. Yet.

Made in the USA
San Bernardino, CA
26 August 2018